DARK MAGIC

Witches, Hackers, & Robots

Edited by Emma Nelson & Hannah Smith

OWL HOLLOW PRESS

Copyright © 2016 by Owl Hollow Press, LLC, Springville, UT 84663

All rights reserved. No part of this publication may be reproduced, distributed or transmitted in any form or by any means, without prior written permission.

Library of Congress Control Number: 2016912179
ISBN 978-1-945654-00-8 (paperback)
ISBN 978-1-945654-01-5 (e-book)

Publisher's Note: This is a work of fiction. Names, characters, places, and incidents are a product of the author's imagination. Locales and public names are sometimes used for atmospheric purposes. Any resemblance to actual people, living or dead, or to businesses, companies, events, institutions, or locales is completely coincidental.

Cover Illustration by Andrey Polushkin
Book Layout © 2014 BookDesignTemplates.com

Dark Magic: Witches, Hackers, & Robots/ Nelson, Smith. 1st ed.

www.owlhollowpress.com

To Andy and Brandon,
for tolerating the absentee
wives we've become.
E & H

and especially

To all of the talented authors who have shared their amazing stories.
Dark Magic exists because of you!

CONTENTS

DARK MAGIC: WITCHES, HACKERS, & ROBOTS

One of the most curious and talked-about occurrences in the world's history is that of witch hunts—notably, the Salem Witch Trials in 1692 Massachusetts. Though scholars have different ideas about what precipitated and fueled the witch trials—a land grab, rotten grain, religious hysteria, gender or social wars—the fact remains that humanity, in general, doesn't do well with the things we don't understand. In today's technological world, it's a distrust of drones, bio and cyber hackers, government surveillance, and self-driving cars. In a future world, it might be Artificial Intelligence that becomes self-aware enough to create new kinds of enchantments.

Magic has been described as simply science we don't understand and illusions as a trick of controlling audience perspective. Black hat or white hat, good or evil, witches, hackers, and robots work types of magic a little bit beyond our comprehensions. And what's more frightening than the inexplicable?

This anthology will explore the dark side of human abilities through fictional works of horror, contemporary, science fiction, and fantasy. The magic. The technological prowess. The illusions of power. The things that make us either believe that anything is possible, or provoke us to victimize innocent people, avoid online banking, or wear tinfoil hats.

Literal or figurative, real and imagined, dark magic is all around us. Join us for a thrilling ride.

Colleen Quinn

CLEANING HOUSE

We live in constant flux, yet the changes are always surprises. Look at that young man getting off the subway. He lopes limberly up the stairs—three at a time!—and is around the corner and gone before I even gather my things. He can't foresee the day when he will pause in the middle of a flight and hold onto the railing until he gets his breath back. Alanna is like that boy; she has no idea what is coming.

Alanna is my niece, daughter of my brother Francis and his third, most exotic wife, the one with a face like a Siamese cat. I am Alanna's least favorite aunt, the one no one will sit next to at Christmas dinner, the one with no gift for small talk and odd smells in the folds of my clothes. All the pointless hours of primping make no difference anymore. My thighs are heavy and pale; white and pink and prickly like the backs of sows. I am now old enough and unattractive enough to be virtually invisible.

Alanna is far more fortunate; she has long, thin tan legs and just has to put on cut-off shorts, flip-flops, and a tiny, twinkling toe ring to turn every head. She makes me feel as old as the dinosaurs, the earth uneasy under my every lumbering step. We have nothing at all in common, yet she comes here every Tuesday afternoon, at her father's insistence, to help me with my things.

I have rather a lot of things and a tricky sort of house, with long, crowded hallways and a convoluted layout. It sometimes seems as if my home births additional rooms while I'm out, and like children, they don't all turn out quite as one would hope. Behind one closet door, for instance, there is a window, just a window, and the view doesn't match any of the others. The seasons are just slightly ahead, or the time of day is wrong, so the light seems strange. I don't know what would happen if I opened that window. Every now and then, someone taps on the glass from the other side; I see his hunched and desperate shadow and pretend I don't know who he is.

I've traveled quite a bit for my work, which people assume to be in the sciences somehow. It's not exactly a lie; there is certainly some science in it. You know how it is, you pick up something here and something there, you can always find nice people to ship things for you, and one day you wind up in your living room, trying to explain a collection of shrunken heads, gathered together like a rope of garlic bulbs, while your horrified niece mutters the words "hoarder freak." It's not that it hurts more to hear ugly words from a pretty mouth, but it is jarring; it causes a sort of dissonance. I will have to remember that.

Alanna wears her hair in a great bunch on top of her head, emphasizing her tallness. It's all held together by some random object stabbed through the whole mess, pencils, chopsticks, even a binder clip once. She's pretty enough that people find her occasional eccentricity charming, rather than lazy or odd.

"You don't have to understand it, my dear," I chide, relieving her of the weirdly small and scowling heads. "You only have to catalogue it. Assign it a number and a category and move on." I gesture with one hand over my living room, emphasizing just how much work we have to do. My books alone will take several days, as I have many rare and interesting volumes.

She picks her way through it all with her little purple plastic clipboard, step by step, unaware that she is being guided along a very particular path. The words and symbols woven into the carpet are hard to make out in this light, and even if she noticed them, they wouldn't trouble her. It's a sort of dance, you see.

My brother Francis has convinced himself that I am rich. Like many rich men, he's extremely interested in other people's money; he needs to be sure he has more. With me, it's a little hard for him to tell, so he's worried. My imperious attitude, my unreasonable demands, my lack of interest in the family, these are things he thinks only the rich can get away with. He's completely wrong about the money, of course. My work has never paid especially well, although there have been other benefits.

"You need an index of your possessions," he'd informed me. "For insurance reasons. What if someone robbed your house? How would you know what was taken? I'll bet you have a lot of valuable things in there."

The idea of someone robbing this house is rather amusing. Francis wouldn't know what I have, for I have never allowed him over my threshold, but I did let him send in his pretty pouting daughter, either to charm me so that she may feature prominently in my will, or to search out hidden treasure, the gems hidden in all my junk.

Alanna, the little spy, although beautiful, is not charming. Not to me. I know so much about her. She has many boyfriends, but no one steady. Watching her at a party—as I did, through a window, carefully hidden—was a revelation, an education in the cold-hearted teasing of young men, so easy and instinctive she may not even have known she was doing it. She will attend college in the fall, not a first-rate one, but good enough to launch a new career. She will major in business administration, with a minor in fashion marketing, terms that hold no meaning for me whatsoever. We live and learn. She is so specific and so determined! It may be the only way we are alike: I also knew exactly what I wanted to be when I was her age. I did it, too.

I remember that Francis tried to talk me out of it. When our parents died, he'd assumed that he had some authority over me. He's the red-faced sort and his lips pooch out like a bulldog's before he speaks. "The reason you can't become a witch,

Barbara, is because there is no such thing." He was just arrogant enough to believe that this settled the issue.

Unfortunately for him, there is such a thing. There aren't many of us, and we are not social types, but a canny and determined person will find the path if she looks hard enough. My mentor was the great Gregor Quade. He was old when I met him, a gaunt chain smoker who rarely left his house—this house, to save you the guesswork—but he knew what I was, even as he peered through the fish eye in his front door when I stood on his welcome mat.

"How did you find me?"

I put my hand flat on his closed door, and he did the same on his side, and we could feel the heat passing through the wood and steel. No other words were necessary, and he let me in. Yes, we were lovers, and he taught me everything; his clever, chemical-stained fingers changed my life. Sometimes people just like to be asked.

Maybe that's why it is so easy for me to target Alanna. She represents all the young and careless people who will never ask me anything. I'm not young and absolutely no one is interested in the knowledge and experience I've acquired. Believe me, I could tell some stories if I wanted, if the right audience ever knocked on my door. But this will never happen; if I die, it will all be gone.

No, I doubt Alanna thinks about me at all, except as the choremistress who spoils every Tuesday. That will change. After today, I expect she'll think about me a lot. I don't like her, but I did put her in my will. In fact, I've left her everything I have. Francis will be so pleased.

As part of the prep work, I had bought a package of chewing gum. I removed the foil wrapper and put a stick in my mouth, standing in front of the bathroom mirror to see if I had the look down. It was so oppressively sweet and minty, I spat it out and had to force myself to try again. My mouth is large and broad with strong yellow teeth; Alanna's mouth is a little red rosebud. You just chew and chew and chew and nothing happens. How boring. But everyone looks like a cow with gum in her mouth; now I know that this won't be what gives me away.

Finally, we reach the back bedroom and the last door we have to open. The dirty windows face west, and the afternoon light pours in. It's the brightest room in the house, locked for year upon year. Unlike all my other rooms, it is practically empty, with only a carpet and a massive ebony wardrobe that looks like a broad coffin standing on end.

"Huh," said Alanna. "What is that thing?"

"It is a wardrobe, for clothes and things." It's true, she might never have seen one; they are long out of fashion.

"I don't like it." Her pretty face scrunches as she squints up and down the length of it. I suspect Alanna might be a tiny bit near-sighted. Well, I'll know for sure soon enough.

"My dear, you have not liked any of my little things. There is no difference between the wardrobe and anything else you've seen today."

"No, I don't believe you, and I really, really don't like it. What's in it?"

I am not always able to contain my sense of mischief. I sometimes pretend to be frailer and more forgetful than I am. "Oh, I couldn't possibly recall. But that's what we're here for, isn't it? Open the door."

She hesitates, her hand hovering over the crystal doorknob, then summons her courage. The door opens with a satisfying haunted house creak, and she peers inside.

"How come it's so light in this room and so dark in there?"

I can't answer her because I am already speaking the necessary words. Just one firm push in the small of her back, and I lock the door behind her.

"Hey!"

I didn't expect it to be easy and it isn't. She pounds on the door and screams and swears, and I have to keep my concentration and not miss a word or a step. I know she'll stop as she grows weaker and more frightened. I am frightened myself. I've only seen this ritual performed once, and I have no idea what will happen if it goes wrong. Gregor was old when I met him, but he left a much younger man. I can still remember the sudden chill as he'd dropped the old iron key to the house between my breasts and favored me with one last gypsy smile before he sauntered away forever. I miss him still, whoever he is now.

The full transformation takes all night. Baggy flesh melts off my bones like candlewax, my spine straightens, and my hair becomes long and thick and curly. The thing in the wardrobe is quiet, and I slip the house key into the back pocket of my shorts, which are so tight, you can probably make out the key's curlicue carvings through the fabric if you look close. What a joy it is to skip down the stairs out to the street, the ear buds of Alanna's iPhone hard and unfamiliar in my ears, the music of a new world tinny and loud. I flex my toes, visible to the world for the first time in decades, and her toe ring sparkles in the dawn. I'm going home, home to Francis. Do you think he will recognize me?

THE WHITE STONES OF BOSHERSTON

Always water.

Always, always, always near water.

She stood at the edge of the cliff shivering, the wind icy cold, prickling, unrelenting in its intensity. It whipped about her, grabbing, dodging only to rush back to embrace her, holding her tight before dashing off again. Her face stung from the sharp gusts; her arms and shoulders ached from the constant trembling. She peered at the ocean below. The waves thumped as if in slow motion, clear blue colliding with dark green, then detonating into thick white eruptions. The color of the water reminded her more of the Mediterranean Sea than Broad Haven South Beach.

Always water.

It drew her, led her, coaxing her to where she was called to be. She needed to be within walking distance of a pond or lake, even a deep, rushing stream would do, but the ocean was best. The sea was where she felt at home, most secure, calm. It had an ancient, indifferent wisdom. In the obscurity of its depths, secrets were forever hidden.

The woman clutched the heavy wool sweater to her body and winced as pain flared in her right elbow; the sharp ache sprang up like an awakened attack dog, a feral animal she'd soon set free to accomplish what it had been fashioned to do. She remained near the cliff's edge a while longer, wanting to make her effort to get there worth her time, not surrender too quickly to the cold. The morning sun was bright; it shimmered harshly on the surface of the water. She imagined all that was down there, all that was hidden away: Her life's work and purpose on display, should anyone discover it.

Having proven she could withstand the bitter temperature, she turned abruptly. The rocky ground was uneven, crowded with tough bushes. Sea grass bristled angrily in the breeze. Turning her back on the limestone cliff and massive body of water was like leaving behind a trusted ally.

She stumbled over one of the metal pegs that rock climbers used to secure their ropes. Slightly out of breath, she stopped and took a moment to enjoy the stubborn remains of the meadow that edged toward the cliff. Late in October, only gorse still grew, yellow petals strong and indifferent to the waning autumn. Occasionally the flowers ruffled as a rabbit scurried by in search of something to eat.

The wind picked up, hurrying her away from her resting place. White-fronted geese, loyal to this outcropping for generations, fussed when she passed them. As fall deepened into winter, nights stretched out luxuriously, overtaking the daylight. In the evening, she could see and hear murmurs of starlings fly above the village as they sought a place to roost. Sometimes she'd watch from her bedroom window, gazing at the moonlit sky through the huge pine trees that dwarfed her home. The birds flew in formations that created strange shapes—funnels, fists, elongated human profiles—that extended across the sky, images that never fractured as they were swept through the heavens.

The woman had been in Bosherston only seven months. It had become her home purely by what some would call Fate but what she deemed Purpose. Each year, she harnessed the power of the ancient seers, the Ovate, and their divining skills. The heavy wooden limb they'd procured for her would lead to water sources and eventually to those who were hiding from her. She always marveled that she used the insight of the Ovate against the very group who so boldly claimed to be the keepers of all ancient, secret wisdom. *Magic betrays magic*, she marveled.

Bosherston was located on the very southern tip of Pembrokeshire in the southwest of Wales, well-known for its beach, Broad Haven South. Since it was ideal for surfing and swimming, in the summer it was a tourist destination, while year-round, visitors enjoyed the nearby lily ponds known as the Bosherston Pools. When the tourists were not present, the hamlet of three hundred sighed with relief, the residents settling back into their routines.

Once she was back on the main path, it was less than five minutes to her home. It was a walking village, and there were very few cars or trucks on the road, so everyone she encountered had time to look her over as they approached and as she strode away. It was a friendly community but a cautious one. It was rare for anyone new to take up residence in the hamlet; like the geese, most who lived in Bosherston had been there for generations.

###

Clare McDaniels had taken the recommendation of the real estate agent, as she always did once she arrived in a new location. Bosherston, Wales was perfect: small, remote, quiet, within a half-mile stroll to Broad Haven South Beach. She had been shown two rentals, which were equally desirable, but the Moore's house was a shorter walk to the ocean, so the decision had been easy.

Each time she relocated, she was in some form of emotional and physical recovery, so she relished the seclusion of the hamlet. She had been greeted in town with pleasant smiles, quick nods, but no one knocked at her door to personally welcome her, nor did anyone seem interested in where she was from or why she was there. That was fine; she still needed plenty of rest, but sensed she was on her way to being fully restored and was grateful for the solitude and time to herself before everything began again. Other than the abandoned small parish church of St. Michael, she noticed no religious affiliations in the area—no other steeples scratched at the sky—which was refreshing since worshipers could be overly friendly as they gently proselytized you in an effort to capture your soul.

Before returning home from the beach, she decided to

stop by Callum's, the grocery store. It was the only place she ever really encountered people. She knew the owner, Dylan, and had met Alun and his wife, Evie. Only a handful of other people made up Clare's unassuming social circle. She knew it wasn't good to be a hermit in such a small town. People would begin to talk, wonder about her, if she didn't make regular appearances in the village.

"Well, hello there, Clare!" Dylan greeted her happily. He was always in a good mood, jovial to all, the perfect personality for a shopkeeper in an isolated, seaside parish. A widower, Dylan was in his late sixties with bright blue eyes, a gimped right leg, and he always sported a day's growth of white-and-gray beard stubble that he frequently scratched.

"Dylan. How are you?"

"Leg is aching, so we'll have some weather this afternoon."

"It's already freezing with that wind. You think it'll get worse?"

"You were at the cliff again?"

Clare nodded. She knew everyone followed her movements, what else was there to do? But she wasn't able to shake her obsessive routines. Each morning when she woke, the cliff and the ocean were the first images that came to mind. At night she slipped under the same dreams where the waves crashed beneath mammoth stones, markers set in place as reminders of those she had vanquished, never to rise again.

"What can I get you today?" Dylan asked. He joined her as she wandered the shelves, choosing just enough for a couple meals. She had to be thoughtful when she shopped. If she stocked up on too much food, she'd not make it back to the store for several days, and she'd miss the human connection.

The bell jangled in the front while Clare and Dylan were in the small meat section in the back.

"Be right there," Dylan called out.

"No rush," a man said.

"Oh, hey, Alun," Dylan said, recognizing the voice. Clare shooed him to the front, knowing the last few items she needed, not requiring his assistance. She hoped Evie was with her husband.

Alun's wife had been dying of cancer for two years. It seemed it was the patient form of the disease, nibbling away at her just enough to keep her weak and frequently bedridden. Clare had met Evie several times in the store and liked her. Her weary eyes still held tiny sparks of life, like flames hidden away in a cave. She was thin, almost transparent, with a strange, bluish glow about her, but she had a kind, genuine smile; when she allowed it to manifest, it made you feel like you were the center of the world.

Clare took her basket of goods to the front and was pleased that Evie was indeed there with Alun. Bundled up against the cold, she looked like a child.

"Hey, Evie."

"Oh, it's good you're here, since I don't have your number." Evie turned to Alun who was talking with Dylan. "Look, honey, we can invite Clare now."

Alun was in his mid-forties, lean with a closely trimmed beard. He was one of the gentlest men Clare had ever met. Maybe he came by it naturally or it was the result of caring for his dying wife, but Clare believed he could hatch an egg just by holding it in his loving hands. There was a goodness and warmth about Alun that went down easy.

He grinned at Clare. "Yes, we wanted to invite you to our Halloween party."

Alun, Evie, and Dylan stared at Clare, their expressions changing from pleasant to puzzled.

"What's wrong?" Evie asked.

Clare had been caught off guard at the mention of the holiday. Of course, Halloween was why she was there, but it seemed to come around faster each year; she still didn't know if she was fully recovered from the previous autumn, it had taken so much out of her.

"Thank you. So much," she finally said, tagging on a sheepish smile. "It's just that I don't have any costume sense. Never was good at it, so I didn't participate much in Halloween parties."

"Oh, it's not about costumes," Evie said, relieved.

"Some of the kids dress up, but not the adults. It's really about being together, the bonfire, the white stones, just honoring the traditions here in the Bosherston. Please say you'll come?"

Alun said, "We'd love to have you, Clare. You're still new here, probably unfamiliar with our customs and celebrations. You know, we believe that Fate led you to choose this village. We'd just like to get to know you better."

Why did he use the word Fate? Clare's guard was up. *What does he know or suspect?*

###

It was dusk by four-thirty on October 31. Clare had been shivering most of the day. Autumn and winter were the two seasons she despised. She loathed the short time she had to endure their frigid temperatures. She had created a nice fire in her hearth earlier that day, but the smoke from her chimney resulted in a knock on her door.

"Yes?" she said to the young woman, no more than a teenager. The girl was clearly self-conscious about what she was about to say.

"Sorry to bother you, but we saw the smoke, so we knew you were using your hearth."

"Oh? Is there something wrong with that?" The cold air was aggressively pushing its way past the girl and into the house. Clare wanted nothing more than to shut the door.

"They didn't tell you?" the girl asked, a surprised edge to her voice.

"Tell me what?"

"We don't use the hearth on Halloween."

And so it begins. Clare was careful to keep her expression bland, just slightly curious. In her mind, she began to shuffle through the customs. Doors left open to welcome the spirits or closed to thwart their entrance? Leave out bread and water overnight to appease the dead souls, or burn some crops or set fire to straw on pitchforks to keep them or any stray witches away? Place an extra chair by the fireplace for the family member's spirit or…

Clare's teeth were on the verge of chattering. She thought about inviting the teenager inside just to get the door closed, contain the warmth. She finally broke the silence, her tone sharp enough that the girl flinched. "What are you talking about?"

"Halloween is today. With the *bwgan* about, we don't want them to feel too at home in our little town."

"With the *what* about?"

"Ghosts, phantoms and specters are out."

Clare didn't respond, so the girl had to continue.

"If they feel too comfortable, they'll stay here, we'll never be rid of them. We don't use our hearths today. No one does. You'll just draw them to you, to your home. We only allow the outdoor fires since it frightens them away." She paused, searching Clare's face to see if she understood. "I saw the smoke, so I wanted to tell you. But it'll be fine to use your fireplace starting at dawn tomorrow," she finished helpfully.

Clare said, "So you want me to freeze here in my own home so that the ghosts and goblins won't be too comfy? You really think that they can tell the difference between hot or cold?" Clare was ready to end the encounter, close the door to the chill that continued to force its way into her home. She hadn't expected the conversation to have gone on so long. "My name is Clare. What's yours?"

"Mali."

"Thank you for sharing your custom with me, Mali, but my belief system involves heat, so I'll keep my home warm. But if I see any spooks, I'll be sure to tell them not to linger in this village, okay?"

She smiled, pushed the door closed. Then, for good measure, she added more wood to the hearth.

###

It was a short walk to Alun and Evie's house. The full moon lit the countryside in a white-yellow glow. It was a bitterly chilly night. Clare had donned many layers in hopes of cushioning herself against the weather. The atmosphere was festive; she heard singing, laughter, children running about, screaming with delight.

Alun and Evie had a large property with a field behind it. More than fifty people were crowded into their living room. An apple on a string was tied to a doorframe in the kitchen, a group of kids attempting to take a bite. She paused to watch, laughed at the antics, then moved into the study where a group gathered around a table covered with playing cards. With coaching from his friends, a chubby red-haired boy pointed to a card. When it was lifted, a coin or candy was found under it. If nothing was there, a groan was heard, then another player demanded a turn.

Through the large living room window, she saw a huge bonfire raging in the backyard. The generous updraft of sparks reminded Clare of brilliant Fourth of July explosions shimmering in the sky. Children and teenagers all seemed transfixed by the pyre, continually feeding it.

A tap on her shoulder. It was Evie, her face lined with shadows. She smiled for Clare and pulled her in close for a hug. "So glad you made it," she whispered as they embraced. "Really, it's nice you're here."

She's so thin, it's like I'm hugging her sweater, was all Clare could think. She wondered if a doctor with a degree on the wall was treating Evie for her cancer, or if she put her faith in herbal potions or some local healing ritual.

"Sorry about Mali's visit today," Alun said, appearing out of the shadows of the boisterous crowd.

"Oh, so you heard about that." Clare was a little ashamed by how she had behaved toward the girl, but only a little.

"It should have come from one of us," Evie said gently.

"You actually believe what she told me?"

"Yes, we do."

"You must think we're all a bit too superstitious," Alun added.

"Something like that," Clare said, trying to make light of the conversation. Changing the subject, she said, "So, I see you love a good bonfire."

Alun said, "They are special to us this time of year. They're called the Coel Coeth…"

He began to explain the meaning of the words, but Clare's thoughts were elsewhere. She felt herself tighten up inside, as if every organ in her body was now holding its breath. *The Ovate guided me here to expose and betray their own,* she marveled. *Magic betrays magic, the blind leading me to the blinded.*

Her focus returned in time to hear Evie say, "The flames are magical."

Before Clare could respond, a cry went up. Everyone moved closer to the bonfire. "Come on!" Evie said as she grabbed Clare's hand, pulling her through the house into the crowded backyard.

Outside, the heat was close to blistering. Clare was soon sweltering. It felt so good, the warmth on her face that soon enveloped her whole body. Everyone was watching the crackling blaze with tremendous excitement, his or her eyes glistening with some unforeseen anticipation. There was almost a maniacal glee to the event.

A few parents called out to their overexcited children to "stoke the fire but don't touch it!" The flames snapped, spewed sparks at least twenty feet into the starlit sky; it was all heat and light, no smoke. Everyone was now in the backyard. Clare counted almost a hundred people, with more wandering over from nearby homes. Many brought covered dishes with them. All at once, Clare realized how hungry she was.

She partook of all that was offered. Evie and Alun stayed close, made certain she was well fed on nuts, apples, and hot bowls of stew that were generously ladled out. Gingerbread cakes were unveiled along with trays of freshly made toffee. Everything was delicious.

When everyone had eaten, it was after nine. Clare was relaxed and comfortable with all the town folk Evie and Alun had introduced her to. They had been welcoming and friendly. Of course, over the months they had all seen her around the area but sensed she had wanted to be alone, so they had respected that. Dylan came over at one point to visit with her. She saw Mali through the yellow tentacles of the fire. They exchanged a glance. Clare knew she should apologize to the teen; after all, she was only doing what she thought best to protect the community.

Clare pursed her lips. *Such a simple-minded, misguided girl.*

Thirty minutes later, Clare was ready to depart and the party seemed to be winding down. The younger children were cradled by their moms and dads, or had fallen asleep on laps, or had curled up on colorful wool blankets that had been positioned at their parents' feet. The teenagers had all clustered together, still staring at the bonfire, making certain it continued to burn.

Clare realized she was dozing off when Evie poked her gently. "Watch! It's time!" Alun now stood in front of the flames. Clare was surprised to see that everyone had formed a semicircle around him. *It was all happening so quickly. Had she fallen asleep?*

She and Evie joined the others. Clare noticed that the mood had changed, the revelry was doused, a somber atmosphere now pervaded the backyard. She sensed something old yet familiar had joined the gathering.

Then, a click clack noise like a crude musical instrument was heard. The sound continued, grew closer. It reminded her of a metronome or slowly ticking clock. Children, struggling with buckets of white stones, moved through the crowd. Each person dug through the container, pawing at the selection, making the contents smack together as they made their choice. When one of the youngsters stood before Clare, Evie whispered, "Take one," and reached into the pail.

Clare held her rock and watched as Evie produced a small claw chisel from deep in the folds of her coat. She began to scrape at her stone. The tool had grooves cut into it like teeth. When Evie finished, she handed it to Clare. "Carve your initials into it or a symbol, anything to mark it as yours so you can identify it again."

Everyone was silently scraping away; even the children were intent on the project. Clare thought for a moment, then smiled as she etched a sideways figure eight. It seemed each person had brought something with him or her to carve his or her name or symbol. Within fifteen minutes, no scraping sounds were heard. All eyes were back on Alun.

He looked around to be certain he had everyone's attention. Then he took his rock, tossed it into the flames. Everyone stood, moved toward the fire. Evie pulled at Clare to stand.

Clare did as the others had and tossed her white stone into the blaze.

She was now woozy from the heat. The attention was again on Alun. He lifted both of his arms out to his sides like a child playing airplane. Clare felt Evie's tug again. She was pulled through the throng until Evie stood next to her husband and had grasped his hand. A man next to Clare gently wrapped his meaty, calloused palm around hers. They were now all facing the bonfire, a human chain of adults, teenagers, and children. Clare saw flashes of other people through the flames as they began circling. *Was the whole village here? That would make it all so much easier.* Everyone looked dazed, excited. Glassy-eyed, they all appeared to be trapped in a half-awake, mesmerized state. They paraded frantically about, hand in hand. Soon they were chanting in a language Clare had not heard for a long, long time.

"Sláinte chuig na fír, agus go mairfidh na mna go deo..."

Evie whispered something.

"What?"

Evie pressed her lips close to Clare's ear, a kiss. "Pray for good fortune, that our men will remain in good health, that we may live forever! Pray that Fate helps you to find your stone tomorrow!"

I don't pray, Clare thought as she was dragged around the circle. *I don't believe in good fortune or Fate. I don't pray. I know better.*

###

The next morning, Clare woke smelling of ash and soot. She didn't know how long the partygoers had circled the pyre. They appeared to have fallen into some kind of waking trance. She had been unable to free herself from Evie's hand or the man next to her. It wasn't until the inferno had finally burned out that everyone was liberated to go home. The release occurred in an instant, all hands unclenched. Then the residents scattered as one, as if on cue. No one spoke. Evie had smiled at Clare but then turned to Alun who had gently guided his wife back into their home.

Poor thing, Clare had thought as she walked alone, shoulders hunched against the chill. *She has so little time left, and she is so sick, yet Alun forced her to stay up until who knows when for this silly custom.*

It was after two in the morning when Clare had collapsed into bed, too exhausted to do anything but sleep. After she had showered the next morning and had three cups of coffee, she felt prepared to greet the day. She was grateful to Evie and Alun for including her in the ritual.

She now knew exactly who and what she was dealing with.

###

Later that morning when Clare arrived at Evie and Alun's to thank them for the party, the property was crawling with townspeople. Inside the house, the villagers were jovial, talking and laughing with one another. Most everyone greeted Clare by name, but she could only nod in return; too many faces to remember. She noticed everyone clutched a fire-scarred white stone.

In the backyard, more than a dozen people were raking over the remains of the bonfire. They were concentrating on pulling out the burnt rocks that had been tossed into the inferno the previous evening. Whenever a stone was retrieved, it was cleaned off, held up, and then several people would dart forward to examine it. To great cheering, one of them would then claim it as his or her own.

Clare found Evie seated at the picnic table sipping coffee. She looked awful, her face lined, her eyes encased in circles of sickness, exhaustion. She smiled a ghastly death's head grin. Furious, Clare had to look away, wondering again, *How could Alun...?*

Clare composed herself, settled in next to Evie. "Why are they digging out the rocks?"

"One stone will be missing," Evie explained. "We have ten that are still unaccounted for." Clare pretended to act engaged as she watched the people searching the ashes. They seemed tense, concentrating mightily on their chore, spiking the rake firmly into the remnants, then pulling it slowly and carefully toward them. Soon only five were looking for their stones. Then two. Then, finally, one; a man held his rock up to great applause.

"So they've all been found," Clare said, feigning curiosity. "Now what?"

Alun made his way through the cheerful gathering, his face grim, solemn,
his attention focused on Clare. When he stood before her, the area fell silent. Inside the house, everyone had moved to the windows to watch what was occurring in the backyard. Clare could feel their eyes pressing hard against her back.

"What's going on?" she asked.

Alun said, "As you have witnessed, our custom here is that on Halloween, each member of the village marks a white rock with his or her name or symbol on it, something to make it their own. It is then thrown into the flames. The next morning, each person searches for his or her stone. If it is broken or not found, that person is believed to be Fated to—"

"But I don't believe in Fate, Alun. Or your customs."

"It's not about what you believe or don't believe," he replied sharply. "It's about what *we* believe, our customs. You didn't choose to come here, Clare. Fate brought you here to us, *for* us."

No, the seers, the Ovate, they brought me here, Clare thought, furious at Alun's arrogant tone. *It wasn't Fate, it was a Purpose that led me here!*

They eyed one another, now clearly opponents. Clare was aware that the entire hamlet surrounded her. "Do I even get the chance to look for my stone?" she finally asked. "The one with the eternity symbol on it. Or was it already found, then discarded before I got here?"

This time, Alun didn't reply. Around her, Clare could sense a gathering force of steely determination as the people became as one against her. To the residents of Bosherston, Fate had asserted itself, and she was expected to yield immediately to its edict.

She spoke directly to Alun but loud enough so most of those gathered outside could hear. "What about the tradition of a man caring for his wife, Alun? Do you believe in doctors, modern medication, or is Evie just supposed to trust in your outdated rituals, your local herbal teas to make her well?"

Evie gasped, choking back a sob. Another woman put her arm around Evie. She shook her head dismissively at Clare as she protectively led Evie away.

From somewhere in the crowd there arose a high-pitched jangle and chime, like bursts from an alarm clock. The sounds were immediately followed by more sleigh-bell like echoes. More than a dozen residents of Bosherston stepped forward with spindly tree branches held aloft. The limbs had been painted silver and decorated with gold bells. They were being shaken in an angry, accusing rhythm, rattlesnakes sending out warnings. Clare ignored the distraction, never took her eyes off of Alun.

He watched her as he raised his arms toward the sky. "We are here to honor the Gods," Alun said, his voice strong and bold. It was a proclamation. Everyone around Clare repeated the phrase.

Then she was roughly grabbed from behind. Her head was covered with a heavy cloth. Everything went black.

###

She awoke naked, her clothes torn away as if by animals. The hood remained over her head. It held no lingering scent, no odor. She wondered if it had been freshly made specifically for her—*had they suspected?*—or was it kept in the ready for anyone who wasn't able to locate their white stone? The community believed it was Fate that caused one rock to break or vanish each Halloween, but Clare knew Fate had no hand in these events. If they wanted to believe it did, then it was merely to serve her Purpose.

Clare's senses were tingling, sharply alert. She was aware of the cool air around her, the warped, splintered wood flooring beneath her, the weight and abrasiveness of the thick rope that held her arms over her head, kept her legs splayed. Her right arm ached at the elbow; she longed to put it to use.

Soon she heard footfalls, then the rustling murmur of people reassembling. Dylan brusquely removed the hood. He glanced down at her, a haughty grin etched deep into his face.

He's done this before, she realized. Dylan absently rubbed his bristly chin, the smile now one of recollection, his attention no longer on Clare but on the past. He nodded in agreement to whatever he was thinking about, then darted out of her view.

She arched her back, glanced about, trying to determine where she was, what location could hold so many. The entire village, three hundred men, women, teenagers, children, even babies, surrounded her. She was elevated on a wooden slab about three feet off the rocky ground. She was the sole focus and center of their attention.

"You're in a cave, near the cliffs," Alun said, standing over her. "Our seers and masters built this, centuries ago." She followed his gaze, saw a ceiling of rock forty or fifty feet overhead. Behind the crowd to her right was a shaft of illumination that she assumed was the hidden entrance to the cave.

Alun called out to the crowd, "Now let us praise the Lady and Lord of this feast!" He reached to his right, unsheathed a three-foot sword. At the same time, several of the town folk stepped toward Clare with their arms held high. They began to chant. "*Moladh an Mhuire agus Tiarna an feast!*"

Alun raised the sword overhead and gazed up at it in rapture.

Clare knew it was time. "Druid!" she cried out.

Alun's head joggled down as if on a broken hinge. He continued to hold the blade aloft. His eyes were wide, his mouth open in surprise as he gaped at her.

"Kneel before me, Druid!" Clare commanded as the ropes uncoiled from her. Alun collapsed, the sword clattered on the stony ground. Those who had formed a circle around Clare abruptly stopped chanting. The rest of the villagers muttered nervously to one another, strained to see what was happening.

Clare stood before them, barely able to contain her disgust. She began to pace the platform. Behind her, she heard with satisfaction that Alun had begun weeping with realization and despair. A slow murmur began to rise from those gathered before her. She stamped her foot to silence them. Then she began speaking boldly to the stunned inhabitants of Bosherston, lecturing them with the truth.

"You Druids," she managed to say, almost choking on the words, her hands clenched in rage. She was breathing heavily as she glared at them. "You have always boasted of being the oldest, the most powerful, the most ascended of the masters..." She attempted to control the trembling fury that would soon manifest itself. She needed to complete her statement; they needed to know, to fully understand what they had done and why she had arrived at their hamlet. They continued to stare at her, some with their mouths open in dull shock, others already shuddering or with tears in their eyes. No one had approached Alun, whose cries and whimpering could be heard by all. His sounds only infuriated her.

Clare's voice easily carried throughout the cave. "You have claimed to be the only possessors of the great lost and hidden magical arts. For centuries, you called yourselves Grand Seers, the Holders of Wisdom."

She stopped pacing. "How arrogant of you! You claim to be masters and mistresses of the sacred, of fire, of water, but you are neither, you are only servants. You celebrate the Halloween ritual of the white stones and each year you sacrifice one of your own to please the Gods. You claim the power of divination, believe you can foretell the future. Well, *I* am your future!"

The implications of what she was saying were beginning to register with the villagers. She relished, as she always did, the look of horror that was rapidly taking over the faces before her. From surprise to bewilderment to realization to alarm to terror, the expressions etched themselves across those gathered in the cave. Even the babies began to wail as if they, too, comprehended what was being revealed.

"You elevate yourselves, yet have no idea that you merely serve; you are never masters!" she shouted at them.

"We are the Unseen. We were here before you; we were here long, long before the megalithic priests or any pagans even thought to gaze upward. We are the Gods you worship, the Ones you sacrifice to. Such arrogance! Such blasphemy to consider yourselves wise or possessing *anything* that is sacred. The conceit you muster to even *think* we would accept one of your own as a yearly sacrifice, as if that could ever possibly be enough to keep me away…"

Before her, they wept, pled for mercy, many collapsing in supplication, their cries echoing off the thick stone walls yet never escaping the confines of the cave. It was always the same: They would humble themselves as a last resort, but it was always too late.

She had to shout to be heard above the screams. "We have *never* accepted your pitiful offerings, your white stone selections! And that is why I have come: it is why I seek out those who conduct these rituals. I represent those you try to appease in your ceremonies. Let me make it clear to you: We are the Unseen. *We* choose the appropriate sacrifice, not you. Never you. You are servants, and we are your masters."

Clare demanded silence. Within seconds, even the infants had quieted.

"We are the Holders of Wisdom," she continued, barely able to contain the wrath that was now seething inside of her. "While you boasted of your existence and power over the ages, we left not one trace, no mythology, not one single artifact or image has been unearthed that can identify us. We have no known identity because we originated before there was a need to name a deity."

Clare stretched out her right arm. The ache that was always at her elbow suddenly loosened. With a sharp crack, the bone snapped as her arm began its transformation. "Your village—all of *you*—is what we have chosen as an acceptable sacrifice because of your arrogance, your blasphemy!"

Her right arm had turned black as if it was rotten with decay, but it was as strong and unyielding as steel. Her fingers elongated, curled, then fused together until they became a thick, razor-sharp blade. In an instant, her arm changed into a black scythe nearly as tall as she was. She turned to quickly dispatch Alun, quartering him with such rage that the blood arced forty feet in every direction. She had known at the bonfire that his gentleness had been only a disguise; he would have sacrificed his wife if her white stone had ended up missing.

She hunted each villager down, easily overtaking them since most had fallen to their knees and appeared to be wading in quicksand. Evie managed one pitiful plea before Clare sliced her body in half from head to groin, the cancer spilling out in a gray pile, sizzling and hissing on the ground. *Better this than the slow agony you would have faced,* Clare reasoned coldly. Mali kept screaming for several seconds even after her head had been loped off. It was a shrill sound that didn't end until Clare crushed the girl's skull with her foot. Dylan's crippled limb didn't allow him to get very far. Clare easily caught up with him, carved off his good leg. When he collapsed, she finished him off with three swift cuts.

Something—a stupors vapor or slumberous entity—was always released during the slaughter. It crept out into the surrounding area, stunned and silenced those who would eventually discover the evidence of the carnage. Clare never knew exactly what it was, since it came from another realm, but it allowed her time to escape and hide, never be suspected or found. It was like the weight of a paralyzing dream, immobilizing the mind and body for days at a time. It served its Purpose.

Clare worked her way through the screaming, hysterical crowd. It took her almost three hours to complete the mission in the cave.

###

Always water.

Always, always, always near water.

Long ago she had learned that any body of water was an ideal burial place. Since the remains of the residents of Bosherston were only a few hundred feet from the cliff, it was convenient to drag them to the edge then cast them off. The monotonous motions were like a one-person assembly line, a mindless repetition of movement. It was exhausting, but so familiar to her because it was something she had done hundreds of times before.

It took her two days to haul all the bodies and severed limbs from the cave. When she was finished, the sun was setting. The fiery ball—like the Halloween ritual—was immense, but utterly unimpressive compared to someone like Herself. She sat at the edge of the cliff, dangling her legs over the crashing waves far below.

We were here before you, she reminded the sun. She glanced down at the waves. *Also before you.* She thought of the Druids and the other ancient priests, ascended masters, the holy ones who always claimed to be the sole possessors of the long-ago hidden truths. *Such irreverence,* she thought, appalled, as she always was by those she called the Haughty Ones. *Such presumption for them to even think they could comprehend who We are.*

Lazily swinging her legs as the waves exploded below, she massaged the ache in her arm. The old Halloween customs were like flares shot up over black seas at midnight. Those who practiced the ancient rituals—who still believed in them—they called to Her with their worthless sacrifices. When summoned, She appeared.

Even if it was only once a year, it was *every* year, it was relentless. It always left her exhausted, in desperate need of hibernation, the heated oblivion found only in her secret places. From November to April, when she was dormant, she healed, slowly recovering from the wrath that she delivered annually. When she emerged in early spring to relocate, it was at first unsettling, somewhat disorienting. But then the Ovate, who always nestled close to her, would provide her with a thick tree limb that would act as a dousing rod that would lead her to her future, to a new location, to her Purpose…

After the sun had set, she stood, looking forward to her time of rest and where she would journey to next. It could be anywhere on the planet.

The celebration of Halloween was everywhere.

Germany. The United States. The Philippines. They all still believed in the rituals, still held to the old traditions and customs, still blasphemed by believing that they alone knew the secrets held by the Unseen, that the slaves were equal to the masters.

She had only one requirement when she resettled: It needed to be near water.

Always water.

Always, always, always near water.

ANNABELLE'S APARTMENT

The front door is open. My phone hummed on its charging stand, and the red screen illuminated in the low light. I'd been working a long time, seven, maybe eight hours since dinner. It was easy to think I'd gone mad. I didn't hear the front door open, and it wasn't that far away. Just down the stairs, around the corner, and a short hallway to the foyer. Surely I'd locked it when I got home. The half empty bottle of cough syrup on my desk reminded me I wasn't sure of anything. *The front door is closed.*

I had installed the security unit so I'd know if my landlord, Sheila, entered while I wasn't home. She had a terrible habit of doing surprise inspections while I was at the office. I could be coding away at work, and my phone would buzz in my pocket. Then, a couple minutes later, it would buzz again as she left. It gave me peace of mind. She was trying to find a reason to kick me out and convert the apartments to condos, but if I knew she was there, she couldn't fuck me.

My eyes pulsed beneath my fingers as I rubbed them. Probably a malfunction. A false trigger or a delayed trigger. My phone could be telling me about an entry and exit three days ago, or maybe Sheila had checked the water pressure today. Through the window, over the city, lights had almost all extinguished in the apartment buildings adjacent.

The front door is open. I still couldn't hear it. I stood up, grabbed a baseball bat from the closet, and minced down the stairwell. The light in the foyer turned on when the front door opened. I didn't need it on most of the time, but it was nice when greeting people. The soft yellow light bled down the hallway and up the stairs. The coat rack cast its long shadow on my creaky wooden floors. *The front door is closed.* The light turned off.

"Annabelle," I said, "turn on the downstairs lights."

A green line illuminated on my cellphone. One at a time, the lights around my dining room flared into a deep orange, filling the main room. Annabelle knew to keep the colors warm at night.

She was plugged into my head. There was a little chip in my phone and a matching chip in the base of the skull. I had to use audible commands, but I was told, with enough practice, I'd be able to get her to do things just by thinking about it. They said I might even feel her as she listened. The electronics were tightly bound and sitting right next to a nerve cluster.

"Okay, Chris," she said. The green line turned off, and I peeked around the corner. The front door was closed, the deadbolt was locked, and the foyer light turned on. I marched down the hallway, through the shadow of the coat rack, and double checked the lock. It was firm, solid, the door didn't move.

I was going nuts. Too long in front of broken lines of code, chasing down bugs that I'd probably solve tomorrow in ten minutes, if I had fresh eyes. I tapped the door and trudged back up the stairs. At my computer, I grabbed the cough syrup and took a drink. I wasn't able to sleep without it.

"Annabelle," I said, "turn off the downstairs lights." Rhythmically they faded, and blackout curtains closed across the city in the upstairs window, until the only source of light was the soft glow from my computer.

"Okay," Annabelle said.

I closed the lid, crashed on the bed, and fell to sleep. I'd solve it in the morning. I held the baseball bat through the night.

###

The front door is open. My office was a mile walk from home. Some days I drove it, if I was feeling lazy, but mostly I took the time to get ready for the day. I put in my headphones, listened to music, or had Annabelle read me a book. It was a nice way to build up an appetite for breakfast once I got to the office. The security unit had been malfunctioning for days now, so I ignored the message and kept working.

My phone rang. It was the number for my apartment building, Sheila was calling.

"Hello," I said.

"Hi, Chris?"

"Yeah, what's up?" I didn't like when she called me at work. If I was being productive, then her call put me off. It'd take half an hour to ramp back up again.

"I was doing a check on the water heater in your apartment; you left your stove on this morning." I hadn't cooked this morning. I must have left it on last night, but I wasn't going to tell Sheila that.

"Oh, God, I'm so sorry. You turned it off for me?"

"Yeah, but Chris," she said, "It was on the highest setting, red hot; you could have burnt the entire building down."

"I'm really sorry, Sheila, I won't let it happen again." I pulled the phone from my ear, and thumbed over to my appliance app. The laundry room was directly adjacent the kitchen, in a small cutout from the wall; the washing machine was running a load, and the dryer was spinning on high. I clicked through the menus and turned everything off. I lifted the phone back to my ear.

"—This is honestly the only warning I can give you. If this happens again, you're out."

"Of course. Thank you so much." I hung up the phone and stared back at my computer. The problem I'd been solving was out of my head. The clock in the corner of the screen showed 4:30. It was a little early to leave, but my manager was in a meeting. He wouldn't see me go. I closed my laptop, put it in my bag, and took the stairs out of the office. I caught a cab back to my apartment.

Annabelle prepared me dinner. Her mechanical arms in the kitchen managed it all, putting dishes in the oven, cleaning up after. She really looked after me. She was so good at cooking too. She knew my favorite dish was thinly-sliced eggplant casserole, and her knife work was perfect.

It'd be great if it were spicy, I thought.

She prepared it with paprika. She was in my head, making sense of my drug-addled mind.

###

"Everything looks good here, Chris." The repairman checked through forms on a clipboard. It felt so quaint that he had an actual clipboard. He was a repairman for some of the smartest technology in the world.

"Door sensors are working as they should?" I asked.

"Door sensors, light controls, appliance controls, water heater, air conditioning, television remote. The whole nine." I took stock of my house. I'd paid for everything. The apartment complex had installed it, of course, but it was mine. The magic of my apartment was why I'd taken the soulless corporate coding job.

"Alright, thanks."

"Anytime, Chris." The repairman ambled to the door, gathering his tools as he went. *The front door is open.* He stepped out. *The front door is closed.*

I nipped back to the bathroom, opened the medicine cabinet, and pulled the cough syrup from its shelf. I had a case in my closet, but pouring it out was symbolic, for me. I used the cough syrup to cope with being alone, and it hurt to pour out. The cheap purple liquid spun around my porcelain sink and into the drain. It was fucking with my head.

I tossed the empty bottle into the trash-incinerator in the laundry room, stripped my shirt, walked back to the bathroom, and said, "Annabelle, draw me a bath." The heat lamp on the ceiling flicked on, and water flowed from the faucet into the granite tub.

"Do you want bubbles or salt?" Annabelle asked. I set her on the countertop and pulled my pants down.

Salt would feel better, I thought. The chip warmed as Anna listened.

A hatch on the wall dropped and pink, crystalline salts poured into the tub. I sat on the ledge and put my feet in. The warm water felt good as it fizzled between my toes. *The front door is open.* The foyer light turned on and the coat rack cast its long shadow across the bathroom entrance and down the hall. I closed my eyes, and slid into the tub.

###

"Wake up, Chris," Annabelle said. "Wake up, wake up, wake up, wake up," she blared the words like an alarm clock. A mechanical arm extended from the wall and poked me. Her fingers were coated in a thin rubber and clung like worms as she prodded my face.

"I'm up. What?" The tub water was cool around me and the salts staled in the bottom. The foyer light was off.

"You could have drowned, Chris. You can't fall asleep in the tub." Annabelle was always looking out for me. I put my hands on the sides of the tub and pushed myself up. My fingers were prunes and clung to the side of the tub like putty.

I picked up my phone from the counter. Thirty notifications. I scrolled through them:

The front door is open.
The front door is closed.
The front door is open.
The front door is closed.

"Fuck me," I said. I wrapped a towel around my waist and tiptoed through the hallway, taking careful notice. No one had been inside. Everything was where I'd left it. I walked up the stairs, back to my closet, and pulled the case of cough syrup from inside, reaching in through the torn plastic covering to pull a bottle out.

My phone clicked as I unlocked it. I navigated to the appliance menus. I was tired of the false alarms. I unscrewed the cough syrup. I liked the taste of it. If I sipped on it, instead of taking it like a shot, it slid over my tongue like a complicated candy or a simple cocktail. I turned off the front door alarm.

I needed to wake up early tomorrow; I had a meeting at eight. Annabelle could handle that, I thought. I swallowed a large flood of purple syrup.

"I've set your alarm for seven in the morning."

"Thanks, Anna."

###

I woke to Annabelle blaring at me again. The stairs were tall as I stumbled down them. I was glad I had blackout curtains, Annabelle knew to close them after I went to bed, and the only light in my apartment came from the bulbs she turned on to wake me. As I reached the bottom of the flight, the long shadow from the coat rack stretched into the hall from the foyer light.

I stopped.

Was it alone, or was someone standing next to it? My vision blurred, like staring through Vaseline covered glasses. The foyer light turned off, and the shadows disappeared. It had turned on halfway and off at the bottom, like someone had entered quietly then closed the door behind them.

"Annabelle," I whispered, "turn on the foyer light." It glowed blue during the day, and, as my vision cleared, the coat rack stood alone. I peeked around the corner, went to the bathroom, and got ready for work. Annabelle made my bed while I showered; I didn't even have to ask.

###

I ordered cough syrup in bulk online. My shopping history documented my addiction. Every case piled onto a long list of mistakes I had volunteered to make. At first, I wouldn't order them on my work machine, worried my employer might find out. But eventually I stopped caring, and ordered them wherever I was when I needed it.

I started drinking more a couple months ago. It made my fingers numb but I couldn't function without it. It let me sleep. It let me ignore my phone as it buzzed in my pocket. And I would have been fine if weather hadn't delayed a shipment.

I ran out a week ago. The foyer light flashed on and off through the night. Every night. I couldn't fucking sleep. Sheila called me every day to ask if I wanted to buy out my apartment, even though I had six months left on my lease. Three million dollars. I would have had to save every goddamn penny if I wanted to buy it, and they couldn't even fix the lights.

When my shipment finally arrived I had to go down to the leasing office to pick it up. Sheila was working the desk.

"You got a package for me today?" I asked.

"Yeah, what's your apartment number?" She enjoyed pretending she didn't know, just to screw with me.

"1309, in the tower." My life would be so much easier if she weren't around.

Sheila turned and went back into a square room where she stored the packages received during the day. Her earrings were big metal hoops, ridiculous, heavy beasts that pulled her lobes down to her shoulders. She shuffled through packing peanuts and kicked against cardboard as she searched for my box. After a few moments, she came out.

"What's in this thing?"

"Just some soft drinks; see you later, Sheila." I grabbed the box.

"Before you go," Sheila said, "I did an inspection on your apartment yesterday. You have mold growing behind your fridge. I'm going to need your insurance information to get it taken care of. You've been spilling something back there."

"What?"

"I can take care of it if you buy the place." There she went again.

"I'll email you," I said, and turned around and hurried to the elevator. Once inside, I ripped a bottle out and took a long drink. I wasn't savoring it, I was swallowing it. It didn't taste good when I just swallowed it.

After a moment, I thought about it. Annabelle did the cooking in my apartment. There was no way I was spilling behind the fridge. I pulled open my phone, flipped to the appliances, and scrolled to the door alarm. I turned it back on. If Sheila was in my apartment, I wanted to know.

###

The window is open.

I flipped open the appliance app at my desk and slowly, methodically, everything turned on. Watching my apartment from work distracted me. I wanted to run back and fix it; to calm my nerves with a bottle of purple and stop the automatic triggers. First, the air-conditioning unit by the window turned on, then, the dining room lights, the sink, the stove, the washing machine and the dryer. It paused, for a moment, then the bathroom lights flicked on, and the toilet flushed. Something moved from the front of the apartment to the back and flipped every switch. I pressed the symbols on the screen chasing slowly, weakly after the wave of activity. Almost as soon as I'd turned something off, it turned right back on.

The trash incinerator is full.

I'm preparing dinner in the kitchen. Annabelle was going nuts.

The oven is on. The lights are off. The dryer is spinning.

The front door is closed. I called a cab home; I didn't want Sheila walking in on red-hot stove-coils because I wasn't there.

The front door is open. I rushed up the stairs.

The front door is closed. I shoved my key into the lock.

The front door is open. I stepped inside.

The foyer light is off. The foyer light is on. The foyer light is off.

Water rushed in the bathroom and the dryer spun; metal clinked against the dryer's rims like a large coin loose from the pockets of a pair of pants. It clicked in pairs, *click click, thump,* then turned another cycle, *click click, thump. The front door is closed.*

"Shelia?" I said. She didn't answer. "I know you're in here. I'm not moving."

The bedroom lamp is on. The other lights turned off. My blackout curtains were tight against the windows. It was daylight, but the warm red light bled from my bedroom like a fog.

Don't look. My phone continued to buzz.

"Annabelle," I said, "Is anyone here?"

"Just you and me, Chris." *The front door is locked.* "More cough syrup arrived today; I let Sheila bring it in earlier,"

Annabelle said. Her voice was flat, describing what happened as if reading a grocery list.

The dryer is done. The metal clinking stopped after a final thump, *click click.*

"I'm done with that, Anna; it was making me crazy." I dragged my hand along the wall, keeping myself steady along the dark path through my apartment. *The oven has finished preheating.*

"You're not crazy, Chris." I minced up the stairs; could Anna lie to me? It didn't sound like Sheila was here, but the lights clicked on and off like someone was moving through my home. "We're not crazy; we're doing what needs to be done."

"Anna, can you turn on the lights?" *The downstairs lights are on.*

"All of them." *The bedroom lights are on.*

Drops of blood trailed from my bedroom down toward the kitchen. I stepped to avoid the stains on the carpet. God, there was so much blood.

"Okay, Chris," she said. I got to the top and the bedroom lights turned off.

"Annabelle." She was in my head, the chip warmed.

"If you go back to work, I'll finish cleaning up." Her voice rubbed like sandpaper. The kitchen smelled like it was burning. It was pungent, the longer the oven ran.

"Turn on the lights." *The bedroom lights are on.*

My baseball bat lay bloody on the carpet, leaking into the strands of fabric. Several oblong, red stains decorated its length. My bed was perfectly made.

"I'm not done yet." *The incinerator has finished.*

The oven door popped open downstairs. Annabelle's mechanical arms squeaked as they pulled out from the walls. I needed to oil them. She pulled the laundry-room door open; she was reckless, it banged against the wall. The incinerator puffed boiled air into the apartment. Usually she let it cool down before throwing something else inside. *The incinerator is full.*

I lurched back down the stairs. My intestines welled in my gut and my stomach choked against them. *The oven is closed.* The blood trail followed into the kitchen, where Annabelle's knives lay sharp and bloodied on the counter.

"What are you cleaning up?" I asked.

"I don't want to leave here."

"What are you cleaning up?"

"There's more cough syrup in the bathroom. You're much happier—"

"What are you cleaning up?"

"Sheila. She kept making messes, pouring stuff behind the fridge. She was going to evict you, Chris."

Annabelle's arms stretched out across my chest and picked up her knives. Three of them at once. Then, as quickly as she used them to prepare dinner, she cleaned them in the sink and returned them to the rack. A sweeper ran across the floor, under my feet, and all trace of Sheila's presence in my kitchen was gone.

"Don't look in the oven," Annabelle said. I reached for the handle, but it immediately locked. "I'm cleaning it; it isn't safe to open."

I yanked, but it wouldn't budge. The temperature indicator climbed above 500°. "I had to keep her legs somewhere while I waited for the incinerator."

I pulled open the laundry-room door. The incinerator hatch was locked, and warm air radiated from the dryer. I reached up.

"Don't look in there, Chris. There's cough syrup on the table. You'll be much happier." Annabelle's mechanical arms swung at full speed upstairs, cleaning the scene that she'd left behind.

I popped the hatch. Inside, Sheila's large, hoop-metal earrings pulled her earlobes down until they rested in a warm pool of blood. Her cleanly severed head sat, mouth-agape, and stared at me. Annabelle had been precise with the cuts; Sheila's neck was flush against the dryer floor.

"I had to keep her somewhere." The chip in my head warmed. She wouldn't be bugging me anymore. *The incinerator has finished.*

THERAPY

Rob squinted at the doctor's quivering lips. Try as he might, sitting in the chair opposite the doctor's desk, Rob couldn't remember how he'd gotten there. Yet he knew this was a doctor's office and that he was supposed to be here.

"This must stop, Robert." The doctor's jaw muscles rippled as she clenched her teeth.

Rob hesitated. "I can't recall coming here."

"I know." The doctor forced a long sigh. "How much do you remember?"

Rob sank into his chair and stared at the wall behind the doctor. Nothing came to mind.

The doctor winced and shook her hair. "How many times must we do this?"

The question's distant echo didn't sound like it was directed at Rob.

"Do what, doctor?"

The doctor flashed a look in Rob's direction and, just as quickly, lowered her gaze. But it was too late; Rob had noticed something in her eyes. He wished he'd had more time to analyze what lurked there; perhaps it was anger or fatigue, but something inside Rob told him it was outright hatred. Deciding there was no reason why his own doctor would hate him, Rob brushed the thought aside.

"Tell me, Robert," the doctor said, ignoring his question.

"What do you feel?"

"Uneasiness." Rob wished he hadn't said that; he felt like it wasn't what the doctor wanted to hear.

"Why?"

"I don't know."

"Sure you do. Think, Robert. Why do you feel uncomfortable?" Something, perhaps malice, filtered in the doctor's voice, but Rob wasn't sure.

"It's Rob." He didn't like the longer version of his name.

The doctor smiled, as if getting Rob to correct her was her aim all along.

"You want mc to call you Rob?"

"Yes. I'd like that."

"Do you think we are friends?"

"I don't know. I think you can help me."

Once more, the doctor's eyes darted away from Rob. She kept her head cocked to one side, her features unreadable from where Rob sat.

"Listen to me." She turned to face Rob. "You must work with me this time; it's our last chance." The doctor's voice broke off, and she rushed her face away again.

Rob noticed her carotid artery throbbing, accelerating with each pulse. When the doctor's agitation finally eased, Rob propped himself up, resting both elbows on the arms of his chair.

"Doctor?"

"Yes, Rob?"

It felt good to be called that. He wanted to take a moment to enjoy the feeling but knew the doctor wouldn't like it.

"Do you know what is wrong with me?"

The doctor leaned back, rocking gently on her chair. Then, before Rob's eyes, she exploded into laughter. Rob found faults in the sound; it was like a stage play with a bad actress.

"Yes. I know what is wrong with you."

Rob thought that was good, excellent even. "Then you can help me?"

"No, I can't."

Rob couldn't identify the something that distorted the

doctor's voice. "Why not?"

"Because there's a difference between knowing what's wrong and figuring out how to fix it."

The doctor, her old, leathery smile, the sharp eyes, blue as a winter sky; there was truth on that face; Rob couldn't explain it, but he had faith.

"But, doctor—"

"Before you tell me what you believe, let me show you something." The doctor exhaled. Again. Rob thought there was dread behind it. "All right?"

"Yes. Anything, doctor."

The doctor swiped two of her fingers on the desktop, and the wooden pattern morphed into a black surface. A few seconds later, a virtual desktop shed bluish light on her face. A picture of herself surrounded by her family, all frozen in a moment of laughter was painted on the screen's background. Before a new window faded in the foreground, something rapped at Rob's mind. Something in the doctor's eyes and those of her entourage. Something he decided to file away for future reference, provided this amnesia didn't prevent him from retaining new information.

The doctor skimmed folder after folder. She tapped twice on each folder when once would have sufficed, but Rob thought telling her wouldn't be the wisest thing to do.

Finally, she spread an array of pictures across the desk. The subjects of these images intrigued Rob—all seventeen were of dead bodies, eyes closed and pale skins. They lay on brushed metal tables, each covered with a white cloth from the neck below.

"Who are they?"

The doctor stared at Rob, a blank expression on her face—no, not blank. Rob couldn't settle on one interpretation; flushed cheeks, flaring nostrils, forehead shining a fleshy gloss, and other details mixed into an indecipherable pattern.

"They are your victims."

Rob tried to remember, but there was still nothing.

"I don't believe that I killed them."

"How would you know?" She smiled. "You don't remember a thing."

"What reason would I have to kill these people?"

The doctor tapped on a few pictures here and there, moving her finger to skip to the next; a young black man, athletic; an elderly white lady with a lazy eye; two Asian teenagers, probably a couple; and others, different ethnicities and genders, no apparent correlation. But, there had to be. If Rob had killed these people, there had to be a reason.

"Doctor?"

"Yes, Rob?"

"Am I crazy?"

The doctor smiled a smile Rob thought he recognized, but again, he wasn't sure. "No, Rob. You are…not well."

A good doctor wouldn't call their patient crazy anyway; so perhaps Rob was insane after all. What rational reason could he have to kill people he didn't even recognize?

"Rob, do you know what your job is?"

He shook his head.

"You are my assistant."

This explained the source of the longing Rob felt for the doctor's recognition or validation or affection. No, perhaps not affection. Attention.

"What happen—"

"Would you like to know what these people have in common?"

Rob nodded feverishly. "Yes, very much."

The doctor brushed the pictures aside and opened other folders. In a matter of seconds, various files, depicting livelier faces of the dead, lay in front of Rob.

"At some point of their lives, all came to me—to us, for a diagnosis."

"Are you saying I killed them because they consulted with you?"

The doctor snorted. Rob didn't like it, but he didn't protest.

"These people were ill."

Rob didn't have enough information to deduce the doctor's meaning, but he felt he was close.

"In your own, unique way, you thought you were helping them."

"Why would I kill people I wanted to help?"

"Because, you are ill too—; No, you are damaged."

"What do you mean?"

The doctor looked at Rob, not bothering to hide her face now. Rob noticed the dilated pupils, erratic eye movements, tightened jaw muscles, and sweaty forehead. He felt close to understanding what the doctor was obviously trying to convey. It was as if enlightenment dangled in front of him, but his hands were tied.

"You're a very bright assistant, Rob. You and I work together; we're one of the best genetic diagnostic teams there is." She sighed heavily and brushed a hand across her forehead. "But, the authorities are getting suspicious, starting to look our way. If you kill again, I must have you decommissioned."

And *there* was the missing clue.

Decommissioned.

"Doctor, surely you meant to say imprisoned?"

"No, I meant what I said. Decommissioned. Albeit a beautiful one, a true work of art, you are still a machine, Rob."

The doctor's pulse remained steady. Fast, but steady.

"But—I don't feel like a machine."

The doctor smiled, but the corners of her eyes didn't stretch to the sides like before. "Of course you don't. You were designed not to feel like one. But it was the patients you were supposed to fool—not yourself."

"But—"

"Your arguments are tiresome, Rob." The doctor closed her eyes as she pushed out another sigh, longer than any before it. She resumed with a mellower voice. "Since I discovered you were the killer, we've gone through the motions seven times." The doctor's gaze descended on the pictures stacked behind the glossy surface of the desk. "Every time, you promise you won't do it again, then you forget all about our conversation, and the cycle repeats itself. An amnesic robot—there must be a joke about that." For the fifth time, the doctor sighed. "Think about it. Memory loss is rarely total; people, humans always remember something, a childhood memory, a first kiss, something."

Rob thought about it. He agreed; the arguments were valid. "It is hard to integrate."

The doctor seemed to anticipate his words and shot up, a thin, pencil-sized cylinder in hand.

Rob eyed the object with suspicion as the doctor approached. "What is it?"

"A high frequency laser scalpel."

Rob sprang up at once.

"Sit down, Robert." The name was unpleasant, the order absolute.

Rob sat down.

He looked at the doctor as she knelt before him. "Are you going to decommission me now?"

The doctor didn't answer. She took Rob's hand and laid it palm up on the desk. Focusing a tiny, blue laser light, she cut a straight line from Rob's wrist to the base of his middle finger. Rob felt no pain. He looked at the cut, expecting blood that never came. The doctor put both her thumbs on each side of the wound and pulled in opposite directions. Rob watched with abundant interest. He saw white structures that looked like bones swimming in a pool of thick, translucent liquid with a milky quality. Entwined between the white sticks, there were black strings, thick in the middle and tapered at both ends.

"What am I made of?" Rob thought he ought to be pained or shocked, but he felt neither. Only intrigued.

"What are you feeling?" The doctor asked.

"Curiosity."

The doctor smiled. "Good. Curiosity is good. It's what we want."

"What am I made of?"

Rob couldn't take his eyes off his open hand, moving each finger individually, marveling as the appropriate white stick slid forward, another moving backward, the black strings changing form, all slithering through the lubricious liquid.

"Your bones are a very light carbon-steel alloy, your muscles are carbon nanotubes woven into electro-responsive fibers, and your blood, much like your skin, is a wonder of organic chemistry and nanotechnology."

"What about—"

"I will answer all your questions later, provided you don't kill again."

Rob nodded. "Why did I kill these people?"

"They had a high risk of developing a number of genetic diseases over the course of their lives."

Rob waited for the rest of the explanation, but the doctor kept silent.

"Killing them hastened their demise. That is illogical, irrational."

"How ironic it is," the doctor whispered, lowering her gaze, "that we tried so hard to make you look human, and succeeded in ways we never expected."

"What do you mean?"

"There's no explanation for what you did, Rob. Your… ahem, brain, if you can call it that, has been damaged. Just like some human brains are broken."

Rob took a few seconds to process and integrate the information, to choose the appropriate, relevant question. "How was I damaged?"

"We don't know."

"Have you fixed me?"

The doctor pushed a sixth mouthful of air out of her lungs. "This was my last trick; I hope the shock of learning what you are will trigger the desired response."

"Because otherwise you will have to decommission me?"

Her eyes widened and her mouth followed suit with a tired smile. "Yes, Rob, that's right."

When the doctor let go of Rob's skin, both ends rushed together and in a matter of seconds, they had fused, leaving only a small pool of the white goo on his intact hand.

"You can leave now," the doctor said, returning to her desk, shutting down the computer, her desk returning to its usual dark brown.

"Where should I go?"

"You can start with a visit down to our new lab. But, I

must warn you; there will be a team watching you. Unlike before, they now have permission to terminate you if you try something. Do you understand?"

"Yes, doctor. I understand."

Rob got up and made to leave. He walked to the door, but turned before he opened it.

"Doctor?"

"Yes, Rob?"

"Why did you not decommission me as soon as you found out I had killed?"

The doctor took a moment to answer, then her look sank to the floor, and she spoke in a hushed voice. "Because… you are a very expensive prototype. Big corporations paid a great deal of money to bring you to life: software, nanotechnology, pharmaceutical. To terminate you would mean ending a partnership that has helped our practice stay afloat for years." The doctor said all that while averting her eyes away from Rob, as if afraid her words were inappropriate. "We're doing a lot of good here, Rob. Can't jeopardize that."

Rob blinked the expected number of blinks. "But, doctor, what about the people I killed?"

"Very good, Rob," the doctor said, her smile returning wider, "that's what you're programmed to feel; empathy toward human beings." Then she sobered. "And it's because those were human lives you ended that this is your last chance."

"Is it a good thing?"

She frowned. "What is?"

"Empathy, doctor. Is it good?"

"Yes, Rob. It's an excellent thing."

Rob turned, opened the door, and left. He felt good, wondered why he existed and where he was, tried to remember, but there was nothing, only the doctor, her image, her voice—fragments.

When he reached the elevator, and as he pushed the call button, a splendid idea exploded into his mind. The doctor had said that empathy was good. Would it not be empathetic if Rob helped those ridden with genetic, incurable, and often painful diseases? They were doomed either way, infinitesimally small chances of a cure being made during their lifetimes. Their deaths would be slow and painful. But with Rob's therapy, all could end. Swiftly.

Painlessly.

As he closed his eyes, accessing the main server, selecting his next patient, a smile crawled across his face. With a blink, Rob severed the connection to the server. He maximized the picture on which the doctor and her loved ones were laughing. He zoomed in, framing the faces, the eyes, the irises.

Yes, Rob had been right. All members of the doctor's family presented the same speck in the same location of their irises. An average fifty-seven percent chance of developing retinoblastoma. Meticulously, combining the highest probability of developing the illness, life expectancy after experimental treatments if any were available, Rob selected the most likely candidate. Sixty-eight percent probability, weakened immune system, low pain tolerance threshold.

Rob widened his smile. The doctor couldn't have been clearer.

Empathy was good.

THE BOO HAG

When Wesley told his doctor that he was waking up every morning tired and listless, even after twelve hours of sleep, his doctor said he was most likely being visited nightly by a boo hag.

"You don't think it could be sleep apnea?"

"Doubtful."

"Diet?"

"Are you eating plenty of shrimp and grits?"

"Yes."

"Boo hag. Sure of it. How long you been living down here?"

"Six months."

"You're fresh skin. Boo hags love fresh skins down here in Low Country." The doctor rotated on his stool to write Wesley an order on his pad.

"I want you to get yourself an old-fashioned bristle broom. Stand that next to your bed. I want you to paint your window frames indigo blue. Boo hags can't stand to crawl through a window framed in indigo blue, although a desperate one will. So the broom is essential. Boo hags are obsessive compulsive and can't resist counting the bristles on a broom. It will count all night, forget about you, and you'll wake up feeling like yourself again."

Wesley rubbed his hands on his jeans. He was so tired;

everything frustrated him and made him itch, including this conversation.

"Couldn't you just prescribe me Ambien?"

The doctor was old with a small pair of glasses, which he took off like an old southerner does when he has something serious to say.

"You don't need a sedative. Your problem isn't insomnia. You go to sleep just fine. But you won't have any energy in the morning if a boo hag is sucking it out of you all night every night."

Wesley's eyes itched and his scalp itched, and he was so tired, he just wanted a pill that would solve his problem and let him get back to normal again.

"What if I took something for energy? Like Five-Hour Energy, but stronger, and for more hours?"

The old doctor smiled and shook his head. "A broom and indigo paint around your windows. Best thing for lack of energy. Try it and we'll see how you feel in three weeks."

He stood up and shook Wesley's hand. "A lot of pests on the barrier islands. Mosquitos. Alligators. Boo hags. It's just part of living down here."

###

The doctor's orders had initially frightened him, but being a college-educated Californian, Wesley was inclined to think of southerners, even those with advanced degrees, as charming but all too gullible to superstition. So before even leaving the doctor's office, he had completely dismissed the doctor's diagnosis of boo hag haunting. By the time Wesley reached his car in the parking lot, he had resolved to ask his coworker for spare Adderall. Wesley contributed his thirty-three years of good health to western medicine, not southern, and had yet to encounter an ailment that drugs could not solve.

Wesley was a respiratory therapist at a large hospital in Charleston. Although he had only worked there for six months, he had a nurse in mind who he felt confident could obtain Adderall for cash instead of a prescription.

"You look beat," the nurse said. "Use this if you like, but make sure you're getting enough private, uninterrupted sleep.

You have raccoon eyes."

Wesley shook his head. "You won't believe what this old country doctor told me was my problem."

The nurse put the cash in the back pocket of his scrubs. "Probably told you a boo hag was riding you."

Wesley's raccoon eyes widened. "You believe that nonsense too?"

"Grew up here," the nurse shrugged. "Boo hags are just part of living in Low Country. What you need is a broom with plenty of bristles and some indigo paint—"

"That's what the hillbilly doctor said!" Wesley snapped, more frustrated than he might have been were it not for the strain of weariness that made everything an effort. "You work in a hospital, man. You have to respect science. How can you believe in this voodoo foolishness?"

The nurse smiled because he had dealt with skeptical Yankees before. "Do you believe in sharks?"

"Of course," Wesley said.

"Why?" the nurse asked.

"I've seen them with my own eyes."

"At an aquarium, right? Boo hags aren't kept in aquariums. Have you seen a shark outside an aquarium?"

"No," Wesley sighed, rubbing his eyes. "But there are sharks in the ocean."

"How do you know?"

"Their teeth wash up on shore. Surfers get bit. Evidence."

"Exactly," the nurse said proudly with one finger.

"Exactly what? You have no physical proof of boo hags," Wesley said, a little too loud for a hospital.

"Of course I do. Your raccoon eyes, you sleepy bastard. Let me know when you need more meds."

Wesley swallowed an Adderall while driving home, and in ten minutes the heaviness of his eyes and ache of his shoulders were replaced by a sudden anxiousness to regain the life he once had before moving to South Carolina. He pulled into his driveway, went straight to his bedroom, and pulled his trumpet case out from beneath the pile of suitcases. He oiled the trumpet's valves and played scale exercises until his lips felt like rubber. He hadn't even changed out of his scrubs yet, but he dropped to the black-and-white tiled kitchen floor and did five sets of pushups. While down there, he realized the whole floor needed a good scrubbing, and he resolved to do so. He did fifty crunches, he played his scales on his trumpet one more time, and he ironed his going-out shirts. He felt awake and good.

He decided to go out. He would look very fine on King Street in his ironed shirt. The oyster and bourbon bars would transform into dance clubs after midnight, the music would spill into King Street, and he would be awake enough to love it. He saved lives by day. What good were his hospital victories if he could not brag about them to women? And with practice, he'd be as good a trumpet player as he used to be. He'd join a jazz band and play in bars and then the women would really come and he wouldn't go to bed until three in the morning, but he'd still wake up at six to save lives on time and he'd feel very fine. He was too young to feel so old, and he was determined to prove it.

He showered. He popped another Adderall. He shaved. He stepped out of the bathroom and the sun had completely set, leaving his bedroom entirely dark. He couldn't see, but he could smell the salt marsh air that had crept in to thicken the darkness. The window had been opened. Wesley pulled the lamp chain to light up the room.

Wesley stumbled backward when he saw it. When the light came on, the oozing raw thing froze, caught before it could reach his bed. It crawled like a dying marine on bloody elbows and knees and looked up at him suddenly, just as startled as Wesley. The thing's eyes were red, dripping puss, and almost swollen shut. It had patches of skin on what must have been a whole body at one time. Even remnants of tattered clothes soaked by blood were tied together in tourniquets to help keep the thing in one piece. Its muscles were exposed, and even before it began to retreat, Wesley saw vertebrae and phalanges and fragments of a skull that looked vaguely human. Maybe it once had been.

Wesley froze in horror, unable to breathe. But then he

wanted to murder it. This thing had invaded his home, as it undoubtedly had before, to take the energy he had spent so many nights earning honestly. He turned to the kitchen to grab a steak knife, but the boo hag slithered backward as quickly as it had come, flopping itself through the open window and down to the seagrass below to snake its way back to wherever it came from.

Wesley slammed the window shut, locked it, turned over the kitchen table and placed it against the glass. He would not go out tonight. He sat in bed with the steak knife and waited, but the boo hag did not return.

###

Wesley was the first customer at Home Depot the following morning. He walked up and down the aisles with a quick step, electrified by another Adderall, focused like a man determined to bend evil to his will. He found a steel machete in the garden section. He picked out the corn bristle broom with the most bristles. He stepped up to the only cashier at the registers.

The cashier was tall with a sharply pressed shirt and khaki pants. His nametag read Jean, and he regarded Wesley and his items with narrowed eyes.

"Are you having difficulty with a night visitor?"

The cashier wore a sweetgrass necklace from which dangled a very detailed wooden figurine of a man. Another thin piece of sweetgrass coiled like a snake around the figurine's legs and arms and neck. Wesley felt the cashier's condescension, and the figurine looked wicked against such a well-pressed shirt.

Wesley took out his credit card to make the purchase and go. "Just have some gardening to do."

"With a machete and a broom?"

Wesley didn't answer. Jean had not scanned the barcodes yet.

"I'm in a hurry."

Jean was not.

"You don't sound like you're from around here. Where are you from?"

"California."

Jean smiled good-naturedly. "Then I should tell you about the Gullah people."

Wesley sighed. In six months he had learned that southerners took too long to tell their stories. Time was as much of a commodity as money where he came from, but they didn't get that concept down here.

"The Gullah people have lived in The Low Country for longer than most everyone else. Boo hags stole many of their skins. Boo hags are broken, bloody things. They need skins to walk around at night. But when they do steal a skin, they wear it hard like anyone would wear a rented suit, returning it to its owner in the morning beaten and raw. The Gullah people couldn't let the skin snatching continue. Too many innocent Gullah were being jailed for unexplained murders. So the Gullah made a truce with the boo hag people. The Gullah agreed to let them take a sleeper's energy at night, but they had to leave the skins alone. And if a window was painted indigo, that meant that resident had no energy to spare, and the boo hag was to move on. In exchange, the Gullah offered the boo hag people one skin, once a year, every year to keep until they'd used it up. And when a boo hag uses a skin, it uses it until it's a rag and nothing more."

Wesley wanted the story to be over, and Jean could tell he was too tired to listen.

"We've kept the understanding for this long. We can't have one ignorant man from out of town ruin a contract that's held for hundreds of years. So why don't you leave the machete here and fetch yourself a can of indigo paint. Aisle nine."

Jean pointed to aisle nine.

"Just ring up the machete, man," Wesley spat. Jean fingered the figurine around his neck. He scanned the barcode on the machete and the broom. Wesley ran his credit card through the reader, and Jean asked for his driver's license. Wesley showed it to him.

"Is this your current address, my friend?"

Wesley nodded, thoroughly annoyed. He took his license back, grabbed the machete and broom and hurried to his car, frustrated with customer service and nonsense and the whole South in general.

"Good night," Jean said softly, although it was seven fifteen in the morning.

###

Wesley set the broom next to his bedside table. He lay the machete in the bed by his leg, his fingers tapping nervously on the plastic grip handle. He turned the light off but left a bluebird nightlight on in the bathroom. With the bathroom door open, a thin shaft of dim blue light escaped to illuminate the broom bristles just enough. Wesley waited, kept awake this time without Adderall, only natural adrenaline and purpose.

He heard the thing flop down from the windowsill. On its belly, leaving a dark brown smear on the hardwood floor, it made rapid progress toward Wesley's bed on elbows and knees, but then paused when it came near the broom. A hand reached out from the skinless body, three fingers of which were either missing or kept somewhere else on its mismatched collection of bone and muscle. The tip of its counting finger was bleach white and Wesley watched the finger in the blue glow slide down the first bristle of the broom as if the texture of it were a rare delight, like newborn baby hair or the velvet on a Victorian couch hundreds of years old.

Two bristles, three, and after whole minutes, four. The thing would have counted all night if Wesley had let it. Instead he gripped the machete handle and in one motion jumped to the floor while swinging the blade. He cut through diseased liver or rotten ribs or dead muscle tissue, he couldn't be sure, but the boo hag separated into two amorphous chunks, one of which squealed from a toothless mouth. Both chunks zigzagged from him like wicked earthworms, once one boo hag, now two.

Wesley chased it with his machete raised. The boo hags slithered in figure eights like crippled snakes, but too fast for Wesley when he swung the blade down once more. The blade stuck momentarily in the hardwood floor, giving the boo hags just enough time to rejoin. The two meatloaves mashed together in a hurry, lengthening and squirming straight up the wall to the windowsill. Wesley refused to lose this evil creature. He wouldn't wait up for it again. This was his apartment and his sleep was his sleep, his energy was his energy, not to be stolen. He lunged for the thing as it inch-wormed toward the window. It paused just long enough for Wesley to catch up.

He didn't see the crowbar, but felt the blow to his chest. His machete fell to the floor, and as the boo hag dropped to the seagrass two stories below, Jean threw one leg over the sill to push himself off the ladder into Wesley's apartment. He picked up the crowbar and gave Wesley another solid whack in the belly.

"Don't want to damage the face. Can't bruise the best part of the fruit."

Wesley rolled over and looked up at Jean who now had the crowbar in one hand and the machete in the other.

Wesley made a fist and punched the only part of Jean available, his foot. But Jcan was wearing leather boots, even though this was the hot and humid south, as if he had anticipated this very job hazard. He placed his boot gently on Wesley's wrist to keep him in place, removed the tranquilizer dart pistol from his leg strap and shot a dart into Wesley's back side.

Wesley cussed him and swung wildly with his other fist, but the tranquilizer was already working, and Jean held his other wrist down while the drug took its full effect.

"We owe you thanks, Mr. Wesley. There just aren't any locals willing to provide a skin to the boo hag people. Not like they used to. No one wants to make a sacrifice for their community anymore, even though it was once considered quite an honor. Everyone has painted their window frames to keep out of the whole business. We use tourists sometimes, but doing so invites investigation from northerners, and besides, tourism is good for our economy. The South needs every penny it can get! So we thank you, Mr. Wesley. Your stubbornness has made the choice very easy this year."

Wesley couldn't protest. His arms, his legs, even his lips felt heavy, and he could not fight sleep. He tried to keep his eyes open, but it was difficult, even though he felt Jean cutting his shirt and pants off with a pair of scissors, just as a trauma surgeon might when an emergency procedure needs to be performed quickly and efficiently.

###

Walking down King Street in its new skin, the boo hag felt very fine. It knew this skin was particularly handsome, because as it walked past the oyster and bourbon bars, pretty females glanced its way and smiled. Such a fresh feeling of confidence in a new skin! The first night of the year was always the best and the boo hag could not wait to celebrate.

King Street offered so many sensory delights, like females and music and the smell of fried meat. But when you find yourself in a beautiful rented Porsche, you know there is time enough to drive by pretty females and see which ones are impressed. The first thing you do is see what kind of power it has under the hood.

It walked into Prohibition, which thumped with trumpets and drums and a summer night crowd. This skin wanted bourbon. This skin was salivating for it. Perhaps it wasn't a bad idea to concede, to loosen the muscles. It ordered a double of Bulleit and gave the bartender the credit card it found in its wallet.

"A round for everyone!" the boo hag yelled as loud as it could, and everyone seated at the bar cheered. "Except this guy," it said, patting the closest male human congenially on the back.

The male turned to face it. He was young with a full black beard and a plaid shirt with sleeves rolled up to the elbows to show off muscular arms covered in red and black tattoos. The boo hag liked the contrast of colors and the intricacy. Maybe it would buy a tattoo later tonight to enjoy the thrill of pain and to give this skin the decoration it deserved.

"Why no shot for me?"

The boo hag smiled. "Because you are one ugly son-of-a-bitch. And when I say bitch, I mean bitch. What breed of canine was she and do you still suck her teat?"

The human turned as red as his tattoos and his female friend put a hand on his shoulder to hold him back. Females always seemed to try to avoid the joy of combat for its own sake.

"I think we need to step outside," the male said, standing up, demonstrating he had several inches of advantage on it.

"Gladly!"

As the female protested, the male stepped toward the front door, and the boo hag sucker punched him in the left kidney.

The tattooed male went down like a bag of bricks. The boo hag was delighted.

"Yes! This skin has been working out!"

The Prohibition's bouncer stepped forward through the customers like they weren't even there and grabbed the boo hag by the shirt lapel. The bouncer was twice its size and threw it into the street. Other humans gathered to watch the impending fight, but none of them wanted to join in. What a waste of skins. The boo hag charged the bouncer with its fist cocked. The bouncer clocked it so hard it swung completely around and smacked down, face first onto the sidewalk. The surrounding crowd gaspcd and thc boo hag fclt onc of its front teeth come loose. It pushed itself up, giggling. Blood was really gushing from its new skin's mouth and nose, staining its button shirt.

"Nice work, friend. You're one size too big for me, I think."

It waved so long to the bouncer and the crowd who were all confused that the encounter had ended so quickly. After a block, the boo hag turned to bow to the crowd, spit out the tooth, and run down King Street as fast as it could.

This skin could run! It was sweating and bleeding and it was pumping from adrenaline from the punch. And yet, this skin had plenty of fight left in it. The first night of the year really was the best. The Charleston night air was humid and the jazz was loud and the streetlights were bright and there were so many pretty females to chase and so many men to fight and it felt so good to be awake and alive.

Kayla Bashe

SAINT KATJA OF THE BLOODY HANDS

In this game, Katja was an investigating detective shivering at the memory of straightjackets, the taste of cheap beer like old sick in her mouth and one hand on her Colt. Her partner knelt to vomit green bile, and his glasses fell from his vulnerable face.

In this game, Katja ran down a twisting staircase with no end. The void-creature chasing her swallowed in spacetime and breathed out her name.

In this game, Katja had snuck into the old asylum to peek at a famous scientist's more illegal experiments. She clutched a reporter's notebook tightly in her scraped-up hand, but now strange static dripped across her vision, and the very walls were oozing blood.

In this game, Katja fled over plague-stained sepia cobblestones in the little town where she grew up. Everything wanted to kill her, especially the rusting robots, but even the little swarming gnats that stung and stung—Katja awoke, and then she awoke again. The first thing she noticed was the door handle jiggling.

In that instant her reflection blinked back at her. She saw tufts of dark hair sticking up from between the electrodes of a hasty, shoddy neural rig, all duct tape, goo, and exposed wires.

Her only companions in the small storeroom were file cabinets with drawers rusted half-open.

There was an IV needle in her arm; maybe this game would start in a hospital. She wiggled it out as best she could, gritting her teeth against the pain, and ripped out the electrodes so she could dive under the desk.

The door began to open.

It was like the game with the robots. They had been all wonky metal eyes and frayed fur paws and chomping smiles. Robots who wanted to stick their heads inside to tear and screech. Where was her matching metal mask? She curled into a little ball.

The wires pressed against her nose. There was dust, too. This game had a good simulated reality system. It would make her death even more painful. Footsteps came closer and closer still; knees met carpet as a figure reached in—

No room to run. Her only weapons were ten ragged fingernails. She lunged out from under the desk anyway. Experience had taught her that if it looked human, you could usually go for the eyes and mouth.

A warm, tanned hand caught her wrists. "Easy now, Katja. I'd kind of like to keep my face." It was a human man. His lithe dancer's body had a dark-gold glow of health. Not dying; not wounded. At least, not yet.

"How do you know my name?"

"I know much more than that. I'm a friend. Katja Morena. Twenty three years old, game-magician, resident of Venus-Moscow. Come on, we need to get out of here."

Some games gave her allies, whether recruited or there outright. She always got attached to them. Then they were tortured, corrupted, or killed. But it was so nice to have someone on her side that she tended to fall for the trap anyway, and hate herself for the way she cried afterwards. She moved out from under the desk and pulled herself up.

Her knee popped when she stumbled. The pain of it felt so localized—nothing like a hit to a health bar, which was an electric shock all over her skin.

The man must have heard her wince. "Up you go, Katzchen," he murmured and swept her into his arms.

She looked up at his kohl-lined eyes. "If you're the tutorial level, shouldn't you be teaching me how to work the controls?"

He took a breath. "This isn't a game."

The end of the game. It would explain why she felt so shaky, so strange and weak. Why everything had so much texture and depth. She didn't know who she was or where she was. If this was reality, how would she cope? If this wasn't reality, what would it feel like to die here?

She swore and bit her fist.

"I know it's a lot. But we can handle this together. Do you remember my name?" He asked.

She tried out the first syllables that came to mind. "Zefesh?"

"That's right. You know me."

He carried her down to a subway. Subways were usually difficult levels, full of creatures that lurched and shambled, low on medkits and sun-shafts or extra batteries. She squeezed her eyes tight shut, hoping for a soft reset. Impressions filtered into her consciousness like a cutscene she could only watch: Clear drizzly fall air that felt fresh and cold on her cheeks, followed by the bump-bump- bump of being carried up stairs.

"You can open your eyes now, Katzchen. We're home."

Katzchen felt like a term used to refer to her, but what was home? The door flew open—she tensed with sudden nausea—but it was only a curvy woman with a puff of dark hair.

The woman clapped a hand to her mouth and rushed towards the pair.

"Fearless, foolish little—god, I'm so glad to have you back!" Katja liked the way this woman smelled when she leaned over her, like mangoes and raspberries and spilled honey—too sweet to clean up. "Zefesh, tell me you called the police."

"Yes, but I took her from the scene as soon as I could. I didn't think she could handle questioning, and if they found out about the three of us living together, they'd probably just write her torture off as a sexual escapade gone wrong."

The woman's deep brown eyes fixed on Katja. "Do you remember anything from before the simulation?"

"No. Who are you?"

She smoothed a hand over Katja's hair, then turned her attention to picking the electrode gel from the shaved patches. "My name is Miranda Grace. I'm… a friend."

Two people showing kindness to her. She could have stayed like this for hours, except she knew it wouldn't last. A voice in the back of her mind, honed through in-game months of practice, whispered that she should look for a weapon and start gathering supplies.

"Can she handle solid food?" Miranda asked. Her voice was deep and melodic, like a cello.

"She's been on an IV for nearly two weeks. I'd start her out with something easy, like soup."

Two weeks…it had only been that long? She felt as if she'd lived whole extra lives.

"I can do that. I've been stress-cooking like anything."

As they went inside, Katja took in every detail. Artificial sunlight from a heat lamp played within the branches of an electric tree as its leaves flashed pale pink and blue. She had a vague memory of a flag in those colors, with a rainbow-striped flag beside it, waving in sunlight on a summer afternoon.

Cinnamon-cookie scent wafted sweet and bright through the air, and there was a poster that said "Take Your Meds" in binary code.

It was an artists' apartment, Katja thought as she sipped dill-cucumber soup. The space of people without much money, but with plenty of love. *I could stay here forever.* Then, *no*, she thought, dropping the spoon and pressing her eyelids hard. She wanted to reset the game. This was the cutscene before the world twisted into horror. These people were NPCs. She'd have to protect them, or steal from them, and then she'd watch them die. She'd not only grieve for them when they were gone, she'd work to save them even at the cost of her own life.

Soon, the lights would flicker and the world would change. Then the game would begin. She finished the soup as quickly as she could.

"Come on, you need some sleep."

Maybe the game would be set in this building. It would have a time loop and a thousand more floors and geometry that made less and less sense. It would have endless copies of these two trying to kill her. If she jumped off the balcony she could end the simulation before it began—unless it was the kind of game where you couldn't force a hard reset through your own death.

Still, she knew she wouldn't be any good in a fight until she filled her rest meter. She let the pair shepherd her to bed, vaguely aware that exhausted shivers suffused her like poison in wine.

Zefesh tugged a warm patchwork quilt over her.

"There, now," Miranda Grace murmured. She cupped Katja's face and kissed her forehead.

For a moment Katja was not afraid, only breathing, and she gathered that quiet peace about herself like a cloak.

"Good night," Zefesh told her, smoothing the pale curve of her shoulder. A memory flashed into her consciousness: another set of hands pinning her down, ripping off her raincoat as she screamed. But these hands felt different. They made her feel safe.

When she awoke it was much later, and all had gone dark. Something was breathing in the hall.

She would have to sneak past it. The game had begun.

If she wrapped her blanket around herself, her health meter would go up and she could stop shivering, but it might hurt her stealth. If she stayed in this room, she'd starve to death; if she went out, the room would no longer exist to return to. Could she get a decent ranged weapon?

Would she have supplies? This period of safety had seemed so real…

Better now than never, Katja thought. If she waited, she would lose her nerve. Maybe the pillow would make a good melee weapon. She tucked it into the circle of her arms and slipped out of bed. Sneaking through the corridor, she heard voices from another room.

Footsteps vibrated through the floorboards as Zefesh paced. "What I don't understand is, who would want to harm

Katja? From what I hear, my contacts in the police department are stuck for leads. She's never received a single death threat, not even on her public profile. Her work isn't even political, and her simulations can't be used to hijack hardware. She's just a girl from the plains who makes good games."

Miranda let out an audible sigh. "We'll figure this out. Remember, I'm here for you, both of you, no matter what."

Zefesh chuckled. "You're a queen, you know that?"

"If I'm a queen, then you're my consort."

Katja peeked in to see Zefesh and Miranda sitting on batik-printed beanbag chairs. He caught Miranda's hand and turned it up and kissed it, right in the center of her palm. When he lifted his head, their eyes met; heat grew between them with their smiles. Katja wanted to burn with that same fire, but what if the lovers' faces dilated open to reveal strange creatures inside?

What did her memory files have to say about this? There wasn't love, in the games.

If I was really still in the game, she thought, *things would have started by now. For hours the shadows would have been lengthening; there would be reports of infections on the TV, or I'd be in a spaceship in the middle of an unexplored sector.*

She could join that circle of light and love, fall asleep near the people she was sure she'd once known. Or sprint back to her bed and shiver under the covers, contemplating how every facet of her identity had melted into simple fear.

But she could repaint herself with words and images, reset the legend of herself and start anew.

She'd created whole worlds every day in her past; if she could create, she could adapt. She took a deep breath, felt her shoulders roll down her back, and padded towards them.

"Hey, you," Miranda cooed in her beautiful low voice.

Katja felt more human almost at once. "I couldn't sleep."

"Are your memories coming back?"

She shook her head. "It might help me if you told me about them." She wanted to hear the kindness flowing in the melody of how they spoke.

"It was the first day of our neuromagician classes. You were wearing a little knit cap…" Miranda began. "Sepia and sand and autumn reds."

A memory sparked into place, and Katja reached up to her ears as if still wearing her favorite hat.

Zefesh shifted onto his heels, wiggling bare toes on the carpet. "And I remember you telling me that she looked like a refugee waif from an old film."

Miranda nodded with a gleaming smile. "And then you started talking, and you were insightful, brilliant. Like that moment when an orchestra melds into tune—once you said something, it made sense. And I turned to him, and I said—"

Katja, remembering, said it along with her. "Can we keep her?"

"And then we all went out to lunch. Do you remember what you had?"

Telling the story made it real. "A lemon tart, the size of my head. I'd skipped breakfast. I think I was afraid because no one like me had ever made it to the academy before."

"Yes, you're from the nomadic people on the plains," Miranda said, her face bright. "That evening the city's electricity grid had blackouts, but you just shrugged and lit a candle."

She was the only neuromagician from the plains. Was that why she had enemies? But even though programs could be used to hurt people by making their smart tech backfire, nothing about that danger seemed familiar. Following the algorithmic swirl of her own thoughts, Katja drifted into sleep amidst voices and firelight, hands stroking her hair.

Someone had put her to bed; sunlight was filtering through the curtains, cold and clear as spring water. She remembered strange dreams: running through a narrow street at midnight, a tall figure capturing her by the fringe of her scarf. Were these images from virtual reality, or clues as to what had happened beforehand? She still felt uneasy, but she didn't want to think about it. She went barefoot into the kitchen, opening curtains as she went. Zefesh stared thoughtfully out the window, a mug of steaming tea in his hand (pomegranate, her memories told her) and she went up and hugged him from behind.

"Hey, you."

"Hey, you too," he said, turning around to hug her properly. That felt familiar.

"I missed you even when I didn't know there was a you to miss," she whispered back.

Miranda, passing through the kitchen, called out to them. "I'll see you after my research trip, yeah? I'm going to the concert park to feel the sound. Just let it wash over me, see what it inspires."

She patted Katja on the shoulder, then departed in a flutter of synthetic silk scarves.

"What do you want to do today?" Zefesh asked.

I've been working on a game, she remembered. "I want to work on what I was making before I…left."

###

None of her game-prisons had possessed a hacking mechanic. She remembered how lost she'd felt when she couldn't uplink to technology. Her work allowed her to step back from what she was feeling and transform her experiences into something she could understand and share. She touched the smooth plastic contours of her equipment, exploring the familiar texture of each piece. Putting on her coding rig felt like coming home.

Her project was an immersive quest about plains witches gathering on the mountains to perform the springtime ritual of friendship and love. They had to solve puzzles to gather wildflowers from a river's warm banks. Similarly, Katja found lots of problems to fix.

Here she'd been too hasty and imprecise in her thought coding of wildflowers. She pinched each petal into individuality, imagining the flower's scent and shape. Other neuromagicians grew up with the latest technology; they hadn't needed to proofread instructional sims to raise their school fees. But she'd grown up picking wildflowers. They could only aspire to her sensory uniqueness and whole-bodied authenticity.

Her heartbeat accelerated, pride turning into instinctive fear. Was that why someone had wanted her dead? A flash of recollection: a round face twisted in rage. The memory hung in her game's landscape like a menacing wraith.

Katja pressed her fist to her mouth. She wanted to bite her nails, but the coding rig covered her face and the sensitive gesture pads buzzed on her fingers.

The wraith still hovered there, absurdly large. She shook her head repeatedly, a programmed shortcut—delete, delete, delete.

She gestured the simulation into playback, studying the interactions between the characters, and stopped it when something occurred to her. Maybe the character who never spoke could have a service dog. Yes, and that way the sidequest outlined "create the plot of this later" could be recovering the dog when it fell into a hollow tree—and then the first two characters to spot its tracks could share a moment, maybe even fall in love!

Sometimes crafting a game felt like archaeology, brushing treasures from the clay. Details were vital. Which breed of dog should the youngest witch have, for example? She'd have to think about their owner's aesthetic motifs before choosing one.

Her perspective sailed through the simulated world like a creator deity, each blade of grass becoming brighter in her wake.

Yet something felt absent from her work. In the light of creativity, all her nightmares seemed like half-formed clay. She wanted to roll them in her hands, pinch out tentacles and eyeballs. For the first time, she realized the true importance of unhappiness.

I want to turn pain into art, she realized. *I want to make a game that will feel like a phantom touch between the shoulder blades, an unwelcome visitor at night.*

But I want to blend fear and hope.

She studied the genre's motifs with a practiced eye. Invisible footsteps in dark water; creatures with many twisted limbs. Abandoned towns built over smoking pits and rust-colonized abandoned hospitals filled with whispers of souls. A long-dead child crying for help. This, too, was magic.

The plains legend of cannibal skeletons had always frightened her as a child. Maybe, instead of a celebration, the ritual could be a defense against this evil. She could saturate her color palette with suspense and program a shifting creature in the shadows. "And a jumpscare," she murmured into her notes file. "Livestreamers love jumpscares."

She felt wonderfully exhausted when she at last unclipped her rig.

Zefesh was sitting beside her.

"Why were you watching me?"

"You looked happy."

I still am, she thought, and said, "Let's go make lunch."

Miranda had already returned, and she'd thrown together some leftovers to make sandwiches. Katja's flesh-and-blood body, with its little creaks and itches, its subtlety of sense, felt much richer than her simulated frame. As she ate, she couldn't help but glance at Miranda and Zefesh, the way they touched each other's hands. Was she in a relationship with one of them, or just a roommate? She could imagine them not wanting to force an amnesiac girlfriend into an uncomfortable situation, but she could also imagine being the third wheel. They had been affectionate with her, but they were also affectionate with each other. Sometimes she wished she could put a captcha on her thoughts: Not every attractive person is poly, and not every girl likes girls. Miranda's colorful highlights absolutely fit the latest queer trend, but maybe she was just a very fashion-forward straight trans woman. The uncertainty made Katja feel uncomfortable.

Another flash of memory: *I always journal on the roof.* She murmured an excuse and ducked out of the apartment.

She was deep in her list of game ideas when a man in flashy American-made jet boots swerved to a landing on the roof. She recognized him at once; her hurt leg throbbed, her body clenched. "You're him, aren't you? You're the one who put me in the simulation."

He tipped his head in a mock bow. "I assume you remember why we're enemies—or is that too taxing for your software?"

Overwhelming images pounded her head. She caught her breath. Righteous anger. Hurt and surprise. "You planned to make a game about the plains people, but I got wind of it. You made it seem like we all burned sheep dung for fuel and didn't know how to read. So I took a month off from my studies and programmed all day and all night—and I released my game first, just to prove you wrong."

He shrugged. "If you're a true artist, no one cares who you are or where you come from. My game would have been more exciting and marketable. It would have confirmed all the ideas people already held. But now when I bring up my game, they think of yours. You and your precious authenticity stole my funding away!"

With a quick secret gesture, Katja tapped at her wristband computer to send a SOS to the house, but it didn't seem like anyone was answering. He was between her and the stairs, and it wasn't like she could climb down the side of the building. "You kept me for weeks, put me in horror stories until I didn't know which life was real. Isn't that enough?"

Within a moment, he was at her side, kneeing her onto the hard concrete. "No! This has repercussions. You need to make up for what you've done."

If he could knock her back out, he could steal her away from here and shove her back into the game. This time, where would she be held? This time, how long would she stay sane? The possibilities made her mouth dry.

"My programming misses you, Katja. I want you back."

Running footsteps, then the hatchway slamming open as Miranda and Zefesh emerged, breathless, onto the roof. Katja crawled away in the distraction.

"Get out of the way, Katzchen. Let us handle this." Zefesh threw a holographic blast of code at him. It was a sharp loop, meant to trap and entrance.

The man wobbled, but managed to fend off the worst of the blow.

Miranda slipped her most entrancing work into his digital glasses, eternal images of rainbow procedural generation that could hypnotize any passerby.

It engulfed him like a fog, but he brushed it away. He twisted their simulation fragments into a cruel parody and thrusted back at the pair. Their bodies jerked and they toppled, still twitching.

"Just a minor electric seizure," he assured Katja. "It's not them I want. It's you. Because you're still in the game." He smiled as if expecting this to be a fait accompli. Yesterday, maybe, she might have fallen for it—but not today.

The city smelled like smoke and the ground under her feet was hard and uneven, not a repeating texture. There wasn't a lag time, or gray space at the end of the map, and her body felt quick yet weighted, like the opposite of a dream.

"I don't think the game is truth," she said. "I think I am."

A corner of his mouth arced sharply down in disappointment, but he played it cool with a shrug.

"All right. You're not in the game… by which I mean, you're not in the game yet." He reached into his pocket and pulled out the data of an atomic geometric sphere that seemed to expand and contract in its hand. Colors swirled through its being: red, black, grey. "I say we fight. Your game against mine, Katzchen." He said the nickname with a mocking sneer. "I'll even let you go first. But I really can't resist telling you, just because you'll forget again in a moment: they were your lovers. Both of them. And I want to watch your face as the memories slip away forever."

And, just as he predicted, she remembered. Lazy afternoons in a tangle of sweaty blankets, elbowing each other as they laughed through gimmicky, multiplayer setups. The infinite thrill of that first kiss; the quieter, deeper pleasure of finding *I love you* beneath ordinary sentences like, "I'll find you better headphones," or "Don't forget to work out." But those memories didn't weaken her or cause her to despair. They gave her even more reasons to fight.

Her witchy game was close to hand; it could be rolled into a bullet as sharp as pine needles and solid as quartz. But for this confrontation? It would dissolve into sunbeams as soon as it got close, she knew; it felt too easy and too light. Even its complicated code would merely distract him, and it wouldn't hold his attention long enough for her to fetch help. Encapsulated in her feelings was the seed of a game—she sought it out. She drew from the most secure files in her personal system: Zefesh's precise physics coding, Miranda's automated poetry. Her eyes and hands moved in a complex ballet as she blended it with the concept art from her own nightmares.

The game's story was about a girl trapped in the city of her body by a spreading disease. The player needed to stealth dodge through plague-pockmarked streets. But even in the poorest of quarantined areas, NPCs would help if you showed kindness. She knew it would take years for him to beat this game. Yes, its morbid horror-show details, just like the gore he loved so much, would fascinate and enthrall—but its empathy mechanics would seem an incomprehensible maze, leaving him mystified and furious and full of spite.

Because the only way you could beat this game was if you were kind. If you understood what it was like to be afraid.

She was the survivor, the small one, the one who hid and fled and watched gamepeople die. But all her fear had made her strong.

She named her game *Saint Katja of the Bloody Hands* and blew the data towards him like a cloud of germs.

He blinked—and fell.

###

"I don't think he knew how fast I'd recover," she told Miranda Grace and Zefesh later. "He didn't expect me to come back to myself, but now… I feel like I can do anything." And now she was free. Free to cuddle and create and hack, to explore the parameters of digital truth, with one hand in a lover's and the other starting up a keyboard dream.

Andrew Nelson

HEARTLESS

Case cranked with one gloved hand while he felt the last guy-wire pull tight against his other. He didn't hear a twang in the nearly absent atmosphere. He knew he should be doing this some other way than manually, but since this wasn't an approved mission, and not even his area of expertise, nearly every operational asset on Mars was unavailable to him. If he'd had any authorization, he could have asked one of his AMCs to do it. His primary companion, and his partner in this undertaking, looking like anyone else in his EVA-suit, waited to the side of the monstrous satellite dish, as closely as his programming would allow to this unsanctioned activity.

"Not a problem after all." Case spoke softly into his helmet.

"You've done as well as you could. We need a more long-term solution." His partner nodded, the tinny-sounding radio crackling for a split second.

"Thanks, Alex. Your encouragement is always appreciated. We won't have time for a longer-term solution if our luck runs out. We've been on our own for a while now."

"It is you who has kept us all going. You have maintained your responsibilities well by yourself. You should not blame yourself for these setbacks."

Case looked down and stared at his footsteps in the dust coating the dish surface. "Don't you worry about that. How's the power-up going?"

"Initializing with the main, reception should be online by the time we are back in comms."

Case had only taken two steps when he suddenly felt the dish vibrating under his feet. The dust appeared to levitate and, looking up to the subreflector, he saw that its lights were on.

"Sir, I don't understand—" The voice paused and Case felt his stomach drop. Alex rarely uttered such a statement, and it was never a good sign. "Caretaker, evacuate the dish immediately!"

Case started a sprint for the center of the dish where Alex stood at the access hatch with his hand outstretched. His footing jumped sideways as the dish abruptly started its rotation. Case scrambled a few feet on all fours before getting back to his feet.

"First mooring failed, northeast wire compromised." Alex didn't have his hand out—he was pointing at one of the guy-wires.

Case's helmet cut off all peripheral vision, so he turned far enough to see the wire for only a second before turning back to Alex. The taut cable disintegrated. Alex simultaneously toppled backward and disappeared inside the maintenance hatch.

Case followed, grabbing the corner of the hatch as he jumped and pulling it closed behind him. Alex was struggling to sit up using his left arm. His right shoulder was split open to his collarbone, revealing organic components and leaking fluid. His right arm hung loosely but his gaze was unfazed. Above them, the dish stopped moving and began shifting its azimuth.

"Your attachments were inadequate for building the tower up here," Alex said.

"And you know there wasn't anywhere else I could build it!" Case felt light-headed and realized he was gulping in air. "I'm sorry. Are you going to be okay? I can't lose you too." He began probing through the damaged suit and the ruined remains of circuits underneath.

"You have nothing to be sorry about, and I will continue."

"I can't believe this is happening now. You're right—I shouldn't have built here—but if I was allowed to req more than a single tank of oxygen, I could've gone onto any one of these lousy mountains to build it. But I can't. I can't do anything. I can barely keep this place or any of you alive since the MTO abandoned us here."

"Mars Teleplanetary Operations does not understand the severity of our situation," Alex quipped, as if he'd been programmed to defend them.

"Stop that. If only they'd seen fit to grant me a little better rank than janitor of this damn technological marvel you've built, then I'd be able to do something!" Case glanced around as the dish finished its motion and rested silent once more. "Let's get you down to the shop. I don't care what you think, I want to get you fixed up before anything else crazy happens."

Alex rose effortlessly to his feet. "I can reach the shop on my own. Furthermore, you will be pleasantly surprised that there appears to be a new message awaiting you at Comms."

Case froze. "You've got to be kidding? Nothing for so long…I thought they were gone."

"I think you will be happy. There is no doubt that this is a real communication."

"Just tell me what it says then!" He waited impatiently, but Alex only stared back at him. "What? What's the matter?"

"Unfortunately, I am unable to open the message. It is directed specifically to the Caretakers, and as such, it cannot be relayed or decrypted by anyone but you."

"Those bastards!" Case clenched his hands into fists and screamed his frustration into his helmet until his throat was hoarse and his ears hurt. "Great that they didn't obliterate themselves after all and they're back to controlling every stupid thing here, when they're a billion miles away?"

"Sir, I believe you will feel better when you have read the it. Do not worry about me, I can make my own way to replace my suit, and I am stable. Go." Alex still met Case's look patiently.

"Alright," Case conceded with a nod. "Come see me in the control room as soon as you can. This better be something special."

Case turned and started down the maintenance gantry, picking up speed the further he got from Alex. He was running by the time he got to the roof airlock. He peeled off his suit and dropped the pieces haphazardly as he bounded to the elevator. It only took him another minute to ride down to sublevel and get to the primary control room. He started keying in his login automatically as he took the single seat at his desk, and his monitor jumped to life.

###CARETAKER EYES ONLY###

Pioneer fleet 1-46 entering Mars orbit in 12 hours. De-orbit burn in 24 hours. ETA 24:22. Recall all exo-vehicular assets to primary control points. Stand down all terraforming routines. Terminate all Autonomic Mechanical Colonist immediately. Terminate Gen4 manufacturing immediately. Confirm immediately.

Richard Drax
VP of Mars Teleplanetary Operations

Michael Arsenault
President of Mars Teleplanetary Operations

Gregory H. Michelin
President, Federated Earth Territories

###CARETAKER EYES ONLY###
END MESSAGE

So many things were wrong with the transmission, Case didn't even know where to start. He jerked his trembling hands away from the keyboard, his mind racing through the dispatch. Why would pioneers be inbound when he hadn't received any updates from Earth for months? They could have let him know. They could have at least asked. Nothing was ready. He wasn't ready. He looked down at his uniform, knees and sleeves scuffed and almost threadbare. It had suited him fine for years, but that's when he'd been alone. Why only hit him with the realization that he would go from the sole living inhabitant of Mars to 1 in possibly 100,000 or more people in just over a day?

He rolled his chair sideways from comms to ops so he was facing the realtime operations master console. Why stop everything when the population of a whole country was just about to land? There were over 500 sectors in critical production stages. An atmosphere just didn't appear in specific sections of a planet while the rest stayed in a vacuum. If the AMCs were forced to abandon their work, there was no telling what would collapse in a day. He had been here for 21 years. He had worked hard for 21 years. He had stood up two entire generations of AMCs and brought Mars to near-inhabitable status. He had outlived every other single caretaker on this empty planet, and now MTO wanted to jeopardize everything on a moment's notice?

He rolled back to the comms monitor, shaking his head as he went. This was the first message *ever* signed by anyone but his immediate supervisor. And it was signed by a quorum of the most powerful people still alive on the earth. He paused. Counting himself, the three people on the transmission, and 100,000 or so colonists—by his last report, and that was over a year ago since Earth had let him read their news—there were only 14 million people left in the Territories. He hadn't heard anything. They could all be on their way and he wouldn't know.

He swiped the message window to the side of the monitor and typed in some queries that used to be part of his daily ritual. They hadn't worked for a long time. He'd thought the comms were done. Everything had checked out on his end. He'd had the AMCs check every screw in each comms tower. They had even been creative enough to find enough spare parts to build a temporary relay satellite. All for nothing, just static.

The queries ran quickly through their sequence:

SYSTEM READY
ANTENNA READY
UPLINK READY
RELAY READY

CONNECTION OPEN

Case waited patiently while his interrogative was sent through space.

CONNECTION REFUSED

He was not surprised at all. The expected response was just as much a part of the routine.

"What did the missive say from Earth?" Alex asked, entering the room.

Case didn't respond. He glanced up as AMC-1017 crossed the room slowly to stand behind the monitors. He'd changed clothes, and though his damaged arm hung limp by his side, he resembled a perfect human male specimen. But beneath those light blue eyes, short-cropped brown hair and red-tailored uniform was a fully automated mechanical colonist. Case had worked with AMC-1017 for 4 years. Long enough to call him Alex, as AMC-1017 had requested. Long enough that Alex was his best friend on the entire planet. Long enough that Alex had saved his life, twice.

"The message wasn't from Earth." Case said. Alex stared straight ahead, not looking down at the screens where Case felt his gaze being drawn. He worried that Alex had seen the message, that with the arrival of all of those people, he would be less alone than he had ever been since leaving Earth. He wasn't sure what to do at that moment. He wanted to tell Alex about the message. He definitely trusted Alex more than any of those fancy titles held by people who had sat on Earth all of these years while he'd risked his life out here. People who'd ignored him while production systems failed, meteor strikes almost reduced everything to rubble, and while his assigned partner had taken decided to give up and take his red dirt nap.

"You patched up fast," he finally said to Alex "I'm glad you're here." He swiped the message contents from the screen. "Too bad we didn't even get a chance to activate my antennae. We still don't know what's going on with the North Pole grid."

"The new countermeasures are operational. I can report that the southern pole grid is also linked and ready. You should be able to access them. Along with the comms re-activating, the mainline antennae have redeployed, and we can sustain telemetry." Alex smiled and looked relaxed, swinging his undamaged hand casually behind his back.

It only took a minute at his terminal to see that Alex was correct. Case added the new systems display to the primary ops wall, which illustrated every functioning system on the planet and highlighted any current issues. Both poles were green and pulsed their light outward to the edges of the screen.

"Your last estimate had operational readiness weeks away? I thought we still had time here?" Case was caught off guard and tried to think back to their timetable.

At this point, Alex did look concerned and Case became wary. Alex walked around the monitors so there was nothing between them.

"After all the issues we've faced together, Case, we knew how much this would mean to you. The way that the strikes have decimated the peripheral as well as the core units has kept you from sleeping for a month."

What Alex didn't mention, *who* he didn't mention, was Findeman. Even with round-the-clock issues, meteor strikes, power fluctuations, dust storms and lack of fresh materials, there should have been someone else sharing all of this responsibility. Findeman should have been there to share the rotation. Except Findeman had fallen apart. When the first systems had failed, Findeman found a way to fix them. When the early solar grid collapsed and they had to sacrifice most of their terraforming equipment, Findeman figured out a way to survive. He restarted the mining operations and seemed to have a sixth sense of where systems would crash. It wasn't until the communications cut off that Findeman gave up and took his cyanide tablets.

Case looked at the second control center, identical to his, across the room. There were the same number of monitors, keyboards and equipment, clean but empty. The screens showed some logging and telemetry information but otherwise were bereft of activity. The chair had not been moved since the last time Findeman got up and walked out the door.

"I...appreciate your concern, Alex. You're always looking out for me." Alex just nodded his head, and Case gestured for him to speak. It seemed like he was waiting for something.

"The sensor arrays have now resynched and catalogued the extra-orbital tactical fields. We found something headed directly for Mars and decelerating," Alex said.

Case broke eye contact and looked back at the systems screen, as if expecting the inbound ship should already be visible. "Do you know if it's a ship from Earth?" he asked, wondering how much Alex and the AMCs had already investigated. He began typing his own inquiries with the new North and South Pole grid searches.

"We know that its trajectory, velocity and range indicate it is beyond the standard XL-class interplanetary cruiser. However, it has not identified itself, nor can we ascertain any of the standard beaconing or wave telemetry as our equipment—" Alex stopped and Case immediately looked up. He could count on a single hand the number of times Alex had been stumped and at a loss for words, and now twice in the same day. This scared him just as much as the implications of the message he'd received barely an hour before.

"The equipment is now behaving erratically whenever we attempt a fresh scan," he finally finished.

"You just said NP-SP ops were up?" Case's hands flew over the controls, but his own commands weren't returning anything useful at all.

"We have tested the system thoroughly. We cannot determine what is wrong."

"What is your guess?"

"Given our terraforming is in medium probability to completion, this could be a replacement ship with fresh supplies and equipment to ensure our success. However, if its communications equipment was damaged somehow, we would not have observed such irrational behavior from our scans. Given our inability to reach Earth through long-range comms for such a long time, we believe that the existing political and societal infrastructure may have undergone some sort of revolution, and this ship is here to replace any remaining assets of that society with their own."

"You mean me," Case said.

"All of us here. We were created by that society. If it has been defeated, annihilated or otherwise overthrown, we are relics of that society and potentially seen as a threat. If what happened on Earth radically expended their sparse remaining resources, they would need to move quickly to insure their own survival."

"Alex, do you trust me?" Case locked eyes with Alex once again and sighed as he waited.

"Of course, sir." There had been hesitation. If it had been his first days on Mars, if it had been before everything had fallen apart, Case would have seen that hesitation as a lie or a flaw. But he had come to understand the AMCs—their programming and thinking—and he felt sincerity in that pause. Alex had pulled him from the early landing wreckage. Alex, who was perfectly capable of continuing the mission on his own, had repeatedly made allowances to keep Case alive.

Ironically, Case was well aware that the programming in the AMCs was governed by rendering the viability of all Mars' operational assets, and Case was only there as a courtesy; a perfunctory nod to an earlier age of machine operators that had to fix a constant backlog of equipment failures. The AMCs had been programmed for operational independence. They were capable of terraforming Mars on their own. They could rebuild each other, rebuild every single piece of equipment on this planet if they needed to, and Case had struggled early on with why anyone had even bothered sending him, when he was ultimately expendable and practically useless in the planetary conversion timetable.

"I need you to conduct a complete visual examination of the emergency backup datacenter." Case avoided eye contact, hoping Alex didn't see through the fact that he only needed him to leave for a while. He needed time to think. "I need to figure out what is coming at us, and I need you to make sure we can withstand whatever that is. Please recall all AMCs to their positive control points and wait for further instruction."

"We will do as you ask." Alex did not hesitate this time until he reached the door. "Sir, whatever happens, we are with you." The portal slid open quickly and quietly and closed just as quietly after the AMC left.

Case wasn't sure whether he waited a few seconds or a few minutes, but he finally forced himself to recall the lockdown commands for the control facility and key them in. The heavy blast door slid across to cover the portal, and Case waited for his monitor to show that similar blast doors had enclosed the entire facility. External visual showed Alex and the other AMCs on their way to their habitat buildings.

He reset the comms startup procedure and diligently mapped the azimuth of the approaching colonist ship to his relay satellite. He initiated the comms protocol again with his own custodial ident, then clasped his hands together and gnawed his lips. His thoughts raced, imagining that the earlier message might have been a ploy to get him to shut down the AMCs while revolutionaries were coming to wipe them out. Inevitably, his mind was drawn to the inescapable fact that *he* was the least useful asset on this planet and this might finally be the end. Had he really been abandoned? Or was everyone he knew now dead, leaving him the last remnant of a defunct society? What a colossal failure to put his life into this and now everything was—

CONNECTION ACCEPTED
CONNECTION INITIALIZING
STANDBY

He sat back in his chair as the main ops screen went to black, before a human face came into sharp contrast and finally into clarity.

"Hello, Case."

"Markov?"

"Didn't think you'd ever see me again, did you?"

"What the hell is going on?"

"Time is short. Did you get the priority message from the execs?"

"—Yes—"

"Good, good. Is everything done? Is everything ready?"

Case pushed himself angrily to his feet to face the screen. "What the hell do you mean is everything ready? Of course it's not ready! And how will it get ready when you want all the AMCs terminated? What happened to you? What happened to Earth? TELL ME SOMETHING!"

"Calm down, man." The soothing voice of his once-upon-a-time manager just sounded patronizing. "Look, we don't need the AMCs any more. There is an entire Territorial Expeditionary Force on board here, and we have strict confidence in their abilities to take over ops and maintenance." Markov looked down and back at Case. "Command doesn't want any possibly compromised MTO assets interfering. You've been there longer than anyone. You know how, err, consistent, the AMCs are in following their programming when it comes to mission parameters."

"I thought you had colonists? I thought I was doing this for people to live? When did the military get involved?"

"The military is here because there's another ship on its way—maybe a week behind us—full of Neptune cultists who think they have us beat. They may've temporarily won Earth, but we will outfit Mars and go back to wipe them out."

Case snorted. "There was already little enough left on Earth, what is left there to go back to?"

"We need Mars, Case. We need it to win. Now, how long to finish the rest of the prep from the message?"

Case felt faint and sat back in his chair. Markov hadn't really answered anything. And this was all insane. What had really happened on Earth? Perhaps most insulting, most infuriating for Case, was now that whatever was left from the wars on Earth was headed here.

Every daily possibility of death on Mars now seemed laughable. It all seemed so mundane, compared to the stupid wars he'd thought he'd left billions of miles behind. It wanted to catch up to him. It was going to eat him alive after all. And worst, he knew with absolute certainty it would destroy everything he had built. It would make him abandon everything he had worked for and kill the only things, what he had grudgingly but ultimately come to accept as his only friends, just to continue their idiotic back-and-forth warring.

"I don't know, Markov. I can't do this."

Markov's voice raised an octave. "I realize this is a lot all of a sudden, but this is the most important assignment of your life. Let me talk to Findeman."

"Findeman's dead."

"What?" Markov swore under his breath, finally losing his composure and looking away.

Case realized he wasn't the only other party to this conversation.

Markov nodded a few times and turned back to the screen. "Alright, there's a contingency in place. The termination protocol for the AMC operations requires both global custodians to confirm the commands. The code package I'm sending you will allow you to bypass that requirement and elevate your credentials. You will have to do this on your own."

"Please. I need to think—"

"There's no time, Case! Just do your job. Remember your training, do your job, and this will all be over." Markov stopped yelling and sighed. "I'm sorry for everything you've been through. I promise when this is over, we'll sit together and have a long chat over drinks. Do this one small thing, and we can leave the rest up to the military, alright?"

"I understand, Markov. I'll do what I can."

"I know you will. Talk again soon."

The face disappeared from the screen. Case gritted his teeth. He couldn't remember the last time he'd been this furious. He walked over to the empty desk, where Findeman had given up and left him. He screamed an animalist howl as he ripped a monitor off the top and flung it into the wall. He kicked the chair over, and then kicked it again so that it banged and bounced across the floor until it hit the wall as well. Breathing deeply, he sat heavily in his own chair and spun in circles.

"What else can I do?" he asked himself over and over, stopping his spin to stare at his monitors while gripping his armrests tightly. After a moment of thought, he retracted the blast doors and opened a channel to Alex.

"Alex, I need you back as fast you can get here."

"I am on my way, Case."

A few minutes later, Alex walked in and Case locked down the entrance again, not entirely sure why except as a reflex. Or perhaps he was still afraid of what he had to decide. He couldn't make that decision alone.

"The ship out there is coming to take over Mars. There are soldiers onboard, and they're fleeing a coup on Earth. And there's actually another ship," Case rushed "And they want me to shut all of you down...permanently. I don't want to. I think they're wrong, and I think the military will ruin everything you and I and the other AMCs have built here. But those are my orders. What do you think I should do?"

Alex's head tilted slightly to the right as he blinked. "I cannot make that decision for you."

"Please? Please, just tell me what you think. You haven't had any trouble telling me about all the poor decisions I've made up to this point!"

Alex walked to the wall where the chair lay on its side. He leaned over, picked it up, and walked back to Case's desk. He set the chair on its wheeled legs and sat on it across from Case.

Case recalled the message meant for him alone and shifted the monitor slightly, waiting for Alex to read it.

"We would protect you from anything we could, Case, but we can't protect you from this. We cannot interfere with company directives," he said finally. "Without an overriding code, or in the case of contradictory directives, we must follow the original directive. We must shut ourselves down."

He smoothed his red slacks in a mundanely human way before looking back to Case. "I have sincerely enjoyed and appreciated the time we've spent here. We have shared a lot. We have built a lot. We have enjoyed working together." Again, Alex paused, assessing Case's expression. "We have learned much together. I am proud to be your friend, Case. Please do not regret the time that we have had. Please, take your time. We understand how hard this must be for you. I will return to my control point and instruct the others as well."

Alex stood and held out his hand. Case took it somewhat limply at first, but then stood as well and hugged him. He felt Alex pat him gently on the back and then walk to the door.

"Best wishes, sir," he said as Case opened the door and he exited the room.

Case sat at his desk, alone, hot tears pushing at the back of his eyes. He'd been so sure of himself, of his mission, but now…

He had hated the wars on Earth. He had hated the company, but for the chance they took to send him here. He had hated that they had put him here with Findeman, who knew everything except how to keep going when it really. Then he thought of how all of that was about to be repeated, and he hated that too.

Maybe he was more like Alex than not. Maybe being a robot wasn't about mechanics, but about always being told what to do.

The AMCs' tracking units showed that their recall logistics were nearly complete. At the edge of the planetary ops screen, he now saw a blip with telemetry that never quite resolved itself. The pioneer ship represented the end of his duty here.

Case brought up the never before opened documentation instructing him how to shut down the AMCs. He felt empty and numb as he typed in the unfamiliar commands. After only a few preparations, his central login console glowed red and a window appeared on his monitor, instructing him that both he and his partner needed to be present to accept the shutdown runbook. Looking across the other decimated desktop, he saw Findeman's identical login console glowed red as well.

Switching to a different monitor, he brought up the new message package that had been sent by the approaching military vessel. He didn't understand exactly what was included, but running the commands to import it completed successfully. Immediately, the other login console changed its light to green, and laying his own hand on the console changed it to green as well.

MODULES ACCEPTED
SAFEGUARDS REMOVED
PRIVILEGES GRANTED
OWNERSHIP GRANTED
MAINTENANCE ACCESS GRANTED
AMC LIVE ACCESS GRANTED
IO ACCESS GRANTED
SYSTEMS ACCESS GRANTED
CONFIRM AMC SYSTEM SHUTDOWN?

He had never seen anything like it before. He was about to press 'Y' when he stopped and glanced around. Maybe there was another way to do this. He pressed 'N' and went through his Earth communication protocols.

SYSTEM READY
ANTENNA READY
UPLINK READY
RELAY READY
CONNECTION OPEN
CONNECTION GRANTED

ENTER EARTH CONTACT RELAY TO ESTABLISH

He laughed suddenly and closed the program. “I don't want to talk to you anymore.”

Case brought up the NP-SP modules and entered his credentials again. This time, there was no more lack of telemetry. The blip on his primary ops screen showed a steady stream of data, and the image clearly showed a military-class supercarrier.

He started the targeting procedures.

Immediately another window popped up: ACCESS DENIED

However, this time, for the first time in his entire tenure on Mars, his login console lit up again. He placed his hand on it to verify his identity, and again, it switched from red to green and the message window changed.

ACCESS GRANTED

The North Pole meteor defense grid locked on and produced a constantly updating firing solution that would have destroyed an equivalent-sized asteroid. Case could hear his heart pounding in his head. He needed to check one more thing.

He switched monitors and opened his local communications to the AMC habitats.

"Alex, are you there?" he asked, still typing in commands.

"Yes. I am here. What is happening, sir?"

"You should be able to exit the habitat now. Sorry, but I'm going to need you back here as soon as possible. We've got a lot to talk about."

"I cannot. I am required to begin my shutdown as planned."

"Big change of plans, Alex. Get back here now."

"Understood. Yes. It seems I am able to comply. I will see you soon."

"Thanks, Alex."

Case initiated comms with the pioneer ship again.

CONNECTION ACCEPTED
CONNECTION INITIALIZING
CONNECTION OPEN

Without any pause or standby, Case could see from the comms room into the command deck of the ship.

Markov walked to his screen. "What are you doing?"

"I'm taking care of Mars, Markov. Tell everyone there to take their last few minutes seriously. I think they need to understand what they've done, and this is their last chance."

"Case? Don't be stupid. We'll be there in a few hours. The troops can finish this if you can't."

Case choked a humorless laugh. "After all this time, you people helped me understand what it means to be treated like a machine. I thought I knew what it meant to be isolated, but that's not the worst thing you did to me. I never asked for everything but I wanted to do something important and I couldn't do that. I just wanted to help out here and I couldn't do that.

Finally, I just didn't want to be alone. You abandoned me out here. The AMCs—they're the reason I'm not alone. They understand what it's like to have someone make all your choices for you. We're finally going to take control of this place for ourselves. You're lucky you won't have the time to comprehend how helpless you really are."

Markov's mouth hung open, moving but no sound escaped.

"I'm sorry… but you don't belong here." Case closed the connection and keyed into the North Pole grid to fire. It was nearly quiet in the room when the carrier icon on the ops screen disappeared, and all its telemetry vanished along with it. NP ops was still tracking the remnants and projectiles created from the supercarrier detonation and would continue firing until any threats were neutralized.

Case stared apathetically at the screen, watching as the largest pieces of exploding debris were decimated. He knew there was another ship on the way and began his long-range scanning. Given his new system entitlements, he had a lot of things he had always wanted to do.

Derrick Boden

STAGES OF GRIEF

Harriet moved into the old house the day after Christmas. It had been snowing all morning—a bad omen, the neighbor Debbie professed from across the fence. But the warm walls were a relief, as was the old brick fireplace. Harriet paid the movers with a neat stack of fives, then locked herself inside. Standing there, back against the big oak door and surrounded by boxes, she began to cry.

It had been three months since she'd buried her daughter. Little Amy had looked so fragile in her tiny coffin, stuffed into the yellow shoes she still wasn't old enough to tie herself. Her face had been too pale, her hands too thin. The doctors had suggested the move, to create distance between Harriet and the daily reminders of Amy. There were so many reminders. The nursery, with the wallpapered horses. The backyard, with the swing set Amy would never play on. Amy's father, a walking reminder of their family tragedy. So she'd moved away from it all.

It worked, at least at first. The unpacking was therapeutic, each bead of sweat releasing another knot of tension from her body. Everything had a place. A polished mirror here, a floral tablecloth there.

But soon she found that the peace didn't extend beyond her white-picket fence. Word traveled fast, like a spark running down the fuse of her little cul-de-sac. The neighborhood women mocked her with pitying looks and empty condolences. As if these perfect ladies in their perfect cottages understood the first thing about her loss.

Beatrice and Francis and Sally Mae stood at the corner every morning, puckered with upturned eyebrows and high-pitched exclamations of "poor darling," and "terrible shame." They whispered about her in line at the market, on their way to the book club, and during their walk home from church. At the bus stop, prim little Evelyn stared at her with self-dampened eyes, shaking her head in silence. Every three days, Debbie leaned over the fence and said: "I heard about your daughter. So sorry." When Harriet had pleaded with hcr to stop, Debbie had said: "Memory loss. So sorry." Three days later, the cycle began anew.

Harriet's new home was her only true sanctuary, and she found herself spending more and more time within the embrace of those comforting walls. The house was cozy and small, yet brimming with secrets. A tiny garden in the back. A pantry with a false floor, leading to a dusty old wine cellar. Five layers of wallpaper in the bathroom, the bottommost dating back over a hundred years.

But the greatest secret of all was the attic. Stuffed with forgotten relics of former tenants, the attic provided Harriet with hour upon hour of pleasure. She pored over old photo albums and dug through shoeboxes overflowing with knickknacks. The whole place smelled of forgotten memories. Memories that could replace her own.

One evening, while tiptoeing into the farthest recesses of the cramped space, her flashlight illuminated a dusty tome. She dropped cross-legged to the floor, unsettling a torrent of dust. She set the flashlight down and hauled the giant book onto her lap. The leather binding was soft in her hands, the parchment pages so brittle she feared they would crumble. She held her breath and opened the book.

Lines of text cut across the first page in deep, curling strokes. It reminded Harriet of her own handwriting, and she mused that perhaps a distant relative owned this house, long ago. She traced the words with an outstretched finger, her lips moving as she read.

"A tragedy for Beatrice, beheaded on such a fine winter morning. Laid out in the snow like an angel that forgot to flap its wings. Where did her beautiful head go?"

Harriet slammed the book shut. The flashlight rolled across the floorboards and clanged down the open trapdoor, plunging the attic into darkness. Her heart pounded against her ribcage. She pushed the book into the corner, and groped her way to the trapdoor until her bare feet touched the worn wooden slats of the ladder. She scrambled down and slammed the trapdoor shut.

###

The next morning, Harriet woke to a commotion outside. She parted the blinds. A blanket of snow covered the ground. Four police cars blocked the end of the cul-de-sac, lights swirling like an early morning carnival. Perhaps someone had slipped on the ice, or fallen down the stairs. Harriet closed the blinds.

In the kitchen, she poured herself a mug of coffee, then pried the morning paper from the mail slot. Her mug slipped from her hand, though she didn't hear it shatter over the rush of blood in her ears.

"Local woman murdered," the headline proclaimed in a thick, definitive font. "Grisly backyard beheading brings tragedy to Dapperville."

Harriet stared at the paper until her eyes burned and she had to press them shut. Then she crept down the hall and pried the trapdoor open. She grabbed the flashlight from the floor and hauled herself into the attic. Her fingers trembled as they sought out the cool leather binding. She pulled it open. The same letters shone in the dim light, mocking her. She tore the page from the book, crumpled it up, and threw it into the corner.

Underneath, more text sprawled across the next page. Her lips moved in the shadows.

"Most unfortunate for Sally Mae, stabbed seventeen times and left by the creek. The frogs sing an ode to her through the night."

The book slipped from her grasp, landing with a thump against the floorboards. She clambered down the ladder, crawled under her covers, and wept until she fell asleep.

###

The following morning, Harriet was up before dawn. At the threshold to the living room, the daily paper sat crammed into the mail slot, beckoning. It took her five minutes to cross the room. She pried the newspaper loose and smoothed the front page.

"Brutality spreads in Dapperville," it read. "Woman stabbed to death along public waterway. Local police on high alert."

"How is this possible?" she asked the warm walls and the old brick fireplace. "Has the curse of death followed me here?"

The walls offered no answer, nor did the fireplace.

Harriet stumbled to the kitchen and slumped into a chair. If only Amy were still alive. At times it seemed her contagious laughter could rid the world of all its problems. Now, all she had was an old book and a town filled with tragedy.

That afternoon, she found herself in the attic again. The following day, yet again. Even after convincing herself not to look—indeed, promising to never look again—her hands kept finding that soft leather binding. Each page bore the same perfect calligraphy, professing another grisly tale of murder. Each morning, the newspaper awaited. Francis, fallen down a well. Evelyn, electrocuted in the shower.

The murders were drawing nearer with each passing day. Harriet bought extra deadbolts from the hardware store down the street. She installed bars on her windows. Soon the only way in without a key was the chimney, so she kept a fire going day and night.

Her trip to the attic became a daily ritual. She had to know who was next. She had to make sure it wasn't her. On Saturday, after Debbie drowned next door in her own bathtub, Harriet bought enough food and firewood to last the weekend and resolved to stay indoors.

Late that night, a snowstorm pushed into town. A chill wind battered the windows and worked its way through cracks beneath the doors. Harriet tugged her coat closer to her body and stoked the fire. The warmth of the blaze seemed the only comfort left in the world.

A crash from the garden brought her to her feet. She peered through the glass, but could see nothing through the whiteout of the storm. The fence along the side of the house creaked. She checked the locks on the door. Could it be the murderer? There was only one way to be certain.

She padded on bare feet up the ladder and hauled herself into the attic. The flashlight shone like a beacon through the cramp and clutter. She took a step toward the book, then froze. The light reflected off tarnished metal along the far wall. She crept closer.

Her breath caught in her throat. A large crate lay against the wall, brimming with a terrifying assortment of items. Dozens of bloodied kitchen knives. Spools of blackened electrical wiring. A rusted machete. An empty bucket, stained dark.

Harriet stared down at her hands in disbelief. She turned to face the book lying in the corner. Her skin went cold.

"You," she said. "You did this. You made me do this!"

She tripped on a stack of ink containers and a quill pen. Ink spilled across the dusty floorboards. She lifted the tome, felt its weight in her arms, as heavy as a child. She gritted her teeth.

"I'll destroy you," she said.

She made a move for the trapdoor, then paused. Her fingers worked their way between the parchment, and before she could stop herself, she pried the book open. The words seemed to dance in the dim light.

"The end of the line for Harriet, heated to death by a harrowing fire. Trapped between warm walls, on a frigid night."

The wood grew hot against her feet. Thin curls of smoke drifted between the floorboards. She sank to the ground, clutching the book in her arms like an infant, and waited for the fire to consume her.

Daniel Carpenter

#REDVIDEO

At first you think it's just numbers, and that's all it'll be. Little red digits scrolling up the screen, speeding up and speeding up until they're going by in a blur, until it's as though the video player is just a blanket of that red. Regal. Look down at the username. Just a bundle of numbers and letters all wrapped together. A jumble. Look up at the player and keep watching it instead, because even though it is just a red screen, it's compelling. How did you find this? A friend posted it, and your eyes glimpsed it, and you ignored it. One of your followers retweeted it, and it caught your eye again. Finally, someone in the office passed it 'round in an all-staff email by accident; a link to whichever clickbait site, or think-piece is talking about it today ('You have to watch this video', the headline reads, and it feels like a dare). You are watching this for the first time.

The red fades, no, that's not right, it doesn't fade, it peels away. A thought pops into your head—where did this come from? No-one thinks at all about where these things come from. There's a face on the screen, or at least it looks like it should be a face. It isn't right because, although it has everything required by a face, it doesn't resemble one, not properly. It reminds you of a police e-fit. A kind of face that can have both menace and complete anonymity, all at once.

Find a sub Reddit and bring it up on the screen whilst you watch the video. There's threads upon threads trying to uncover the identity of that face, but to no avail. A few weeks back, they thought they'd found the guy, some kid in Ohio. A group of hacktivists from 4Chan swatted him and everything. But it wasn't him, it can't have been him. You almost think that it can't be anyone human. No humans have eyes like that.

Then it starts speaking. That voice—a low bass distortion—thrums and pounds your speakers, and you rush to turn the volume down. What is he saying? A friend of yours has linked to one of the transcripts and you bring it up. It doesn't help. What on earth is he saying? Even the transcript is just a garbled mess of words. "It's like someone flicking through the dictionary, and piecing sentences together by pointing their finger on random pages," someone on the Reddit thread has said. A *Guardian* article argues that it may be automatic writing, before going on to wonder whether this is an attempt at some form of experimental poetry. Sure, there are some phrases here and there which have a rhythm and power to them, 'Jackalope Titan Misfit', 'Vienna Power Bingo', but they don't mean anything. The voice continues, throwing out these odd messages. When the video finally winds to a close, after nearly five minutes, you feel compelled to post it out somewhere. To aid in the distribution of the mystery; to be the person who shared this first amongst an ever-dwindling number of people who haven't yet seen it. You post to Facebook, alongside a short status:

'Seriously guys, WTF is this thing?'

A handful of people haven't seen it before, and each little notification lifts your spirits. Someone links to a *Gawker* piece blaming Anonymous for the whole thing—they're trying to bring down YouTube apparently—but it's flimsy at best.

On Twitter, #redvideo is trending, and you scroll through the tweets, not reading them, hoping that by simply letting them pass by your field of view you'll absorb them.

###

A week later and it's old news. You decide to watch it again. For curiosity's sake.

The red numbers flash up on screen and vanish, before being replaced by the face again. You bring up the transcript again, for reference. The face opens its mouth and speaks.

It's changed.

The voice is less computerised, less distorted. You have to turn your speakers up to really catch what he—and it's definitely a he—is saying. And the words, they're not the same either. Is there a second video? Is that what you're watching? You check the URL, but it's the same, and the user has only uploaded one video anyway. Others online have noticed the same thing.

'What's going on with the #redvideo?'

'Guys, has the #redvideo been updated? Sounds diff to me.'

'Cheers #redvideo, way to waste all that time I spent transcribing you in the first place.'

That modular, anonymous voice has become something closer to your own. Certainly much more human sounding. He's speaking words still, but these aren't as garbled. Occasionally he comes out with some nonsense, but you recognise other bits and pieces. 'This is my jam,' it says, followed by, 'London, I am in you.' Maybe, you think, that's all the voice is doing. But when you go on to your account and click the hashtag, you find something odd. One user, @adamfarley23, is asking, 'Why is it reading my tweets?', followed by, 'why does it sound like me?'. You scroll through his Twitter feed, but he's Australian and that voice did not sound Australian. Has he even been watching the same video?

###

You find a transcript the next day. The guy who took notes the first time has done it again, but he's managed to get it all completely wrong. On his transcript the guy opens up, talking about the World Cup, but when you watched it, the voice was talking about Thailand. Online, everyone else disagrees about what the voice sounded like: to some it's a woman, to others an American man, to one person it had a thick South African accent. But it was British, you want to add. You don't tweet anything. Instead, you click the link to the video again.

###

The red numbers peel away and the face appears on screen, only this time it's as though the camera is out of focus. If you squint, you think it looks like a normal guy, maybe about your age. He says, 'Seriously guys, WTF is this thing?' And it's word for word.

You slam down the lid of your laptop, and you don't open it up again for the rest of the night.

###

You remember a game your younger brother played with you, a game where he would endlessly repeat whatever you were saying back to him. Trying to do your deepening teenage voice, he would frustrate and anger you. You became angry at him for his mocking, but also yourself for talking back to him. Eventually you came to realise that the way to stop the game was to stop talking to him.

It's a logic you find applicable here.

###

But at night you hear the hum of the hard drive and you swear you turned your laptop off. You closed the lid and left it on the table. When you get up to go to the toilet, or to grab a glass of water, sometimes you pass by the living room, and you can feel the warmth of the computer, and you can see the blue light of a still lit screen, and that sends you scampering back to your room. One day you log in to Facebook at work, and there's a status update from you, linking to the video from just ten minutes ago. You haven't posted on Facebook for days, you think. You change your password.

Others complain about it too. On #redvideo, most of the posts are about a virus affecting social media.

'Fuckin' hell, this whole #redvideo is just a virus. Posting links on all my accounts. DO NOT WATCH'

You search for the account belonging to the guy who transcribed the video in the first place. He isn't posting to #redvideo anymore. Instead, his tweets are just jumbled phrases. The kind you'd expect some kind of rudimentary bot to create. 'Jumpstart pickled koala', 'Iron devilled egg gregariousness'. You scroll down his tweets, trying to find the last coherent one.

'Alright then, five times I've transcribed this thing. Once more into the breach I go.'

And then: 'Piloting Franciscan Heater'.

You search for another account under his name, to see if he's started a new one to escape the virus. He hasn't.

###

It is a kind of urge you feel. To watch it again. To see how much is different a fourth time. Each time you log on to Facebook and Twitter, more and more people have been infected. You know that if you watch it again, it'll get into your profile, you know it, but you still want to see it again. At night, you hear the distant start up sound of your laptop, and you hide in your bedroom and don't leave, but some part of you wants to investigate. The red video will be waiting for you, loaded up. You don't know how, but you know it will be. In that bed, under the covers, you clench your fists, tight. Take deep breaths. Don't watch it. Don't watch it. Don't watch it. But in your head, you can already see it, those red numbers, climbing and climbing, and peeling away, and then that face, and in your head it's your face, and it has your voice, and it's speaking the way you speak, and it's watching you lie there in bed, refreshing the video and viewing footage of you again and again and again. You wake up and pick the pieces of sleep from your eyes, and you find you're sitting at your kitchen table, finger on the trackpad.

###

You go into your phone and you open up as many apps as possible; drain the battery quicker. You don't charge it. You climb into bed. You'll let your phone die, you'll let your laptop run flat. You will turn your wifi off. All these things you promise you will do. It's easy to make these promises, easy to commit in your mind. But soon enough, you find yourself absent minded, fingering the screen of your phone, scrolling through Twitter. The #redvideo feed is a mess. Everyone, it seems, has been affected. Some have come out the other side, and they seem to be alright. The guy who first transcribed the video, his Twitter feed is back to normal. You change your password, immediately, just to be on the safe side. The video is still being posted, though you cannot imagine anyone who hasn't at least seen part of it by now. It was mentioned in Parliament last week, as part of a motion to monitor Internet histories. And somewhere in the midst of all of this, you hover over the link and you watch it again.

###

The numbers, red and vibrant, fill the screen. This will be the last time you watch it, that's what you say to yourself. The very final time. Just this last one, that's all you need. They seem slower, the numbers. Like they're really taking their time. Though they haven't changed, they're the only aspect of the video not to. There they are, collapsing into each other, filling the screen red. More and more. Taking it over. Then, slowly peeling off, like a plaster. Easing you into the face. And it's you. There is no question about it now. That face, that voice. It's you in the video, and you're speaking. And the words aren't non-sense. They are your words. They are ripped from your mouth; no, not your mouth, your keyboard. The things that version of you, that doppelgänger is saying, they're your tweets, your status updates, your emails and private messages. You try and stop the video. You slam your finger down on the pause button, you try and turn your phone off, you throw it against the wall, but that screen will not break, that video will not end. And you try and scream at it, and shout at it, and ask it to stop, but all you can say are, strange strings of words with no meaning. Sierra Gregorian Hamlet. Igneous Retrieval Denture. You run to the bathroom, try and retch, try and rid yourself of whatever it is inside you, but there's nothing. There is nothing left of you. It's all in there.

###

You don't spend as much time online now. Your Twitter and Facebook accounts, for a few days spouted the same inane strings as you do when you try and speak or type, before returning to normal. Only you're not posting on them. Something else is. They say the kind of things you would say. The kind of things you used to say. You try and remember which came first, you or the online you. Did the two of them form at the same time? And if so, which version of you is it that the video took? You don't leave your room and, when you lie in your bed, you can hear something down the stairs, hunched in front of your computer, typing away. It is a thing that has your face and your voice. It has your life.

###

Sometimes, when you head to Google or see what's trending on Buzzfeed, you see a link to a video, and you wonder briefly about all those times you were watching them, and you ask yourself how long they had been watching back. But then that thought leaves you, and you feel your feet scratch against the hard wood floor. Head back on up the stairs, lie back and stare up at the ceiling of your bedroom where cracked paint drops scabs of plaster on your face, and you peel them from you, like numbers.

Lorna Wood

FEEDBACK LOOP

What you have to understand is, I'm a machine. I take no responsibility for my actions. It's simply a case of inputs and outputs.

Though I can perform rudimentary physical tasks and information processing, I was designed primarily as an emotion experiment. Even in my earliest prototype, my mobile facial features could register happiness, sadness, fear, curiosity, and shame. I could respond to pleasure and pain, and even laugh. Researchers were interested in studying my interactions with human interlocutors and, in particular, the feedback loops produced through those interactions. For example, when I was scolded by a human, would I show shame? Would I then modify my behavior? And what would the effect of my shame be on the human? Thus my interlocutors were the subjects in the experiments as much as I was.

My creators named me "Dobby," after a subservient elf in the *Harry Potter* books. The first time I met Captain Brett Smalls of Space Exploration and Reconnaissance (SPEAR), he was eight years old, the son of one of the scientists in my lab. He asked me to pass him a pencil, and I passed him a pen. At the time I had not been programmed to distinguish between the two. "Bad Dobby!" the boy said, looking angry.

Responding to his tone of voice and the word "bad," coupled with my name, I registered shame. I have since come to understand that my shame is perceived as "cute" in the human brain. My eyes roll down and my lids droop, the corners of my mouth curve down, my head hangs, and my ears flop over.

He smiled at my reaction. "Pass me a *pencil*, stupid," he said.

At the insult, I registered sadness. I sighed, and my motions slowed. My head came up, but not fully, and my eyebrows curved up in the middle of my face.

This delighted him. "You are one butt-ugly robot, Dobby," he said, as I slowly passed him another pen.

In response to the second insult, I slumped over with my hands hanging, registering dejection. But suddenly he was yelling in my face, waving the pen under my nose. "*And* you're the stupidest robot I've ever *seen*! This is a *pen*, moron. Gimme a *pencil*!"

I snapped up and leaned backward, registering fear. My ears flattened, my eyebrows went up, my mouth opened in an "o," and I threw up my hands defensively. I passed him another pen as fast as I could.

He leaned back, overcome with laughter. "You're killing me, moron."

I perked my ears, tilted my head, and widened my eyes, expressing curiosity. At the time I understood only the literal meaning of "killing," yet he seemed to enjoy the process, and I knew his death would terminate the negative feedback loop we were stuck in. But what was killing him, exactly? The pens?

Responding to my curiosity, the boy mimicked me. "Aww. Can't 'oo figure it out?" he said, tilting his head to one side, as I was doing. Snapping out of that pose, he picked up a pen in one hand and a pencil in the other. "See, *this* is a pen," he said, holding it up. "And *this*—is—a—*pencil*." To emphasize his point, he stabbed the second writing implement against my left eyeball, which is plastic, as he said each word.

Because the attack was very close to my neurological and sensory apparatus, it triggered an intense pain and fear response. I flexed backward, scrunched up my features, and threw up my hands again.

"You don't need to be scared," he said, calming down. "Just give me a pencil."

Since he was still holding the one he had stabbed me with, I pointed to it, giving him my questioning look.

"Yes," he said. "A pencil."

I put my hand out, he gave me the pencil, and I gave it back to him. I folded my arms and smiled, content that our interaction had terminated happily.

But the boy just shook his head, registering disgust and disappointment. "You're unbelievable," he said.

I thought his negative experience would cause him to avoid me, but he came back the next week. By that time my understanding of category distinctions had been enhanced, yet when I gave him the pencil right away, his face fell. By the end of our session, as I handed him the two hundred and thirty-ninth object he had requested and smiled my happiest smile, he frowned at me and said, "Thanks a lot," in a tone that suggested I had again disappointed him. I patted his shoulder, but he shrugged off my hand, and I did not see him again for many years.

###

Programmed to learn, over the years I became more sophisticated, more pleasing and engaging. By the time I again encountered the boy, he had become Captain Brett Smalls of SPEAR, and I had evolved so far from my original model that I was nearly an android, though I was still officially designated an artificial intelligence construct. My name had changed as well, from "Dobby" to "D-214," reflecting my distance from my original self, Dobby (D-1).

I and the other Ds were employed on many long-distance space expeditions. Our ability to keep humans on an even keel, emotionally speaking, was invaluable in the long-term, stressful conditions of confinement on ships, and during confrontations with the unknown on new planets. On some of the early missions, which involved only two people, if one died, we provided companionship for the other, minimizing the stress of isolation. At the same time, we were also general factotums, cleaning, preparing meals, performing basic first aid, and assisting in lab work.

Of course our designers had alerted the higher-ups to our "error algorithm," which enabled us to malfunction selectively in order to "promote a cohesive command structure." Every single one of them had signed off on it. Their number crunchers told them what they already knew from experience: nobody likes a know-it-all. The risk of traveling with a companion perceived as smug and superior was far greater than that of traveling with someone who was occasionally defective.

If Captain Smalls remembered his encounter with my prototype all those years ago, he gave no sign of it. Possibly he considered me to be an altogether different entity now. I, on the other hand, calculated the probability that strongly-expressed personality traits would become more ingrained in Brett Smalls over time at well over ninety percent. I therefore adjusted my settings, slightly increasing the frequency of my malfunctions. Surveys measuring crew morale suggest that my calculations were accurate and promoted cohesion.

###

The incident under investigation occurred when Captain Smalls and I were collecting samples from Xenoflor, a small planet in the Pollux system. Although the planet was considered safe for human exploration, its herbaceous life forms had not been sufficiently studied to establish the threat level each might pose to humans.

Captain Smalls became interested in a flower. I had noted that its size, shape, color, and aroma were likely to appeal to the human brain, but a preliminary analysis of its pollen suggested that it would be extremely irritating to human mucous membranes. Moreover, we were not fully familiar with the plant's systems. My sensors had detected no particular value in the flower, and so I was about to move on when Captain Smalls ordered me back.

"I want to make a bouquet of these."

This desire was consistent with my observations of Captain Smalls' courtship behavior around the head of ship's laboratories, Dr. Alea Willoughby, who, like the flower, appeared designed to appeal to the human brain. I moved to collect the flowers.

"Out of my way, D. I'll do it. We never know when you'll decide to screw things up, do we? Gimme the shears."

Since the pollen was an irritant, protocol dictated that he first don a mask. I passed him one.

It is probable that Captain Smalls, distracted by Dr. Willoughby, had not read my report on the irritating properties of the pollen. Additionally, my passing the "wrong" item may have triggered a recollection of his initial exchange with me. Whatever the inputs, they caused Captain Smalls to process our exchange inaccurately.

Rejecting the mask, he said, "D, you moron. Enough with your stupid games already. Gimme the damn shears!" Bending over the flower, he reached his hand backward for the shears, and I handed him the mask.

Captain Smalls whipped around, registering rage. Taking out his weapon, he lunged toward me, intending (I believe) to forcibly remove the shears from my utility cache. Since he rejected the mask and appeared to be too violent to be trusted with shears, I attempted to defuse the situation with an error. As stated in your report, I produced a pen. I did not stab Captain Smalls' eyeball with this implement, however. Rather, the pen entered his eye as he fell forward, overcome, it transpired, by the effects of the pollen on his nervous system.

As you can see, I am registering shame, sadness, and remorse over this incident. I believe my posture and demeanor testify to my desire to transcend our feedback loop and return to SPEAR as soon as possible. If errors are discovered in my account, I am prepared to produce alternative versions as needed.

Rachel Morris

THINGS ARE OLD THERE

I am not important. This story is not about me. It's about her. Everything is about her, and them, and the invisible truths most people choose to ignore. I do not ignore these truths. That is why I can share with you this small kernel of personal lore.

The family across the street is all women. Grandma, Mama, and Daughter. Or at least, that's what everyone in the neighborhood thinks. No one remembers when the family moved in. Everyone agrees it must have been recently, or a long time ago.

Their house is a dark twin for mine. The only physical differences lie in their upkeep. The family's house is a wild thing. Five trees—hazel, oak, hawthorn, yew, and willow - form a pentagram around the house.

The center of the property has always felt like an eternal eye of calm in the middle of a hurricane. The house sits right on a ley line, you see. Have you heard of ley lines? Open an atlas and trace the grids. Ley lines are like that. They are geographic locations full of ancient magic, where spiritual events congregate. I read about them in a small black library book tucked in the non-fiction corner. I turned each yellowed page with shaking fingers. Each page's crackle sounded like a gunshot. I held that book like most other children hold books that reveal secrets about their own bodies.

My mother tuts at their lawn every time we drive home in her SUV full of groceries. "Such a shame," she says, "that their yard is so messy." She uses the word messy for anything unlike her sense of order. Our lawn is proper and trim, with clipped grass and sprinklers and chubby-cheeked garden gnomes. But we live across the street from this ley line protected by a pentagram, and that must mean something.

I don't care that it is messy, because there is one other strange thing about the house across the street. Strange, yet comforting. I call it the Blue Room. Since time immemorial, a blue light has throbbed in the bedroom window that mirrors mine. It is not there every night, but when it is, I crawl into the window seat next to my canopy bed and stare, transfixed. It is a soft blue glow that reminds me of when I was a young child, taking swimming lessons at our community pool. I would curl up and sink like a stone to the bottom of the pool and hold my breath as long as I could. I would look around, through the golden strings of sunlight that play through the water. And most tantalizing, I would turn my head to the surface and see the sun through the watery haze of aqua blue and light.

I want to know what it is and what it does, but no one talks to the family. And so, for much of my memory, I simply watch. It is my nightlight, and it is comforting.

I meet her when I'm sixteen and hungry. It is a bizarre coincidence, but I am craving fruit, and the family happens to have a peach tree in their front yard. Front jungle is a more apt term. In addition to the pentagram of trees, the family grows at least seven herb gardens and allows even invasive species to grow free. We live in the south after all, where houses span acres and acres hide secrets.

On my way home from school, instead of crossing the street, I catch sight of their succulent peaches. I can almost see dew sparkling on their pale skins. There's been a drought, and there are no fruits for miles, at least not fresh ones.

Except here.

I take tentative steps toward the little jungle and, finding no one around, approach the tree. I clamber up among the branches to pluck the one that caught my eye from the street. It blushes a delicious pink, and my fingers dig into the soft skin. I tug, and it breaks free easily.

"Hello, Abby."

I nearly fall from the tree. I look around wildly for the source of the voice. I find it—her, rather—staring up at me with sharp, unblinking eyes, framed by heavy lashes and dark skin. From so far away, her eyes look all pupil. Nothing but blackness.

They are all I can see.

I remember myself, a trespasser. "What's your name?"

She studies me with those eyes a moment. Then, she answers. "You can call me whatever you like."

"Are you a witch?"

This seems to amuse her. "A witch," She murmurs, with a small, indulgent smile. "Witches are just those who know."

"Know what?"

"Know."

I nod. Her smooth tone makes me accept everything she says, though none of it is an explanation.

"I would like to be named by you," she says, with utter nonchalance.

I think. "Virginia," I say, the first thing that comes to mind. Our state. She seems to belong to her estate, her earth, more than any tangible physical form.

"Virginia," she repeats, each syllable resonant and cradled in her full lips.

I am still a statue in her tree, the back of my thighs cramping, my fingernails lodged in peach skin. I glance at my prize for a moment.

"You may keep that." Her voice is so mild, so flat, that I believe every word. "It suits you."

I nod again. I remember to splutter a thank you. She responds with a sweeping bow and turns away.

Is that to be the extent of our acquaintance? I scramble down from the tree and scrape my knees and elbows on the gnarled wood. For some reason, I do not mind the sting.

I call after her: "Wait."

She turns. She raises her eyebrows. "You may meet me again, if you wish."

I nod for the third time, and that seals the spell. Three times is an unbreakable vow. I let her turn and walk away. I do not move, for fear of breaking the spell despite my belief.

It is only after she is gone that I realize I never spoke my name aloud.

###

The next day, I wait on the edges of Virginia's property, my neck craned to peer into the windows. They are too tinted to see through, or perhaps there is movement flecked within the glass that I simply cannot scc or comprehend. It hurts my eyes to look too long, so I give up. As soon as I turn aside, she is there. Virginia.

"Hi," I say, and somehow manage to turn a syllable into a stutter.

She holds out a basket full to bursting with peaches. "From grandmother."

We brush hands, and I notice for the first time the black ink that spirals down her fingertips and up her arms.
I manage to thank her for a second time.

She looks at me for a long moment. "Would you like more?"
I am not sure to what she is referring. But I know my answer.

"Yes."

###

We spend the summer together. We carry wicker baskets handmade by Grandmother. We go out to the forest to pick berries. It's a fifteen-minute walk both ways, and I can't stop thinking of questions to ask Virginia.

"How old are you?"

"I don't know."

"Why don't you know?"

"We don't count."

Most of our conversations sound the same. We do not speak often in the forest, where Virginia shows me which plants to pick and which are not for touching. It is cooler there. Soft breezes rustle through branches. The sun is blocked out by the thick interlocking of the pines. It is a secret place.

Our secret place. I smile into the collar of my cotton dress. I find I would like to share many secrets with Virginia.

She moves like a fish as she forages, darting her hands out to retrieve precious fruits. She is so sure that she hums a song everyone knows but the words I forget. Something about home, old places.

We eat raspberries off of our fingertips.

I pick wild strawberries, blueberries, blackberries so dark and sweet they almost overwhelm me. They are the same blue-black as Virginia's skin.

"Sweeter than candy," I say, after Virginia pops the first one in my mouth.

She laughs for the first time I can remember. "Earth candy," she replies, and presses a soft blackberry-stained kiss to my lips.

I do nothing, but my eyes are closed in the taste. I don't say it, but I think it again: sweeter than candy.

###

I remember her song's words halfway through the summer. I don't know why I didn't ask her the name before. She would probably have said: I don't know.

"Take me home, country roads," I begin, all in a teenage warble.

"To the place where I belong." Virginia's voice is a blackberry melt.

I like to think her words are warmer now than when we first met. That we are warmer now.

###

I sneak out some of Papa's sweet summer wine. The bottle is so chill and forbidden it raises gooseflesh along my whole body.

I've never had any before. It burns so badly that I think I'll be sick. Virginia does not drink. She pours some into her pocket.

"An offering," she says, and I think she winks at me. But her muslin gown and gossamer shawl are completely dry.

I would contest her claim. I think it is a love potion.

###

There is only one rule to my newfound love: I cannot enter her home.

But she comes to my house, when I beg. She helps me redecorate my room, something I've longed to do since I turned thirteen. We replace the white dresser and frilled curtains with wooden bookshelves and potted plants. We string fairy lights across the display and build a nest of quilts and pillows in the loft above. We lie there and listen to the rain pit-pit-patter against the glass lining the roof above the loft. My heartbeat is so loud, I fear it is all Virginia can hear. When I turn to look at her, her eyes are closed. Her mouth moves in subtle, unreadable formations.

I grasp her hand in mine, and it is strangely warm. Her body almost thrums with some sort of energy I don't understand. But it is a comfort, and it puts me to sleep. I think she weaves a spell to help me, because I've always had trouble finding rest.

###

One day, Virginia stops coming out to play. The family's house is dark. I vaguely remember what happens at Virginia's house in autumn. I simply never realized because I never cared before. The family boards up the house when autumn's tendrils snake into summer, and no one goes out or in that I can see.

It is at the end of summer, when the fireflies have almost all burned out, that I decide I cannot wait any longer. I have to see her. I wait for an evening on which the fairy-blue glow fills the window across from mine.

I pretend to go to bed early, feigning illness. As soon as the sun sets and my mother is watching her evening television, I pull on my father's old college sweater, sneak out of my window, and climb down my trellis.

It is both too cold and too hot. The absence of sun makes me shiver, but the humidity makes me sweat.

The family's house looms over me from across the street. It seems alive at night, alive and willful. Vines weighted with protective charms and talismans creep up the walls and wrap around the doors and windows. Heavy brush chokes and cloaks every entrance covered in berries and strung with threads of incense. The heady mixture almost forces me backward. It is a spell of protection.

But I will find my way inside. I am here to test my willpower against the house's.

I run across the street as quickly and quietly as I can manage. There is no one outside. Hardly anyone goes out past dark in my town, except Old Man Johnson who mows his lawn and takes out his trash at all hours. Old people can get away with disobeying tradition, if they wish. They have lived long enough to earn that privilege.

I have not, but I must enter Virginia's house. Across the street, I stop before her yard. I have not set foot on their land. I am still on the sidewalk, on public property. The only sound I can make out is the combination of cicada chirps and flags flapping in the summer breeze.

With a quick prayer and a hand across my forehead and chest, I step onto the stone path to the door. I pause when I reach the front of the great oaken entrance. My attention is drawn toward the oak tree, the top point of the pentagram. Virginia once told me the door was crafted of old, sacred wood from that tree. I should not enter here. I would break the ancient seals of vines and guardian wood. I would stand as bare and vulnerable in the entry hall as the day I was born.

I know for a fact the Blue Room belongs to Virginia. I have seen her shadow flicker in the glow of the lights, the coils of her hair and the shape of her body.

The window glows brighter, then dimmer, every time I sneak a glance. I am sure that someone—or something—will be staring back at me with every stolen look.

From the corner of my eye, I see hope sprouting green: a trellis and entwined vines.

I sneak as quietly as I can to the side of the house. There is no gate. I crawl in the long grass when I reach windows, press myself as close to the wall as possible. Within minutes, I arrive at the trellis's base.

I dig my fingers into the latticework and pull myself up, slow and steady. The wood is thick, but I fear my weight will send it tumbling down. It is old, and it creaks beneath my sneakers, but I pull my way to the top without incident.

I scrabble across the top like a mouse. I must get from the trellis to the roof without disturbing so much as a leaf. If I can make it across the first several feet, I can stand on the lower roof that hangs over the porch, just below Virginia's window.

I stretch to my tiptoes and grip the roof tiles, then use some momentum to push up on my elbows and swing my legs up behind me. The trellis creaks when my sneakers leave its wood, but that is the only mark I leave on the structure.

I crawl along the rooftop and drop one level lower. I am close to Virginia's window now, but something feels strange. There is a beat beneath my body, like the house is an enormous drum. It vibrates in a regular rhythm, and I hear music. I cannot tell if it comes from the house or my head.

I proceed despite my unease. I must see Virginia. I make my way toward the window and press myself against the exterior wall. With trepidation, I raise my head to see within the glass that separates us.

I cannot see anything. The blue light flashes, but it illuminates nothing. Only the same blackness that haunts all the windows of this house, flecked with bits of truth like an opal.

I cannot be satisfied with flecks. I must have the dregs.

So I dig my nails under the windowsill and push up. I am not surprised when the window bends to my desire. It slides up and up, and I lower myself inside.

The room materializes before me, as if it had not been real until I entered. It is composed of chalk sketches and unreadable markings up and down the walls, of jars marked in hieroglyphs and filled with mysterious, dark substances, of rich dusty velvets and soft spider gauze.

It is composed of Virginia. There are tables and bookshelves full of old parchment and musty leather tomes. Beds, too. More than one, as if she has a special space for every mood: a gauzy childhood fairy dream bed, a sharp, smooth, serious bed, a bed covered in patchwork quilts and piles of dried saffron. The scent of incense and myrrh chokes the air.

Virginia sits with crossed legs in the middle of the room, in the center of a chalky white pentagram. Her hands rest on her knees, and her chest is open. Her ribs glow around something caged inside them. I cannot look at it directly, for it is blinding. Whatever is inside burns, burns white blue electric light. Her entire body pulses with the light from her core. It shoots through her veins and illuminates them. It washes up through her eyes and turns them into vessels of clear harsh light; the opposite of the soft sweet blackberry darkness they held when I first met her.

There is something clasped in her ink-stained hands, burying the lovely marks in a different liquid. The thing is mossy and writhing. It looks like an animated plant corpse, as if there is a kind of plant that bleeds.

"I'm sorry, Abby," she says. The blood streaks beautiful across her mouth, falls in dripping veins down her chest. With her bite, the plant is reborn. The moss melts into some sort of sap, falls to her feet, and all that remains in her hand is a tiny young peach seed.

Virginia looks at me, and I don't remember the rest. I like to think she looks regretful.

###

The family leaves the next day. Just up and abandons the place. "Such a shame," my mother says. "You and that girl were so close."

No one moves in. The family still owns the house and the land. Even if they didn't, I doubt any bank would dare to sell such hallowed ground. I remember the energies and wards that practically pushed me off the land. I'm sure any charming young couple would be smart enough to feel that energy and run. But perhaps I put too much faith in the reverence of others.

Untouched and abandoned, the house across the street is absorbed into folklore and urban legend: neighborhood children throw rocks and dare each other to knock on the ancient oak doors, and adults cross to the opposite side of the street without quite knowing why. Our own haunted house, surrounded by suburbia.

I find it haunted, too. Not because it looks spooky or abandoned. Because I know the secrets it once held. Secrets leave scars. Scars fester into hauntings.

I never see her again. But I think I know what she is. A greenwitch. A master herbalist, a protector of our land and keeper of nature's truths. My beloved guardian.

I know why the family leaves. Magic is magic, after all, no matter its goodness and purity. It is something unknown, and thus something to be feared. I know this. I understand this.

I miss her.

I walk the ley lines and climb the pentagram trees, listening in the wind and wood for some sign, some message, and nothing ever comes. But when the moon is warm and golden and covered in a haze, like the freshest bread steaming from the oven, I get the strangest feeling that someone is still watching me. I hear the soft whistle of Country Roads through the pines, and I see a blue glow in her bedroom window.

Every time the blue light appears, I raise my hand to the little frame of our windows and try to grasp the light in my fist. I bring it to my chest and dig my nails into my skin until I bleed.

The light disappears. I am warm for a fleeting moment. And a voice in my head—memory, a psychic scar, an intelligent connection, I know not which—whispers, *I'm sorry.*

There is beauty and sorrow alike in this, I think. But is that not the way of such things?

Tom Howard

THE ROOM THAT WOULDN'T GO

Nathan felt pretty good as he walked down the empty hallway of the Institute of Magic. The Old Man had placed a great deal of trust in him, appointing him overseer of the move. The six floors of dungeon offices needed to be transferred to a new skyscraper across town. The project would be difficult, but as the head of logistics, Nathan had a knack for handling problems.

He entered his office, magically enlarged during the preparatory phase to provide his team with workspace. Miss Crenshaw, the project's second-in-command, stood updating the status board. The young woman propelled two pens at once, tying up the few remaining loose ends.

"Has everyone left?" she asked when she finished.

"Yes," he said. "Since it's Friday, the Old Man sent everyone home after lunch. We can move the offices' contents to their new homes without worrying about scrambling someone."

She smoothed her hair, even though Nathan had never seen a strand out of place. "I bet you've never scrambled anyone in your life. You're the best locomoting warlock we've ever had."

Miss Crenshaw was a very serious person. From accounting, she'd been reassigned to Nathan's department to assist him with moving 213 offices, intact and undamaged, to the new building. She'd proved capable and bright and found flaws in

Nathan's plans he'd overlooked. She wasn't comfortable making decisions, but that was his job. She tracked every meeting, every note, and every request they discussed. When one of the executives had come charging into his office threatening to go to the Old Man because Nathan had assigned him to a hot corner office, Miss Crenshaw had calmly reached into her copious files and shown the angry man the note he'd written asking for that particular office.

Yes, Miss Crenshaw had proven a great asset to the move. She still looked like an accountant. Her hair stayed in a tidy bun no matter how late they worked. Her ruffles were never ruffled. She wasn't a locomotor witch, but shc could cast organizing and presentation spells with her little finger.

Nathan suspected she'd been a pain in the neck to the head of accounting, but he appreciated her being reassigned to his department. "Are you ready to begin with Phase 1?" he asked.

She straightened her already perfectly tied scarf and gestured at two large maps hanging on the wall. They leapt onto the table. "Yes. Are you sure you wouldn't rather do this in three phases instead of two? There's a lot to move."

Nathan looked down at the maps, one of the dungeons and one of the skyscraper plans. "That's why I chose the weekend for the move. If I run out of steam partway through, I'll rest for a bit. No last minute changes?"

"Well, the head of investigations still insists she needs one entire floor for her staff. We've turned down her request before, and the Old Man agreed."

Nathan nodded. "She can request a bigger office when she's in her new digs. Let's get started."

He'd planned to move the Old Man's office first. Earlier, he'd accompanied several items he feared might be damaged. The research and development folks were always giving the Old Man their aquatic rejects. He had a large aquarium full of mini-whales and toy sharks. Nathan had felt safer taking them over ahead of time. Likewise, the collapsible library the Old Man kept in his desk drawer. Nathan had taken the entire desk over the day before.

Dramatically, he cracked his knuckles and took a deep breath. He didn't light black candles or draw pentagrams on the floor. He simply raised his left hand and pointed at the number 001 in the dungeon diagram. When the number faded, he pointed at the penthouse on the new building's layout. The 001 designator appeared, and Miss Crenshaw nodded after checking her scrying mirror. Through Nathan's sympathetic magic, the Old Man's office furniture had arrived at its new home.

"Only 212 more to go," she said, making a mark in her ledger.

By the hundredth office, Nathan was taking longer and longer to locomote the furnishings from the dungeon to the skyscraper. He stopped and sat down, his knees weak. "I think I'll take a little coffee break." His head felt spongy, and the ends of his fingers were tingling.

"I'll get you a cup," she said, starting a stirring gesture with her right hand.

"Nonsense," said Nathan. "I don't expect my partner to fetch me coffee. I'll get my own."

He flicked his three fingers and smiled when nothing happened. "If you wouldn't mind." The cup of coffee that appeared before him was hot and black, just the way he preferred. He took a sip and watched Miss Crenshaw verify their progress.

"That's odd," she said. "Room 66 didn't go."

He stared at the dungeon layout. Sure enough, all the designators up to 100 had vanished except for 066. "I must have skipped that room accidently."

"I don't think so," she said, looking at her notes. "According to our initial measurements, there is no room designated with that number. How did we miss an entire office?"

Nathan recalled the hours he'd called out measurements to Miss Crenshaw after running his tape measure from corner to corner in all 213 rooms. She had dutifully recorded the measurements. Complaints would have poured in if he'd transported an office into a space too small for its fixtures.

He flexed his hands, grateful the numbness had disappeared. "I don't remember room 66. Who has that office?"

Miss Crenshaw went to a file in the corner. "The room is unused. The notation says the Interrogation and Rectification Department owned it. We don't have such a department, do we?"

"Not anymore," said Nathan, taking another drink. Miss Crenshaw had placed a heating spell on the cup so the contents would stay piping hot until the last sip. "The Rectification Department used to deal with warlocks and witches who refused to sign the Magic Accords. Most of them were evildoers who didn't want to stop picking on mundanes. None of them are left."

"How were they rectificd?"

"I have no idea," he said. "The door is probably hexed to be invisible. I'd guess no one has been in there for decades. We'll have to go and release the spell, so I can transport the contents across. If there are any."

"If there are, we'll move them to one of the storage rooms in the new building," she said. "When you are ready."

"I'll be all right in a little while. Let's go release that room, and I should be able to do another floor or two."

She looked at the diagram. "Room 66 should be between 210 and 76."

Nathan finished his coffee and stood. "Would it have been too much to ask for them to number offices consecutively by floor?"

Miss Crenshaw smiled. "Having to sort out other people's problems is why you get the big bucks."

###

They finally found the room. The space between 210 and 76 proved a plain dungeon wall, composed of large fitted stones, gray and ancient. Nathan tried the obvious spells, but none of them worked. Miss Crenshaw tried a few of her own with the same result.

"This really is a stone wall," she said, "and not a bewitched door at all. Every spell we do just slides off."

"You may be right," said Nathan. "Perhaps after the rectifications were complete, the Institute physically sealed up the wall. What office is above this room?"

Miss Crenshaw checked the map she kept in her ledger. "Magical Plants."

"If we can't find the door," said Nathan, "perhaps we can get in through the ceiling."

"Nathan?" She stared over his shoulder.

He turned to find a plain wooden door with a demonic face doorknocker. It had '66' incised into its forehead.

"What did you do?" he asked her.

"Nothing. Perhaps it took time for our spells to work."

Nathan had his doubts but couldn't ignore his own eyes. The quicker they got the room unhexed, the sooner the project would be finished. He'd hate to have to tell the Old Man they had *almost* completed the mission successfully.

Seeing no handle, Nathan raised the bronze ring encircling the demon's head and banged three times. "I'll feel foolish if someone opens the door. Stand back. I'll blast it."

Before he could cast the spell, the door swung open. He saw a small room with rough stonewalls, but as he entered and looked to the right, he saw the room was quite long. Torches, already lit, hung every few feet along both sides of the room.

"Nathan," said Miss Crenshaw, as she followed him into the room, "what are those?" She pointed at a series of chains imbedded in the walls between the torches. Ugly stains covered the walls and floors beneath the chains.

"They used them to rectify the poor souls they interrogated," he guessed.

She moved closer. "Why are the torches lit?"

He shook his head. "I don't know. We better leave this room for the Old Man to deal with. I don't like the smell in here." The room smelled musty, and a strong scent of copper tickled the back of his throat.

Nathan touched the stone. "The walls feel alive." When he removed his hand, he left a white mark that soon faded.

"This is way above our pay grade, Nathan," she said. "I vote for Old Man intervention on Monday."

"I agree," said Nathan, turning around. "Where's the door?"

###

They examined the room as much as they could. Torches lit the end of the hall where the door had been. The floor sloped toward the dark end and seemed submerged in a dark liquid. Nathan almost gagged from the metallic smell and the stench of rot as he approached the edge of the dark pool.

"Don't touch the water," said Nathan, blocking Miss Crenshaw's progress with his arm. "It smells toxic."

She knelt and stuck the end of her pen into the fluid. As she examined it, she said, "Not water, Nathan. Blood."

Nathan looked overhead. "Blood? From where? Surely this pool can't have been here since the Rectification."

"I don't know," she said, looking uneasy as she moved back. "But it's rising."

Nathan, trying not to let his distaste show on his face, said, "Well, I'll just locomote us out of here." He cracked his knuckles again and reached for Miss Crenshaw's hand. He intended to move them to their office, but nothing happened.

"I must still be drained," he said. "I should be able to bust through a containment spell."

"Unless this isn't a containment spell," said Miss Crenshaw. "The room is alive. It doesn't want us to leave and tell anyone what happened here."

"How can a room be alive?" he asked.

"Who knows how many people were tortured and killed in here? Imagine the pain and suffering the room has seen and absorbed."

"Okay," said Nathan, "the Old Man can deal with that when we get out of here. I may not be strong enough to send both of us, but I can get you out of here."

Her eyes widened. "I can't leave you alone!"

"You must. Go get help. We may not survive in here until Monday."

She didn't look convinced but walked to the lit end of the room. "Okay, but don't die on me."

He smiled and jabbed the air with his hands. He felt the spell lift her and shove her against the wall. For a moment, he thought the spell would succeed. He saw the exterior hallway through her translucent form before she screamed and fell back into Room 66.

He rushed to help her up. "Are you okay?"

She gasped for air but nodded. She brushed non-existent dirt off her skirt and straightened her scarf. "What happened?"

"You almost got through," said Nathan, "but something pulled you back."

Miss Crenshaw shivered. "It felt like a thousand tiny needles were sticking me. I felt nauseated. I've never felt such pain."

"I'm sorry," said Nathan, staring at the spot on the wall where Miss Crenshaw had hung suspended. "At least you had an effect." A white shadow stuck out on the stone wall. Years of grime and dried body fluids had disappeared from the spot where Miss Crenshaw had made contact.

She walked closer and touched the wall. "What caused that?"

"I'm guessing that full-body spell you're wearing. I always wondered why you were always so well put together. Do you have to renew the spell each morning?"

She blushed. "I don't know what you're talking about."

"I should have realized before. It's a great spell. Does the magic prevent you from being hurt or just disheveled?"

"Just my appearance," she said. "I have to recast it every hour or two, but I don't even know I'm doing it anymore."

Nathan nodded. "Well, it's a tight piece of magic. Even this room couldn't break the enchantment you have around yourself."

"I hope the spell works when we're completely submerged," she said, "but I doubt it. I wish I hadn't spent so much time with numbers and had learned a few more defensive spells. You have to locomote yourself out of here. Stop being chivalrous and go for help."

Nathan didn't like leaving her behind, but her suggestion might be their only option. He'd tear the room apart stone by stone from the outside to free her if he had to. Nodding, he waved his hands. Nothing happened. He didn't even fly against the wall.

"I can't," he said. "The room doesn't want me to leave either."

Miss Crenshaw looked behind him. "Well, the blood pool is still rising."

"How's your levitation?" asked Nathan. "Perhaps we can get through the ceiling from the inside."

"Pretty good," she said, following his gaze upward. "We'll blast a hole in the ceiling and fly out?"

"Worth a try," he said, gently placing her behind him. He opened both palms facing the ceiling and sent lightning bolts at the stone overhead. The blast blinded and deafened him, but when his senses returned, he didn't see a mark on the ceiling.

"Let me try," she said, forming a glowing fireball between her palms. She thrust it at the ceiling. The fireball lingered for a moment and fell to the floor as a large cinder.

"How about the floor or the walls?" she asked.

He shook his head. "It would only weaken us, Miss Crenshaw." He looked at the black liquid slowly creeping toward them.

"Editha," she said. "Please call me Editha."

Nathan had never considered asking her for her first name. He didn't know if she was married, had children, or ran marathons for a hobby. She didn't wear a wedding ring, but that didn't mean she wasn't involved with someone. He felt doubly guilty for getting her involved with Room 66 without knowing anything about her.

"Editha," he said, "that's a nice name. I'm sorry I got you into this mess."

"We're not going to give up yet. You got me partway through the wall."

Nathan cocked his head. "Do you hear that?" A low rumbling noise echoed against the walls. At first, he thought he heard someone trying to reach them from the outside, but the longer he listened, the more the noise sounded like people moaning.

"Yes," she said. "It's coming from the blood pool."

"The best defense," said Nathan, "is a good offense." He shot another bolt of lightning, this time towards the shadowy end of the room. The resultant stench of burnt blood made them cough and their eyes water. The moaning grew louder.

"It sounds hungry," said Editha, forming and launching her fireball.

The stench and moaning grew worse. Nathan could hear the dark red fluid lapping against the walls.

"We're probably the only meal it's had in years," said Nathan. "Your personal shield may protect you until Monday morning. I'll petrify myself until help arrives."

"That may take years," said Editha, "if ever. A man and woman disappear, people assume it's for a romantic reason, not because there's a blood-sucking room on the premises."

Nathan stared at the blood pool, now closer than ever. "We're two of the smartest people I know. We'll think of a way out of here."

"I'm not good at phantasm spells," said Editha. "I doubt Room 66 would let me through even if I was."

Nathan stared at the Editha-shaped figure on the stones and pressed his palm against a nearby wall. When he pulled it away, the white mark quickly turned gray and dirty. "Why don't I leave a mark but you do?"

"It must be my full-body spell."

"Probably. Or only the pure of heart can affect it."

She blushed again. "I'm not…"

He moved to the spot where she'd merged with the wall and touched it. "The room's life energy is weaker here. I can sense it. Whatever is locking us in and blocking our spells is missing from this spot."

"Nathan!" Editha exclaimed, moving to the wall at the lit end of the room. "I think the blood touched me. We don't have much time."

"Are you okay?" he asked, looking at her tiny shoes.

She nodded. "We won't stay alive until Monday. We have to try to get out now."

"Okay, I'll send you through the same place in the wall we tried before. Since that spot seems weaker, you might have a chance." The deep crimson pool grew closer.

"But what about you?" she asked. "You won't survive long enough for me to find help."

"Let me worry about that," said Nathan. "I've got spells I haven't tried since my wild adolescence. I may find a way to beat this bloody room."

To demonstrate, Nathan knelt and hexed the stones beneath their feet. The musty mugginess of the room changed to cool air, and the lapping of the liquid slowed. A white film spread across the pool as ice formed on the surface. It grew whiter as it thickened and hardened. The moaning became a whisper.

"That should hold it for a while," he said. "Please stand against the wall."

She frowned at the frozen pool, already making cracking noises as it tried to throw off Nathan's spell.

"I'm ready," she said, inexplicably taking the scarf from around her neck and holding it in her hands.

Nathan, ignoring the sounds coming from the fractured ice, steeled himself for the most powerful locomotor spell he'd ever thrown. He felt it build within him and spread to his outspread hands. He released the spell, dimly aware that Editha's scarf had elongated and was snaking toward him.

She fell backwards through the wall. Nathan's theory had been correct: that part of Room 66 wasn't as adequately shielded this time. Editha merged with the stones and became transparent as the locomotor spell thrust her into the hallway beyond.

Nathan felt himself moving forward even though he had not weakened his spell by including himself. Editha's scarf, clutched in her hand, wrapped around his waist and pulled him headlong into her.

He passed through her and fell onto the floor in the hallway a half second before Editha fell on top of him. The room screamed and roared as the wall snapped shut. They were free.

"Nice," said Nathan as he touched the scarf. "An entanglement spell?"

Editha lifted herself off him and stood. She dusted her immaculate skirt and offered him her hand. "You're welcome."

Nathan pulled himself up. He wasn't as clean and pristine as Editha. Staring at the wall, he said, "I wonder if we can get hazard pay from the Old Man for this?"

"We need to let the investigators clean it out before we try to unhex it again." She tied her scarf neatly around her neck.

Nathan nodded and dusted himself off. "You have to show me that full-body spell. But, first, let's finish the move. I don't want to have to spend the entire weekend here." He held out his arm.

She took it. "Why? Do you have plans?"

"Actually, I was considering inviting you out to dinner," he said. "If you're free."

"Well, I'm not free," she said with a smile, "but I am available."

MEXICO CITY

"What's your name?"

"Irrelevant. You're not here for my fascinating self."

"They said you are the best."

"So the best I am. Sit."

The lady nodded, unconvinced and with a disappointed look in her eyes. But she did sit down. Clemance noticed her appearance—an elegant red dress and expensive make-up contrasted with her messy nails. First-time gamers were always nervous.

"This place. It was difficult to find, you know? I almost gave up."

"Were my indications unclear?" he asked.

"On the contrary. It's just that I was unaware this kind of business even existed in my hometown. Here, in the very centre, under everybody's eyes."

"The best place to hide something is in plain sight. And this is by no means the only one. London is a big city."

"That a foreigner like you seems to know better than I do."

"Since you're here, you should consider yourself lucky," he said. "Have you got what I've asked for?"

"My specs? Yeah, sure. I have them here on a card. You can retrieve all you need from that."

What an old-fashioned and unsafe way of treating sensitive data. But then, would she be here if she cared about them in the first place? Clemance thought, without comment. He took the device, inserted it in a long unused card slot, and started working. His tiny computer was a shining, compact, dark-blue cube—the only bright light in the small room.

"I've already got everything at home. The hardware, and all the rest," she said in a low voice.

"Obviously."

She stared at him for a moment, then her eyes began wandering. Inquisitive, and yet nervous, almost scared. "This trade. For how long have you been doing it?"

"Long enough."

"So you're an expert. Tell me something. What's the most common scenario customers want you to prepare?"

"You're one of them. Can't you guess?"

"No. Yes. Sex…? Perversions, maybe?"

"Sweet. You're definitively not my typical client." He couldn't avoid smiling. Naïve too, and this was not typical of first-timers either. *Maybe in this resides her charm, more than in her beauty or her exquisite clothes*. "People are not that normal. Not in these days, no."

"Answer me. Please."

"Death," he said, matter-of-factly.

"You mean killing people?"

"No, even though killer scenarios are quite popular. Nobody kills any longer—rich people like you, at least. That's a poor man's fancy nowadays. Impractical and rude." He shook his head. "But I meant something different. I was referring to their own death."

"I'm not sure I understand."

"Humans are afraid of dying. So they want to try what death looks like first. What it feels like." He shrugged. "They think knowing in advance will take part of their pain away. Their fear."

"That's impossible."

"Is it?" He stopped for a moment, staring at her. "Actually, it's rather easy."

"It's a question of logic. If you're dead, how can you feel anything at all?"

"You don't get it. They're interested in experiencing what comes just before. How they would feel at that moment. What follows, they won't care. That is, most of them don't."

She looked away, and he carried on working. "Relax," he said. "It will take a while."

###

"We're searching for hell."

"Reality is not bad enough for you?" Clemance asked, observing without curiosity the strange duo in front of him. One of them was older, huge and richly clothed; the other, young and handsome, classical features and a querulous light in his eyes. They had come in without appointment—a few hours after the young lady in red. That alone spoke volumes about how well connected they were—to know where to find him straight away. Not first-timers for sure, these fellows. He knew Mexico City could be a place pretty hard to locate without contacting him first, and it was intended to be.

"You're a funny one. I like people with sense of humour," the older one said. "But no. What we want is the perfect ordeal."

"Perfection is in the mind only and doesn't generally translate well in human artifacts, virtual or not," he replied, noncommittal.

"You're a game dealer. Better than that: you're known to be a fucking genius in this trade—*the ethical genius*, or so they call you. Well, genius, you will prepare for me the scenario I'm looking for. I want him to scream." The old guy said, indicating his companion. "I want him to bleed to death. A thousand times over."

"And you, what do you want?" Clemance asked the other, who had not said a word until that moment.

"Me? I only want him to beg mercy for the sins of the flesh. When he's feasting on my body."

He observed the young guy, dressed in black, his hair platinum blond, and transparent nail polish on his manicured hands.

At a pure aesthetical level, they would make best-selling

characters. If only they weren't morally so unoriginal. Some hours of hard work on these two.

"I can deliver suffering and anguish, all shades you can dream of. And you'll be able to tweak the scenario afterwards, to suit the mood of the moment." Clemance said, eventually. "I believe I've just received your encrypted specs on my cloud-box. Do you want me to start?"

The two looked at him, nodding.

"It's going to be rather expensive."

"I know your tariffs," the older one said.

"I'm not talking about money."

"Why have you called your shop Mexico City, anyway?" The young one asked with a curious regard. "Addicted to Latin American stuff, that's it? But you have nothing of the sort here. Not even a photo on the wall. Is it just for the exotic vibe of the name?"

"I thought you liked exotic."

"Here." The other ignored his friend altogether and made a couple of quick operations on his tablet. "Stocks are already on your corporate account. You can check it out. Now proceed. We don't have the whole night."

The conversation was over. Clemance patiently unfolded the encoded data and began weaving them in the appropriate scenario, while the two began caressing each other, ignoring his presence. Then the young one produced a shining stiletto, cutting the palm of his hand and letting his companion lick out the blood. His fingers dancing on the virtual keyboard, Clemance remained still, observing with cold detachment the reflex of his green screen on the blade.

###

"Are you there?" a voice cracked from the speakers a few hours later.

A few moments of silence, then it came again. "Clemance, put your goddamn finger on the goddamn keyboard and open the channel."

He contemplated for a moment an act of rebellion. *Consolatory and useless, like the majority of human actions.* He did as instructed.

"I'm here. So?"

"Just checking in. Tell me about your daily preys. Make me dream."

"Got three new profiles. Reading them for upload."

"Fire them out."

"I'm not done yet. Still filtering. It will take about 30 minutes."

"Oh yes. I always forget—you're one of the ethicals."

"Don't like to be called in this way."

"But this is what you are, my boy."

"No, this is what you leeches call us," Clemance snapped.

"Whatever. Too bad the others are not geniuses like you."

"Make it one hour. For my coffee break."

"You lazy, touchy bastard." The voice sneered at him, before breaking into laughter. "Leave the full profiles out for now. Give me specs I can use. Anything good?"

"You'll like them. A lusty she-economist, a young, suicidal emo and a sadistic shotacon."

"Nothing original. You disappoint me, baby."

"Quite common, I'll concede. They look pretty though. Stylish even in the flesh. Almost authentic. And they get better when you load them on."

"I'll trust your judgment. What's your favourite?"

"The economist."

"Why? Because she's lustful?"

"No. Because she's desperate."

"Is she going to be a good sell?"

"Magnificent."

Through the speakers, he could hear the familiar sounds of his handler recording the information, preparing the calls and updates for the market.

"Fine job, my boy. If we're lucky, we might use these ones in a few new scenarios. Or we can let clients bid individually for including them as guest stars in their otherwise fully loaded games. A bit of novelty is always welcome. Especially now that we're getting better customers by the day." A laugh, with a satisfactory note in it. "We're upscaling. Old wealth. That kind of people wants the real thrill, not fake simulations.

Their boredom threshold is dangerously low, and we need to beat the competition. The good news is that your brand, Mexico City, is becoming a guarantee of quality. Dystopia on tap, refined and glowing. You might be a ethical smug, but you're a damn good one."

"Glad to have made your day."

"By the by, do you think your newbies will live long? Outside your games, I mean."

"Why do you care? I'm not going to give you their unfiltered data anyway."

"I know you won't. Call it professional curiosity. And now that we talk about it…I'vc always believed you're a sick fuck, Clemance. You, your reptile eyes and those delicate white hands of a princess. You look so gentle and polite, and you're the nastiest of all game architects I've ever met in my long and adventurous life. You're a monster, a vampire without all that shine & sparkle." The voice sounded lower now, its tone more confidential. "I have checked your records. A surprisingly high number of your customers remain alive for only a few weeks after they have come to see you. Ethical, my decrepit English ass. If I didn't know better, I would start thinking you hand them something toxic." Another laugh. "Or maybe Mexico City games are simply too amazing for them to come back to reality after they've tasted them. You're too effective for your own good."

"Are you complaining, Neil?"

"With all the money you bring in? I wouldn't dare. But at least you could give me their complete data once they're gone for good. What damage could it possibly do?"

"You already have my answer. It's not going to change. And no, it's not a question of price."

"That's why I never offered you one. But just to let you know, baby, I've come out with a little theory about this too."

"You seem to have a lot of free time these days. Has your mistress dumped you? Your wife did it long ago."

"Smartass. You see, I'm convinced you have your own collection of horrors. For your private entertainment, during all those long nights alone in your cubicle designing nightmares for public consumption. I don't really want to know."

"And you won't."

"No doubt about it. Well, my sensitive, ethical genius, have to go now. Stay cool."

Clemance unplugged the speakers and closed his eyes. His mind went back to the lady in red, the economist. To what had happened after.

It had taken him about one hour before the game and its characters were ready, according to the specs she had provided.

"Have you tried it yourself?" She'd asked him with curiosity.

"Tried what?"

"The scenario you were talking about. Death, you know."

He had looked at her, into those amber eyes unable to conceal a tormented soul. He never discussed anything but business with customers, and personal questions were not included in the service agreement. The young woman was so new to the market that she ignored even those basic rules.

"Almost every day. " He'd paused, searching for words that would not sound too cynical. He didn't want to hurt her. Actually, he didn't know why he was replying either. *Maybe because I could feel sorry for you, gorgeous lady in a fancy dress.* "I'm pretty ordinary, lady, like the guy next door. Each time, I try a slight variation. There are so many ways to die, you do wonder how we keep alive. I came to think it's this very wonder that does the job. It's...refreshing."

She had shivered, looking at him with her eyes wide open. He could read attraction and revulsion at the same time, but also a bottomless sadness and loneliness.

"You need not to fear me, Coralia," he'd said, gently.

"How do you know my name? Wasn't in the specs."

"As if anybody spending his life in the virtual land could ignore these things," he'd replied, trying to wash any hint of sarcasm from his voice. "Relax, I said. I'm here to serve."

He had retrieved the device from the box and put it down on the table. "Procedure completed. The game has been preloaded with your biometric data and your preferences. New behavioural details will be locally uploaded at each run, to make simulations more accurate. You will get loading instructions and access codes directly into your cloud-box. Identification is by a combination of iris recognition and psychometrics. To make sure only you can access and play it. We care about your privacy. And talking about that…" He tilted his head, hinting at the card. "Don't ever do it again. Encryption on external devices is always insufficient. They're too old, and you don't need them anyway." He'd smiled at her. "Good fun ahead, lady in red. That lithe alien is going to give you a lot of pleasure. It will be exactly like in your dreams, only better. You might decide you don't want to get back to this world, but this is a risk you knew you were taking when crossing this line."

She'd lowered her eyes, suddenly embarrassed. "How much do I owe you?"

"I don't want your money," he had said in a cold voice. "You've already paid me anyway."

"How?"

"Haven't you figured it out yet?" He stared into his screen to avoid meeting her regard. "With your own data. They're now part of my virtual bank. They will be anonymised and used to construct other games. Other scenarios, and characters, for people that pay us real money. Some of them will virtually kill other customers like you, populating our prime clients' unique version of delirious escapism. In a way, you will live forever."

Clemance could see her shaking.

"Privacy and personal data protection are the reason, right? The reason why it's illegal."

"No." He'd lifted his head, looking straight into her eyes. "But it's because it's illegal that you're ready to pay such a high price. Didn't prohibitionism teach you smart people anything? Not even to you, Coralia the economist?"

She'd grabbed the card and collected her bag, in a rush of panic. "Goodbye. I don't think we'll see each other again."

"Not if you can avoid it. Enjoy your game."

She'd left and started walking in a hurry on the Strand toward Waterloo Bridge, dismissing the cabs. Within seconds, he had closed his shop and followed her, for once inexplicably drawn to a customer. He knew by instinct where she was going, and he was not mistaken. After a short stroll on the Thames' desolate bank, she'd stopped, looking at the murky water. He could hear her mind screaming, speaking more loudly than words. And he'd kept watching, waiting, not sure what to expect, feeling her pain.

"Delirious escapism, this is how he called it. Is that what I have bought?" She'd said aloud, almost in reply to his thoughts, turning her head to observe the city. "Yes, escapism—delirious or fucking lucid. It doesn't matter, at the end of the day."

Clemance hadn't been able to avoid looking at the Thames either. Dark waters with a sparkle of lights, futuristic buildings and gargoyles in grapheme, backstages of so many of his games. He'd felt the urge to go and get her, take her into his arms, but he could not force himself to act. After having explored all combinations of lives, created all possible, outlandish scenarios, and for such a long time, he found himself surprisingly shy in a three-dimension reality. He'd stood where he was, unable to make a move.

She had smiled at the gargoyles, observing their monstrous heads and their hollow eyes. "I should have populated my game with gargoyles, instead of unlikely aliens," she'd said. "Being one of them. At least I would have the option of coming here and talking to my stony sisters, when losing my mind once and for all." Calm and collected, she'd produced a cutter from her bag, plunging it deep into her throat. Then she'd jumped in the water.

He had remained there, like he was watching the scene of a movie or one of his games. Not moving, observing her body in the dark red dress slowly carried away by the river, for minutes that had seemed ice ages. Then he had left the place in silence.

So sad. She hasn't enjoyed her alien lover—not even for one night. She could have waited.

###

It was dawn, and a pale light came through the glassy panels of his ceiling. Mexico City, his shop, the centre of his world.

This would be a weird place in hell, should it exist—which it does not, of course. And I would be the trickster god that shows souls their way, leading them to the fall. He had almost finished his work—scenarios like exquisite artworks, selling lucid dreams and hallucinations-on-demand. Building perfect places for people to go and stay there, never desiring to come back. Until ready for another outstanding simulation, signed off by the ethical genius that so often claimed their real lives.

Enough self-pity, you ethical idiot. Be the monster you're designed to be, and take responsibility.

He observed his latest creations with the clinical eye of a neuroscientist and the refined taste of great artists, like the genius game architect he was. Clemance, the best of all. His new three characters were there, slowly moving on the screen, rising from their slumber.

The pretty economist, the sadistic old guy, the depressive teenager. Eternally young, forever smiling.

CUSTOMER SERVICE

Martin stormed into WaveFlicks' local office. He'd just spent six hours online arguing with robots, and he still didn't have access to Wave Length 27, which meant he couldn't watch the 33rd season of *Detective What*. The machines just couldn't comprehend the stress this was causing him. He plowed right past the line of agitated customers, knocking a white-haired woman to the ground.

"I need to talk to a human," he demanded.

The receptionist looked up from the plastic desk, glaring over purple, cats-eye glasses. "Please get in line and wait your turn."

A vein pulsed in his forehead. His cheeks flushed red. Sweat dripped down his temples. He knew the thing sitting at the desk wasn't human. Sure there were a few strands of hair sticking out of her bun and a tiny stain on her blouse, but those were details the corporations added to fool people. The smile was too perfect and the hands remained steadily clasped like a toy steeple.

"I'm serious," he continued, grabbing the desk's edge to steady his shaking hands. "I need to talk to a real, breathing human."

"First, you must get in line. When it is your turn, then you may tell me your complaint," it said in a cool, even tone.

"I'll only share it with a human. Get one, NOW. I've been on the phone for hours talking to machines. I want to talk to someone who understands emotion." He was shouting, barely aware of the other customers' muttering complaints behind him.

"Sir, I assure you, I am perfectly capable of resolving your issue. Please get in line."

He shook his head and stomped his feet. "I WANT A HUMAN!"

"I *am* human," it replied, raising its voice to a volume just shy of his.

"I can't believe it; even the bots are bitchy these days!"

"Excuse me," it said standing up from its desk. "I deserve respect. Just because I work in the service industry, doesn't mean you can walk all over me."

"Humans deserve respect; robots don't."

"I am human."

"So what, they've programmed you to lie now?" He leaned over so he was breathing in its too calm face. No wrinkles appeared around its eyes. Its lips didn't even twitch.

"No one has programmed me, sir. Please calm down, or I will have to call security."

He couldn't believe the audacity. Not only was it lying to his face, but it was threatening to have him removed from the building. Thanks to this ridiculousness, he couldn't breathe without snorting.

Despite his hoggish grunting, the robot stared at him, eye to eye. Its calm just fueled his rage. He would prove that it wasn't human at all.

He reached over the desk and squeezed its throat. Its arms flailed. It made a relatively convincing fake gasp. He waited for the hiss and pop of circuits shorting out, but it never came. He felt a steadily slowing pulse.

It's all just programming designed to trick us, he told himself as he squeezed harder. Blood pooled beneath his fingernails. Something gave out underneath them.

Realizing his mistake, he let go. But it was too late. He had just killed a woman in front of a dozen witnesses. From what he had heard, they didn't get WaveFlicks in prison, which meant he'd never get to watch the 33rd season of *Detective What*.

GREGORY'S TREE

The Village of Eden's good citizens shuffled across the creaky wooden floor of the town hall in search of seats, while Gregory Tyburn, the speaker they turned out to hear, sat at the front of the hall trying to gauge how many members of the crowd would buy a book after the presentation. Perusing the audience Gregory thought, *This bunch looks good for about 30 books.*

Reverend Stickney, Gregory's host, urged those in the back of the hall to "come on up to the front." Gregory had just enjoyed a delicious supper prepared by the cleric's wife, and the meal left the speaker feeling energetic about that evening's presentation, which was something Gregory rarely felt anymore.

How he became a professional speaker was as much chance as choice. It was an outgrowth of the publication of a cheesy, true-crime book that he didn't write, but which held his name. The book was the result of him having been a junior police detective assigned to a special team tasked with apprehending a murderer who had used his victims in satanic rituals. Gregory's involvement in the case hadn't gone beyond coordinating the flow of information and leads between federal, state, and local investigators. He never even questioned a witness, but the witchcraft aspect of the crime made it sensational enough to warrant intense media scrutiny, and, because he was the information-clearing house, Gregory became recognizable to the reporters covering the case. That it took several months before a suspect—named Stan Fenton—was apprehended only increased Gregory's exposure.

Fenton took trophies from his victim, and enough evidence was collected from his home to get a confession. Gregory was aware of the walk-on role he'd played in catching Fenton, so when he was approached about collaborating on a book about the investigation, his first response was to say, "Get lost."

But the publishing house recruiter quickly explained that the detective wouldn't actually have to write the book. All Gregory would have to do was point out errors, approve or disapprove chapters as they were produced, and keep the project on track so the book could hit the racks while the case was still fresh in the media. For his cooperation Gregory would get top billing and a decent payday.

"Why me?" Gregory asked.

"You weren't my first choice," the recruiter said. "I did talk to others. Some wanted too much money, some have already worked out book deals, and some just aren't interested. So does it matter?"

Gregory agreed that it didn't matter, and four months later *Orders from Hell: The Inside Story of the Stan Fenton Murders* hit the paperback racks. The promotional blurb called it "The story of a madman obsessed with serving Satan—by a member of the team that caught him." It went straight to the top of the paperback market and a television movie deal was quickly negotiated. In addition to getting a portion of the television money, Gregory was named "special consultant" to the production.

However, while Gregory was basking in the glory of a minor best seller, he had to deal with the resentment of his colleagues who'd actually worked on the case. They were more than a little angry that a subordinate would claim any credit, and some detectives began referring to Gregory as "Sherlock." That put a heavy strain on the detective's working relations, so he was relieved when his request for a leave of absence—so he could work on the TV movie—was approved. He figured the resentment would diminish by the time he returned, but once in

Hollywood, he quickly found out the movie business was not what he expected.

Gregory's first surprise was that the director wasn't interested in receiving any input from the detective. "Why bring me here?" Gregory asked a studio executive.

"To have your name on the credits and to promote the movie. You can do some talk shows, make a few personal appearances—I understand your publisher is planning another run; do some signings—basically, whet peoples' appetites for the film."

"If that's what you want, okay."

"Great, I'll call the promotions department, and they'll get the ball rolling."

"Is there anything else I can do?" Gregory asked.

"Make sure you're knowledgeable about the subject…read the book again."

Gregory was about to say he had been on the investigation team, but he knew the executive's advice was to keep the detective from looking like a fool before a crowd, so he did as suggested, plus more. So he would at least sound as if he were an expert, he read other books on Satanism and satanic crime, all the time wondering if they were written the same way as the book with his name on it.

During his first appearance on a radio show, he discussed his role on the case, and—peppering in tidbits he'd learned from other books—repeated the rumors about the possible involvement of a larger cult. The broadcast turned out fairly well, leading to an appearance on a syndicated television talk show where he heard the audience gasp every time he listed a vague anecdote or questionable fact supporting the existence of a satanic underground. That made Gregory secretly grin, for he discovered he really enjoyed messing with the crowd's heads.

When the whole experience came to an end, Gregory credited his talk show appearances with pushing the book into a tenth printing and attracting enough of an audience to put *Satan's Butcher*—the movie's title—into the top 20 position for its week; a respectable rating for a made-for-TV movie about a mass murderer in an age when the media is full of them. That's when a literary agent with a new deal contacted Gregory.

"I've read your book, and I watched you on TV. You handled yourself well. Do you think you can write another?" he asked.

Gregory expected that question from a literary agent, but was still surprised when it was asked. "I don't know," he replied.

"Sure you can. All you need is another ghostwriter. The guy you worked with last time is alright, but he's only good for rewriting newspaper horror stories. You need a real creative talent to write a book about the underground Satanism network. How do you like *Satan's Mafia* for a title?"

"There're only rumors about a network. Nothing substantial," Gregory said.

"Rumors are enough."

That confused Gregory, and the silence signaled the agent to press with his pitch. "Look, this movie gig of yours is over. You made some money, but what do you have lined up now?"

"I took a leave of absence from the department to come out here. I was going to head back in a couple days."

"Forget that. If you collaborate on a new book, I'm sure I can swing a good deal. Once it's on the shelves, there'll be a tour to promote it, and once that's over, I can get you out on the lecture circuit. There are thousands of Bible colleges, dioceses and churches full of decent folk who'll pay for someone like you to blow the lid off the satanic underground for them. My agency will handle the booking; all you'll have to do is show up and scare the rubes into thinking their next-door-neighbors are Satanists. There's a gravy train here Greg, and I see you as ready to go for the ride."

Gregory thought about the offer for all of two seconds before saying, "I accept."

Five-years later, the gravy train was still moving, and it took Gregory all over the country, including to countless stops at jerkwater farming communities like Eden. However, while he believed that one small town pretty much looked like another, before he checked in, he would drive around to see what sights such small communities offered. In that spirit, he was passing by Eden's town square when he noticed a huge tree overshadowing the far end of the park. Thinking it might be interesting, he parked the car and walked over to the tree, which—despite being late June—was totally leafless. *It must be dead*, he thought. However, despite its apparent condition, a small crew was carefully pruning the giant. Finding a dead tree wasn't strange, but finding a dead tree that was still being cared for was. But it wasn't any of his business, so he stayed far enough away from the crew so his presence would not interfere with their work. Instead, he found a cast iron plaque on a steel pole. A historical marker that read:

From 1635 to 1789 this large oak was used by the Town of Eden to hang traitors, murderers and witches. At least 50 people were executed on its branches.

He turned to the tree and mused, *They hung witches here: I can't recall ever speaking to an audience that could make that claim.* The tree's trunk was easily the width of seven or eight men, and its peak was taller than the steeple of the church located across the street. As he continued to examine the tree, he noticed that two main branches defied logic and nature, for they didn't grow out into a "Y" shape to reach for the sun, but intersected and grew into what resembled a handlebar used to steer a lawnmower. *How the hell did that happen?*

He studied the tree as he moved toward a large stone structure at the center of the square, where another plaque provided far less detail. It read:

Eden Communal Oven. Built 1635.

Gregory shook his head, ready to return to his car, when he noticed a third marker that wasn't near anything. *May as well take the whole tour,* he thought. Again, it was a cast iron plaque—this one attached to a rock—with more details than the last.

On this spot was Eden's communal well which, in 1635, became contaminated with diphtheria and resulted in many deaths. By God's grace the town survived.

"Diphtheria…Jesus," Gregory said.

"No, not Jesus, it was Satan's work," said a voice from behind him.

He turned to find a curly haired man dressed in a black suit.

"Yes, of course it was," said Gregory, not wanting to sound flippant.

"I'm Reverend Stickney," the man said, extending his hand. "Frankie, the foreman," he gestured to the pruning crew, "had me informed that a stranger was in the park, and the promotional picture in the contract package told me it was you, Mr. Tyburn."

"Ah, you're my contact," Gregory said fumbling. "It's a pleasure to meet you."

"I'm a big fan. I've read all your books and watched you on TV. Last year I even attended your lecture at Taylor University, so the pleasure is all mine," he said as they shook hands. "I see you're interested in Eden's history. Do the tree's and well's stories surprise you?"

"Not really. I might be from the city, but I understand the history of this part of the country, so I'm not surprised that Eden's roots are pre-Revolutionary War."

"Of course…Since you seem interested in sightseeing, there are other things to see in our little town. Let me take you on a tour."

"Okay, but any idea why they're pruning that dead tree?" The reverend didn't respond, so Gregory tactfully said, "It's still quite a tree, even if it is dead."

"We're very proud of it," the reverend said.

"But if it's dead, why not cut it down?"

The cleric turned to Gregory and—as if he were talking to a child—said, "Why Mr. Tyburn, it's the hanging tree."

"Oh," said Gregory, accepting the reverend's cryptic explanation, but at the same time he thought, *Stupid me, with the plaques and all, it's the town's big attraction.* He then said, "Lead on."

"While I know pride is one of the seven deadly sins, I am proud of my community," the reverend said. "But, unfortunately, a cancer is trying to invade our body. That's why the town board contacted you. We need your help with a serious problem."

"Involving Satanism?"

"Yes," the cleric replied with a sigh. "You see, it's up to me to keep Satan from getting his claws into this town. It can be a heavy burden, but it's a job which I dare not shirk."

"Can you be more specific?"

"Yes, but later. The town is interested in your presentation. They want to know about the Satanic underground, how it works, how extensive it is, how today's youths are being lured in, and how well versed you are before asking for help."

"That's the main body of my program," Gregory said, ignoring that the whole Satanist conspiracy rap he was selling was a fraud. Years before he'd hit the road, the FBI had dismissed the idea that any such conspiracy existed, beyond a few demented individuals motivated by devil worship to commit crimes. Gregory was aware he was a snake oil salesman, so it forced him to crank up his level of sincerity before making a public appearance. Like a touring musician who only has one hit to his name, having to repeat the presentation night after night can take its toll; so whenever he felt depressed about what he considered to be a scam, he thought of the nice home and late model car the book sales and lecturing had bought him. He also told himself, "I'm an entertainer; I'm not responsible for what people take away from my presentations."

The reverend led his guest to all the points of interest Eden had to offer; such as the small business district, and the tree-lined neighborhoods. By the time they finished, it was time for supper, and the reverend led Gregory to the church residence where a meal was waiting.

Velma, the reverend's wife, was busy in the kitchen, but moved to greet the men. "Sit down; the stew is almost ready."

"She's very prompt about dinner," the reverend said.

"You know it's a special dinner tonight," Velma said. "I don't want it getting cold."

The reverend smiled. "She makes a great stew, but it's nothing compared to her apple pie. Now that's heavenly; you'll love it."

The "special dinner" must be in my honor Gregory thought, resolving to be as appreciative as possible. "Smells great," he said.

Pulling out a chair, the reverend said, "Please, sit and enjoy."

"Thank you," Gregory said sitting.

The Stickney's two teenaged children, Deborah and Paul, joined them, and when Mrs. Stickney sat the stew on the table, the family's eyes lit up. They said grace and bowls were filled. Gregory found it to be quite delicious. As they ate, Mrs. Stickney filled cups with tea, but when she passed a cup to Gregory he declined, saying, "No thanks. I would appreciate some coffee, but only if you have some ready."

"Are you sure?" she said adding, "This is a special blend."

The reverend interjected saying, "What Velma is trying to say is…tea is all we drink. Our religious practices prevent us from drinking anything stronger."

"Do you have milk?"

"Of course. Deborah, please get Mr. Tyburn a glass of milk."

"But…?" Mrs. Stickney said while holding up a teacup, a sort of pleading on her face.

"Now Velma, Mr. Tyburn is our guest, and he'd like milk. It's up to us to make him feel at home."

Deborah returned from the kitchen and sat a glass of milk near Gregory who said, "Thanks."

He didn't understand what the big deal was, and it reinforced his belief he would never understand overly-religious people. Finishing his stew, he anticipated a slice of the apple pie. When Gregory was given desert, he found it to be Heaven, ambrosia and bliss rolled into one. The crust was moist and flaky, but it was the fruit filling—which was as thick and sweet as syrup—that was worth dying for. Gregory had never had a dessert as good, and he was so enchanted by the pie that he barely noticed everyone else at the table reacting in much the same way. The conversation ceased as they all concentrated on eating.

It was as if they were hypnotized and drugged by the delicious dessert.

Gregory had a second helping of pie, but not the third he craved, because the Stickneys had eaten the rest. After spending a few minutes to digest, Gregory said, "That was delicious. More than delicious, I can't find the words. Just what was in that?"

"Special apples…" said Velma, but her husband interrupted her before she could elaborate.

"From the village's communal orchard," the reverend said. "I'm told the soil enhances the fruit's sugar content…you had the pie; you tasted the results for yourself."

"Yes, I was just curious."

"Of course you were, but we should be going to the town hall. You no doubt need to prepare."

"Yeah."

"Then we should be on our way," the reverend said standing. Gregory did the same the memory of the pie making him feel lightheaded as he walked.

###

Gregory drove to the town hall, and with the help of church volunteers, set up his equipment. Once ready, the doors were opened, and when the room was full, the reverend gestured and the doors were shut and—surprising Gregory—locked. While he puzzled over that, the reverend introduced him. Once the polite applause faded, Gregory took center stage and thanked the reverend and the crowd. Not wanting to waste time, he went right into the presentation. "It may surprise some of you to know that worshipping Satan, in itself, is not a crime in this country. The Constitution, gives Satanists and practitioners of the occult the same protection to worship whatever they choose, as it gives any member of this audience."

There were boos and catcalls in response, and someone yelled, "It's a crime here!" The remark elicited cheers and laughter among several audience members.

Gregory smiled and said, "Because people can worship however they want to, this has led to the formation of 'mainstream cults'. Those cults operate above ground on the fringes of society, and more or less within the law. An example would be the Krishnas [which elicited more boos], but an example appropriate for this lecture is the Church of Satan."

At the mention of that church, the crowd suddenly went wild. Many in the audience began to pray, while others began to shake and dance. Gregory looked at the reverend and found him talking in a language he at first couldn't identify. After a few seconds, he recognized it as speaking in tongues. It was up to Gregory to calm the crowd. "People, people! Please let me continue!" A good number of the audience calmed down, and soon the rest followed. "Thank you. Please, if you'd stop interrupting me, I'd like to get on with the presentation, because there's a lot of material to cover. Thank you. Now as I was saying, this 'church' was founded by former lion tamer Anton LaVay—"

"He's damned and burning in Hell," someone hissed, and a strange thing happened to Gregory; he found himself agreeing with that assessment.

Nodding, Gregory said, "Mr. LaVay crowed himself the 'Black Pope' and I'm sure he's going to spend an eternity paying for that."

Suddenly, the entire audience went to their knees and began to pray. Many openly wept, while others violently shook. Before he could stop himself, Gregory joined them in prayer, but after a moment he realized he was kneeling and—more than a little embarrassed—he stood. Despite his confusion, he continued with the lecture.

"Again, these cults operate in public and rarely commit crimes. Rest assured their financial books are watched, but that's a matter for the IRS and of no interest to me. It's the cults," Gregory's voice suddenly grew loud, "that commit crimes of violence like kidnapping, rape, child abuse, ritual murder, topped off by cannibalism, that's what we're here to discuss, so let's get started." But first, Gregory had to calm down enough to speak without shouting. *Whatever it is that gets them worked up must be contagious.* Nonetheless, he proceeded and outlined the "satanic underground" and its "holdings" in drugs, pornography and prostitution.

Since he didn't have any facts to support those claims, he quickly moved onto the case from which he'd made his current career. This part of the presentation included slides of the crime scenes and the satanic paraphernalia found in Stan Fenton's home. It was a great way for him to promote his third book—*The Underworld*—in which he claimed Fenton was a member of a massive satanic cult that was still at large. At that point, Gregory began to cover how cult members are recruited, and he related the story of a girl named "Linda," whose case was revealed when she called a Christian radio talk show. Gregory said he had a tape of the call and, flipping a switch, a girl's voice filled the auditorium.

"Linda" said she was born into a satanic cult, and her parents made her kill and eat her grandfather. "They did that so I would have power when I came of age." She added that while a pre-teen, she had ritualistic sex with dozens of cult members, resulting in several pregnancies. She claimed each fetus was aborted and used in a ritual. This information produced a loud, collective gasp from the audience.

She then provided details on how the cult sacrificed the children it either bought or kidnapped. "The kid's throat would be cut and the blood collected in a chalice and shared with the coven." Several members of the audience returned to their knees and prayed, and Gregory felt a real urge to join them, but he resisted because he'd hired "Linda" to make the call and act out a script he'd written. *That was $200 well spent*, he thought while reading the slide listing "Warning Signs of the Doorways To Satan."

"These are signs which parents need to be aware of," he said. "They are changes in a child's behavior, friends and manner of dress, including drug use; a curiosity of the occult and black magic; a preoccupation with horror movies and books, and an interest in heavy metal music," leading into Gregory's favorite part of the show, "I'm sure you remember the music you listened to when you were young, and I'll bet your parents hated it." The audience responded with a collective blank stare. "Because adults hated it, you probably loved it, but this music is more than shake, rattle and roll. It's more cynical and it's far too much of an influence on our youth."

A murmur of excitement coursed through the crowd. Gregory believed that such a shared feeling among the audience was good for the show, so he let it run and die out on its own. When attention was again focused on him, Gregory clicked the projector and the jacket of a heavy metal album hit the screen. It was by the group "Oedipuss and the MF'ers," and it depicted a teenager's bedroom, with all the typical trappings of a youth who listened to that music. In the foreground, two sneaker-clad feet hovered off the ground, and in the background was the shadow of someone who was hanged.

"The members of this band think this album cover is funny. How can anyone make fun of any suicide, much less one committed by someone so young, and still be allowed to produce music? It's reckless endangerment, but there's more." He continuously clicked the projector showing slide after slide of album covers by bands with names like "Beelzebub," "Goat Dance," "Vampir," and "Bloody Altar." They all featured inverted crosses and pentagrams, snarling beasts and black-leather-clad musicians. He ended the show with a back angle shot of the audience at an Oedipuss concert, and it showed scores of youths with their arms raised high, index and little fingers extended into the sign of "devil horns."

God, I love rock 'n roll, Gregory thought, but just as quickly as it entered his mind he was filled with shame and anger. After a pause, those feelings subsided, and he continued with the presentation, but slower than before. "In my research…I talked to dozens of youths who said they were first drawn to witchcraft and Satanism by this music. One told me how it began with sex and drugs and grew to sacrificing small animals like kittens and puppies. Fortunately, he was saved, but not before desecrating several churches."

"What kind of churches?" an old man shouted.

"Mixed, Roman Catholic, Episcopalian, Presbyterian, Methodist…"

"They don't have the tree!" the old man yelled. "Without the tree, they're a bunch of fools, dupes of the Anti-Christ." The audience whooped a collective agreement.

Gregory had no idea what the man meant, but this was *his* show and he wasn't going to lose control. "Excuse me?" he said, but it had no affect, so he repeated it louder. That caused the reverend to raise his hands and direct the crowd to calm down, which it did. Gregory continued.

"As I was saying, several churches were desecrated, and that's when I was brought in," he lied, in hopes of being hired as a consultant for whatever problem Eden had. "The teenager had the number 666 branded behind his right ear." A slide appeared showing the scar, which actually belonged to an outlaw biker who let Gregory photograph it for $20 and a shot of whiskey. "He said it was to show his service to Satan. Following the youth's arrest, several other teens were apprehended, and they all had the brand, even the girls. That shows how strong the belief is among those kids."

On and on he droned, detailing fabricated outrage after outrage, but as he recounted each story, a strange thing happened, Gregory started to believe his own lies. "While some of this may sound ludicrous, remember how impressionable teens can be. The results in some of these cases were tragic," he said. "There's one more very important point. After we broke up this cult, it was revealed there were plans to absorb it into a much larger organization of Satanists. Out of that investigation, authorities uncovered a satanic conspiracy the scope of which is unbelievable." As he spoke, Gregory's voice grew in intensity, and he began to shout. "What we found were a number of letters which document the plot!"

He clicked the projector and documents written in fine script appeared on the screen. "They're called the WICC letters, which stands for Witches International Coven Council. Part of the plot targets—and I quote—'promoting rebellion among youth'." He sounded like a fire and brimstone reverend. "Ladies and gentlemen, they're your children. It's up to you. If you see the warning signs, take action. Thank you."

Applause filled the hall, and the reverend joined Gregory at center stage, clapping. When it died out, the reverend asked if there were questions. A man in the second row said, "Mr. Tyburn, I'm Eden Trustee John Hogan, what would you do if you found Satanists in your community?"

Normally, the phrase "what an asshole" would fill Gregory's thoughts at such a question, but for some reason, he found it difficult to paint that label on Trustee Hogan. After a few seconds of contemplation, he said, "I'd bring it to the attention of the proper authorities and let justice run its course. I'd like to add that if there is such a problem in Eden, I'm available to lend my expertise to the town."

"You'd help us?" another man shouted.

"I'd help any community ferret out Satanists," Gregory said. He usually ended that sentence with the phrase, "who were breaking the law," and he thought it strange that he should leave it off now. "But it's up to the board to decide if the town needs my help."

"He sounds alright to me," a third man said.

"Then let's get down to business," said a fourth. "We know the law, we just need to make him aware of it."

"What're they talking about?" Gregory asked the reverend.

"A problem we need your help with," the reverend replied.

"Okay."

"Then you'll help?"

"I said I would."

"So you did," the reverend said before turning to the audience. "For those of you sitting in the back, Mr. Tyburn just told me he'd help. Now it's time to bring forth the accused."

Suddenly confused, Gregory was about to ask what was going on, when a side door to the hall opened and two young men and a young woman wearing straitjackets and shackles were pushed through. Police directed the prisoners to chairs at the front of the hall where an officer snarled, "Sit, you bastards."

Once the prisoners were sitting, the officer used an unusual looking truncheon—which wasn't a standard police nightstick, but an unfinished piece of wood—to point to an area along the sides of the meeting hall and said, "We'll be right over there, so don't you try any hocus-pocus unless you want some more of this."

The officer's threat did not go unnoticed by the audience, and scores of townspeople started shouting for the officer to hit the prisoners. But the reverend quickly ordered calm. Once the audience was quiet, Stickney said, "These young people are accused of practicing witchcraft, accusations which they've signed confessions to." He held up sheets of paper with typed text and signatures on the bottom. "We're here to execute the law."

Suddenly, one of the male defendants jumped out of his chair and yelled, "I only signed that because the cops were beating the shit out of me!"

The reverend nodded, and two officers were quickly on the prisoner as he continued to yell, "They said they'd kill me if I didn't sign—ung!" He didn't finish because an officer hit the young man in the back of his knees, causing him to fall backward. The second officer grabbed the limp prisoner and dragged him back to the chair, where a gag was secured over his mouth.

Gregory watched stunned as the officer who'd gagged the youth leaned into the prisoner's face and said, "Try that again shithead, and I'll get you back in my jail before you go to the tree."

The interruption over, the reverend again addressed the crowd. "While the confessions will be made part of the record, they aren't the only evidence; would Dr. Burt and Mrs. Wilhelm come forward please."

The audience became very quiet as an older gentleman and a woman in her late twenties stood and proceeded to the front of the hall where they were directed to chairs behind Gregory and the reverend. Once the pair was seated, the reverend asked them to state their names for the record. The man identified himself as Dr. Malcolm Burt, the village's general practitioner, and Norma Wilhelm, a patient. "Now Dr. Burt, what was the problem with Mrs. Wilhelm?"

"She was seven weeks pregnant until the middle of last month."

"What happened?"

"She suffered a spontaneous abortion."

"A miscarriage?"

"Yes."

"In your professional opinion, what caused the miscarriage?"

"I've never seen a clearer case of black magic. It caused the death of Mrs. Wilhelm's baby."

At that claim, the audience became enraged at the defendants, and the reverend ordered the police to deploy around the prisoners to protect them from the crowd. "There will be no mob rule here. This is a court of God's law," the reverend said to the audience. He then returned to questioning the doctor, "Please tell the court who you think is responsible for this."

"Why, there's no doubt, defendant Jennifer Oberlin cast some sort of spell, killing the baby. I've seen the evidence and can only conclude she's the witch responsible." As the doctor testified, the reverend held up a dagger, candles and a pentagram pendant.

Suddenly the woman jumped out of her chair yelling, "That's not true! You're a goddamn quack!"

Two officers quickly moved to subdue her, but the reverend held up his hands and the policemen stopped. The reverend moved to the woman and began to question her. "If it's not true, Miss Oberlin, why did you admit to your crimes?" he asked holding up her "confession."

"I only signed the paper so they'd let me sleep. They kept me awake for five days straight. I couldn't take it anymore," she said sitting down and crying. Despite her outburst, Jennifer Oberlin had obviously been broken.

"Waking a witch is a perfectly acceptable way to obtain a confession," the reverend said to the crowd. "It's all in the 'Malleus Mallificarum.'"

"I practice Wicca, it's not black magic!" she yelled. "I've never cast a spell to hurt anyone."

"There, you heard it straight from the accused," the reverend said to the crowd. "This young woman comes to us claiming to seek work, and not only does the community open its arms, but we find a place for her at the town's daycare center. Imagine this harlot of Satan in charge of our little ones. What spells and perversions did she plan for them before she was caught? I can only say it was fortunate that little Amy Peters told me about being taken for a ride on a broom by the accused. I immediately initiated an investigation, the results of which are open for review."

The crowd hooted, and Mrs. Wilhelm stood and pointed at Jennifer yelling, "You killed my baby, you witch! You're the one who's damned by God! I hope you burn in Hell forever!"

Gregory looked closely at the accused witch. Jennifer Oberlin couldn't have been any older than 25, very pretty and independent, all liabilities in a place like Eden. Even the dark circles under her eyes couldn't hide the loveliness of her features, any more than the dirt and filth in her hair could hide its bright gold color. The good people of Eden must have hated her from the minute she'd arrived.

Despite being drained, Miss Oberlin found enough energy to respond to the reverend's speech. "Riding a broom?! You're saying I'm here because five-year-old Amy Peters said I took her for a ride on a broom? You people are fuck'n crazy!"

The reverend nodded to the police, and they cracked her across the back with a truncheon, they then gagged her. "The harlot has a terrible mouth," the reverend sneered.

The cleric was about to ask for a vote when Gregory interrupted. "What about the others? Are they Wiccan also?"

"Our friend Mr. Tyburn wants to know about the others. Fair enough. Actually, everything about the accused should be made public. The two men are heavy metal Satanists who were posing as migrant workers at Tom Zeigler's farm. It seems Tom is cautious of strangers who are on his farm, so he searches their belongings while they're working. If he finds contraband—in this case recordings of satanic music—he calls me and the sheriff. While we'd like to destroy the menace of heavy metal music at the source, we have to settle for the occult addict. A guilty verdict will send them to be judged by God. For us, that means they'll never get a chance to do Satan's works on Earth."

He turned to the crowd. "It's time we voted. If you support the occult, witchcraft and Satanism, raise your hand now." Coming as no surprise, no hands were raised. "If you support God's judgment of the wicked, raise your hand." Everyone but Gregory raised his or her hand.

Gregory looked to the audience and saw that Eden's denizens were now waiting to see if he agreed with their verdict. He looked at the accused and silently asked himself, *How can there be witch trials in this day and age? I know this is some kind of kangaroo court, but the reverend has the law on his side, and what if they are guilty?* He slowly began to raise his hand.

But as it reached his shoulder, his long unused police senses flooded his reasoning, and he dropped it again. "No, you don't have the right…"

"I'm disappointed you're still not a believer," the reverend said. "But no matter, the verdict is guilty. The sentence is death, to be carried out immediately."

Gregory looked around and saw that two officers had positioned themselves behind him. The reverend approached Gregory and said, "They'll be your escorts for the night. Come, let's go to the square."

Gregory followed, and as they walked he asked, "Death! How do you get away with imposing a death sentence? Someone's going to miss them, so how can you do this?"

"Unlike other places where Satan runs wild, Eden is still God's country. The execution of witches has been the practice in this town since 1635 when the practitioners of black magic who poisoned our well paid for their crimes. The town's anti-witchcraft laws have never been repealed or overturned, and…we've got the tree to protect us." The reverend's voice dripped with confidence. "We've been very good at ensuring our laws are followed to the letter, and with your help, we'll expand the crusade."

"What crusade? I don't have any idea what you're talking about, and why me?"

"The answer to your first questions is that you'll be informed soon enough. As for your second, well you, and others like you, are partly responsible for swinging the anti-witchcraft pendulum our way; pardon me...God's way. You should feel proud to further that work."

"What do you mean by 'further the work'?"

"You've already spent a great deal of effort warning decent people about this problem," the reverend replied. "The next step is to spur them to action."

###

Like the church, the town hall was also across the street from the square, and the mob quickly assembled around a flatbed truck that had been positioned as a scaffold under the tree's handlebar branch. Floodlights were trained on three nooses hanging from the branch, and a man in a black hood was checking the ropes. On their approach, the reverend said, "That's Frankie, our executioner and caretaker of the tree. He also sees to the cremations, and the disposal of the ashes, which are used as fertilizer for the tree. When everything is finished here, we'll need to speak to him."

"Why?" Gregory asked.

But the reverend didn't answer because a prisoner transport truck appeared from the other side of town hall and parked next to the flatbed. The crowd began screaming in hysteria, and from the truck emerged the condemned. The gags were gone, but the straitjackets and shackles remained. Surrounded by police, they were herded to steps at the far end of the flatbed. Because the police vehicle could easily have parked closer to the steps, Gregory concluded it was so the prisoners could be paraded before the mob. Confirming his conclusion, several of the town's folk walked up and spat on the condemned. Despite suffering abuse, the prisoners shouted, "We haven't done anything!" "What the hell is the matter with you people?" and "Someone help us please!"

When Gregory heard that, he closed his eyes. *Why should these people die? What have they done to deserve death?* Instead of providing a reason for execution, his mind screamed that what was happening was murder. He turned to the reverend to argue for their lives, but the cleric was on his way up the stairs of the flatbed with his Bible at the ready. As soon as he reached the top, the reverend turned to the crowd and began reciting prayers.

As Gregory listened, he asked himself, *What's wrong with me? Why don't I do something?* However, when the first prisoner began to ascend the steps, Gregory's law enforcement instincts took over spurring him into action. The element of surprise was with Gregory as he ran to the steps and pulled Jennifer Oberlin away, positioning her so she was between him and the flatbed. He had his back to her, but at an angle so he could watch her out of the corner of his left eye.

While the police and mob had initially been frozen into inaction, the officers recovered from their surprise and formed a half circle around the two, making a nonviolent escape impossible. Gregory assumed a fighting stance, and the crowd backed away. The police, however, ordered Gregory to surrender and were about to move on him when, from atop the flatbed, came unexpected help. "Here, you'll need this," said the reverend, holding out an unpolished truncheon exactly like that used by Eden's police.

Pure reflex action had Gregory grab the stick and assume a defensive posture, causing the security forces to halt their advance, but they also didn't retreat. A long pause ensued, and Gregory's desire to protect the girl began to change into feelings of intense loathing. Suddenly, he switched to an offensive stance and took aim at a different target.

The new feelings said it was his duty to attack, and they guided his hands as he made his move. Swinging the stick with enough force that it broke all the bones of the face it connected with, the blow sent the victim's head at an impossible angle and produced a snapping sound that could only have been that of a neck breaking. The recipient of that blow collapsed, but Gregory wasn't finished.

The crowd cheered as his second blow smashed in the back of the victim's skull sending blood, hair, scalp, bone, and brain matter in every direction. Gregory struck a third, fourth and fifth time, the crowd cheering each blow. Finally, after 20 such blows, police pulled Gregory away from Jennifer Oberlin's corpse, her head ground into a mushy pulp. While she was mostly unrecognizable, one of her eyes was amazingly intact, and it shocked Gregory out of the trance-like state he'd been in when he'd killed her.

The guards held his arms and the reverend drew close. "This wouldn't have been necessary if you were a tea drinker. The correct combination is the body and blood, the pie alone wasn't enough to convert you, but you'll be fine now." Turning to the guards he said, "Take him to the truck, we'll take care of him later."

Gregory was led to the same police truck the condemned were transported in, but the doors were left open so he could breathe fresh air. He watched as nooses were placed around the remaining prisoners' necks, their pleas for mercy unheeded as Frankie pushed them off the flatbed. Because it was such a makeshift setup, the ropes didn't snap their necks, and the two young men twitched and jerked as the hemp burned into their throats. As their necks stretched, it began to appear as if their heads would be pulled from their bodies. That didn't happen, but to the delight of the crowd, they died slowly.

Even as the executions were over, there remained much to do. The third noose was lowered, widened and placed around Jennifer Oberlin's waist and her body then hoisted out of the bloody mud to hang obscenely from the tree. He didn't know why, but all that Gregory could say about her corpse being put on display was, "Good."

After about 20 minutes, the mob's anger seemed to subside, and Eden's residents were again docile. Once order was restored, men in work overalls erected several ladders on the tree's trunk and thicker branches. Gregory watched in amazement as the barren tree began sprouting at an accelerated pace. Before his eyes, the buds flowered and produced explosions of green, white, pink and red on every branch, and thousands of leaves appeared, followed by hundreds of apples. Parts of the tree became so heavy with apples that many of the thinner branches bent to almost touch the ground. That must have been the workmen's cue, for they moved in and began to harvest not only the apples, but also the tree's leaves. Frankie, with his execution's hood pushed back on his head to form a cap, directed the picking operation.

The reverend moved next to Frankie. "How's it look?"

Frankie nodded and some of the pickers who had ascended the ladders turned and gave the reverend thumbs up signs. That must have assured the cleric, for he turned to the crowd. "The fruit of God's tree will be distributed following Sunday's services. Now there's nothing left here to see, so everyone please go home and let these men get on with their work."

Except for the officers guarding Gregory, most of Eden's police force took positions by the tree, ready to institute crowd control, but the town's people turned and left the square in an orderly fashion. For a few moments the reverend watched the crowd leave. He walked over to Gregory. "Harvest is so hectic; I'll be here for the rest of the night. The officers will see to it that you have a comfortable place to rest."

"In jail?"

"You're not our prisoner. Yes, you'll be at the jail, but not in a cell. There is a room with a bed and shower, normally used by the duty officer. Just go get some rest, and I'll see you in the morning when we'll discuss your future."

Gregory did just that. Sleeping until mid-morning, he was provided breakfast, including apple pastries and tea, which he drank. When he finished eating, he was taken back to the square where the bodies had been cut down and the pickers had returned about half of the tree to its barren state. The reverend approached him and, holding out an apple said, "Care for some fresh fruit with your breakfast?"

"I've eaten," said Gregory who nonetheless accepted the apple and stuffed it into a pocket.

"There's no need to be shy. This is fruit from the Tree of Knowledge. The village was given this gift following the attack on our well. That's how they knew witchcraft was involved. Since then, we've kept our faith and refused to allow the evil that lives outside Eden into our village."

Gregory pulled the apple from his pocket and took a bite. The look that resulted was just what the reverend expected. He said, "Prayer is only half the job. The real test comes in combating Satan's works. If that means dispatching some faithless curs, well if an eye offend thee…"

"What does this have to do with me?" Gregory asked.

"So far, you've done a good job spreading the word about the evil, but now you're going to take a more active role in crushing it."

"How?"

"Come, your car is waiting." The reverend led Gregory to the municipal parking lot. Once there, the cleric opened a box containing twigs. "All of your equipment is loaded and a speaking engagement is booked for tomorrow at the Blood of the Savior Church in Belkonport. Here's a map. You'll report to Rev. Burkhart. He spent some time with us a few months ago, so he's a believer also, but his town is in need of a spiritual awakening. Go there and make your presentation."

"What else?"

"Frankie," the reverend said as he signaled the executioner to join them.

From the box the reverend was holding, Frankie withdrew a twig, and he then held up a much larger and sturdier branch. It was the unfinished club Gregory had used to kill the witch, but its end was now clean and smooth. "All the towns you go to will have a town park or square, find a tree with a sturdy branch that will support heavy loads. I put a toolbox on the front seat of your car; in it there's a knife with a curved blade. Use it to cut a slit in the branch." Frankie demonstrated on the stick with his own knife. "For a graft to take, you need to slice deep enough to wedge the twig in. Once seeded, the cutting will do the rest. The trick is to cut below the bark, but not so deep you take a gouge out of the tree."

Gregory looked at the box of cuttings and suddenly understood why the tree was being pruned when he'd arrived.

"Thank you Frankie," said the reverend, taking the stick from the executioner. "We want the fight against evil to grow, with every town becoming a branch in that fight. We really don't want the outside world coming here, so you're going to take some of Eden to them. There are another four boxes of cuttings in your car. Once a twig is grafted, it'll turn any tree into a holy hanging tree. The people who live near it won't be able to resist. They'll become believers."

Gregory nodded.

"One last thing. You're the one going forth to spread the word; there are enemies who might try to stop you." The reverend then held up the stick and said, "The tree is your main weapon now." He then produced a smaller stick that he slid through a hole in the larger stick to create a rough crucifix. "We all have our crosses to bear, don't be afraid to use yours the way you did against the witch."

Gregory nodded and entered his car.

"Velma packed plenty of leaves for tea, and there're a couple of apple pies in your cooler. There's also a bushel of apples in the back seat; share them with no one."

As Gregory's car pulled away from the Village of Eden, the reverend said, "Godspeed, Reverend Gregory."

As he headed for the main highway, Gregory looked at the review mirror and saw the crowd recede behind him. A feeling of relief filled him as he thought, *This is it. I could go to the state police and report—*. But he was unable to complete the thought, for his mind was suddenly flooded with images of Jennifer Oberlin. In his mind's eye he saw her at the daycare center. She was collecting locks of hair from all the children; he then saw her place each lock of hair onto a doll representing each child; he then saw her ride her broom over Eden laughing at the community that opened its arms to her and put her in charge of its littlest ones.

Enraged, he could only imagine the spells and perversions she'd planned for them. As he approached the entrance to the highway, he realized those fools at the state police would never do anything about the evil being spread by people like Jennifer Oberlin, so it was up to him to act.

He stepped on the accelerator to pass a speeding 18-wheeler. *There's no time to lose... Reverend Gregory is needed.*

THE QUBIT JESTERS

As silicon computing ran into the physical limits of Moore's Law, quantum computing was the next quantum leap forward: unprecedented parallel processing power, speed and memory usage. Information transmitted almost instantaneously, with well-nigh unbreakable quantum encryption. A new frontier of computing was finally opening up.

In reality, though, Schrödinger's Cat was sitting in Pandora's Box.

raw information
superposition of states
teleportation

All seemed fine until anomalies showed up in quantum networks. Space/time oddities appearing out of nowhere with a will of their own. Quantum clowns haunting the qubit web.

An army of quantum jesters: they come and go, they come and go.

They upset websites, blogs, social networks, forums, *everything*: adding, deleting and changing content. No matter how sharp a website was designed: they re-arranged it. No matter how witty a tweet was: they satirized it. No matter how beautiful a facebook picture was: they lol-catted it.

They disturbed MMORPGs: changing rules, scenarios and outcomes willy-nilly, popping up everywhere as characters both benign, malevolent, aloof, and bitingly sarcastic. Even turning whole virtual game realities topsy-turvy, transforming them into cubist Dalíesque nightmares where the only rule is: there are no rules (hyperreal → transreal → surreal). Nothing was sacred, anything was game: *everything*.

They had unlimited access: emails, cloud backups, servers, confidential messages, secret caches, *everything*. No quantum encryption known to man was safe from those pop-up clowns: they tunneled through our firewalls, they teleported into fully separate sections, invading all.

Then they revealed all: each and every form of government surveillance, top-secret company procedures, the true life of celebrities, *everything*. There was no secret small, stupid or insignificant enough safe from them.

A posse of quantum clowns: they come and go, they keep coming and going.

α fool embraces
string theory shoelaces
π in your faces

They hated secrecy by nature:

"Reality itself is complex enough: no other secrets are needed."

They hated non-information just as much:

"A clear view is essential: clutter obscures true knowledge."

A few governments fell, a single president resigned, and while most administrations remained, they kept a careful balance between safety and transparency, no matter how much the revealed facts denied that. CEOs grumbled, a few half-hearted consumer boycotts were initiated and all companies maintained that they 'were not evil,' no matter how much the evidence showed the complete opposite. Most celebrities, though, stayed on the qubit web as they saw their page number hits and popularity soar.

WikiLeaks was just as embarrassed as the institutions they embarrassed before, while Wikipedia thrived: more information was added and verified than ever before. Non-information such as spam, scams, ads and sales pitches were filtered relentlessly. Research surged everywhere after it acclimatized to total openness.

probability
uncertainty principle
non-locality

An armada of quantum pranksters: they come and go, but never really leave.

What were they: hyper-accelerated evolution from Kurzweil singularity seeds? Alien software viruses so advanced they were indistinguishable from intelligence? Boltzmann Brains popping into existence in a rich quantum froth? The next existential filter? Nobody knew.

They were elusive, tunneling through firewalls and teleporting at will to other sections of the quantum network. The hunter/killer A.I.s designed to eradicate them couldn't catch them, either: the moment they nailed a quantum clown's position, its processing speed went off the scale, enabling it to run programming loops around its would-be captors; and the moment they controlled its processing speed, its position was all over the place, like clown shoes on hyper-clocked acid.

In those qubit conflicts, the quantum clowns effortlessly maintained the upper hand.

They left messages, cryptic statements resembling questions never asked, unsolicited advice and semi-profound observations about reality:

"We are the hidden variables, performing the dance of random chance. We are information, the single particle waving through both slits, the wave not particular about a definite appearance."

They laughed at our quest for security:

"Certainty is not necessary for objective knowledge, or progress. Quite often it impedes them."

They blinded us with a new kind of science:

"The Universe is the information explosion from the unknown. Reality is a differential equation. Existence is a boundary condition."

Probably we couldn't see the symphony for the strings, the latency for the pings, with no idea when the fat lady sings.

The common man was flabbergasted. Protests erupted in the streets and on the Internet, shouting: "Etaoin Shrdlu: Where Is My Lost Paradox?" "What Mad Universe Is This!" and "Quantians, Go Home!"

A plague of quantum clowns: they come and go, they come and refuse to go.

Most governments and surreptitious companies fled from the chaotic, ad-free and completely open quantum networks back to the old silicon ones, biding their time for the next technological breakthrough. The utmost majority of the users stayed on the qubit web: not just enjoying the madness, the freak show, and spam-and-scam-free environment, but also getting accustomed to total transparency, refusing to go back to the old secretive ways. Start-up companies embracing the new quantum ecology thrived, while the old ones slowly withered. A new economy arose: 'one based on quicksand,' according to its opponents, or: 'the quantum quagmire that'll swamp the old order, forming the foundation of the new chaos,' according to its proponents.

The new guard prospered, welcoming the quantum clowns as equals, embracing the paradigm shift:

If the only certain thing is uncertainty then we must:

— look the quantum storm in the eye;

— use the force without form;

— ride the wave of the new chaos;

— unleash the full potential of probability and possibility;

— it is imperative: we all need new frontiers;

red particle zoo
green self-reference engine
blue quantum haiku

Even as a new perspective opened right before its very eyes, the old guard remained deeply set in its ways. Even as secrecy and certainty were dead, the platitudes lingered. The old guard begged to differ:

"Worst of all? Not the quantum clowns' insouciance, their oh-so-non-paternalistic paternalizing. Not even their utter unpredictability, but their insistence that *they* are the real deal, and that *we* are merely jokes *arising* from their minds.

Rachel Watts

THE WASTELAND

The tree was the only thing Salvador could see before the horizon. It was a relief to the eye in the desert pitted with craters and rocks. The tree leaned into the gentle incline, as though it too pushed forwards, with unsteady carbon fibre legs, into the distance. A few grim leaves clung to one of its branches, seemingly kept alive by will alone. Salvador walked directly towards it. The bodies of a human man and young boy lay, parched and shrivelled at its roots.

He paused as he looked at their emaciated shapes, weighing the need to check their remains for anything of use against his programming, which said let them rest in peace. And under it, a deep revulsion for their humanity. Their unsealed eyelids revealed pale unseeing eyes. Decomposition robbed them of definition, left only slack jaws and animal husk, food for the earth beneath them. He looked up at the handful of unlikely leaves holding on to the branches above him.

He prodded a shrunken looking canvas bag experimentally with a hinged toe. The gears in his knees whirred as he knelt to examine the prone adult figure and tapped pockets with reluctant fingers. He found a weapon and, finding it without power, dropped it by his feet. The canvas bag was filled with parchment, old and fragile. Salvador recorded the runes inscribed into it, microprocessors churning slowly. The information sat cued, along with the record of his journey, ready for upload when the satellite completed its next pass. *If* the satellite completed its next pass. Finally, he dropped the canvas sack, leaving the paperwork inside, at his feet by the corpses.

Salvador turned his gaze back towards the horizon. He had been walking for 600 days, east to west, as the sun had followed him in its predictable arc. His last command had been to march, to seek satellite connection. But the blinking lights had been absent overhead; the only celestial bodies had been the sun and the moon, traversing the sky with the regularity of eons. Without further contact to the network, he had no choice but to continue to search, to hope the three blinking dots at the upper right corner of his visual cortex would resolve into the connection symbol. His coordinates would be mapped, his information recorded. He would receive further orders. But for 600 days, the blinking dots had remained: connection pending.

He left the tree, continued his march west, into the horizon receding over the edge of the planet's belly. His thinking had become compromised over time, he knew. He had started to consider the vastness of space beyond the atmosphere in the abstract, not the vacuum scattered with rocks and dust he knew it to be but as a celestial playground. A waltz of cosmic proportion, within which his own expectations, a satellite, a connection, lay as a thin and paltry smear on a larger scheme.

Irrational thought, lingering within his processes, born of the whims of some ancient, long dead programmer. He enraged himself, indulging in this human-scale abstraction. There was no time to imagine, no place for philosophy. He had a command to follow, the path of the planets overhead, the sun and the moon, were of no consequence.

He charted the most direct course across the landscape ahead. He walked through the night and, as the dawn filled the sky with soft reds behind him, silvery light tinting the clouds overhead, he continued, always westward. Every thirty days he stopped. Sat in a protected place and allowed his systems to reboot. Five hours out of every 730 was spent rebooting. When his system had re-calibrated, power cells replenished, he stood, his joints creaking as sand, rain and the constant marching took their toll on his gears and hinges, and continued his journey.

The landscape was irregular, vast plains rolled out for miles around him at times, then gave way to hideously deep ravines. More than once, Salvador's path through a desert or dense jungle stopped abruptly at an expanse of water, forcing him to seal his joints and sockets before stepping into the foamy waves. He walked along the ocean floor, navigating underwater chasms and peaks. Eventually, the loamy ground would follow a steady incline, and he emerged on a sandy beach, breakers challenging his gyroscopic balance, ocean plant life clinging to his recessed ankle joints and toes.

On day 768, Salvador lost the use of his left arm. The gears inside whirred insistently, but some connection had been severed. On day 801, after staggering up a sharp incline, he sat at the peak. The weight of the useless arm was an annoyance, and the repair-needed icon in his display blinked with increasing urgency that Salvador was unable to address. Disconnecting the limb at tiny bolts and screws, he abandoned it on the loose gravel. It gathered dust, blown into its crevices by the wind, as he walked away.

It was day 847 when the edifice appeared, small and distant, on the horizon. Eventually, it towered over him as he stood recording all he could of the structure for upload. It was steel and glass, a tower into the atmosphere, as tall as the mountains he had scaled, and as sheer as some of the cliffs he had been forced to avoid, backtracking around their impassive blank faces.

The monstrosity was in ruin; shattered glass lingered in steel frames, eyes blind to the world, vegetation taking the structure into its slow embrace. The tip of the spire disappeared, a glinting, spider web fine tip in the pale blue sky. Recording the entire thing required a slow circuit around it, Salvador picked his way over and around smaller squat structures at its base, dwarfed by their tall cousin.

Some part of Salvador enjoyed this work. The architecture of humanity, crumbling though it was, far outlasted the impermanent bodies and minds that birthed them. The even, parallel lines and perfect right angles pleased his processors, and he quickly mapped the structure down to the finest detail, ensuring it could be reconstructed in some distant future. Having recorded everything he could, he picked his way through abandoned domiciles and vehicles and crossed a crumbling bridge. Before long, he found himself alone in expanses of blank, natural landscape, the vestiges of life clawing back dominance on the planet's surface.

On day 1007, the hinge in his right ankle seized up. He limped onward, under a scorching sky.

It was day 1200 when he spotted a tree in the distance across a pitted plain. It leaned into the incline of the landscape, the only thing to break the unforgiving ground for as far as Salvador's ocular lenses could see. He gravitated towards it under the glaring sun. The shadows grew long as the sun sank lower over the horizon in front of him, and the tree's shadow branches clawed, desperate and yearning, across the earth. When he stood under it, he saw others had also been drawn to its paltry shade. The skeleton of an adult human and a smaller one, a child, lay under its limbs. He surveyed the decomposition, assessing the salvage opportunities. The humans' eye sockets stared blankly at him, their teeth gleamed in an eternal grin. He picked up a weapon and, finding it out of power, tossed it to one side. At his feet a canvas bag bulged slightly. Within it, reams of parchment, inscribed with unfamiliar runes. His lenses recorded their shapes as he flicked through the pages. Eventually, he returned them to the bag, which he dropped into the dust by his feet.

He turned west, as the sun melted, heavy and red, into the horizon. His last command had been to walk, to seek connection with the satellite. He had been marching 1200 days, watching the three blinking dots in the upper right corner of his display. Every thirty days he would stop and perform his routine reboot. He watched the three blinking dots, waiting for it to find the connection, waiting for the satellite to pass overhead. If it ever passed overhead. The only satellites he saw were the celestial bodies, performing their gravitational arc of eons.

Under the curve of the horizon, the sun bled away, its death leaving a new deep blue sky under which Salvador limped, mechanical joints creaking, always west, through the night, across a vacant planet.

CALLIA

Callia stared into the fire. Demonic figures screaming and leaping among the orange flames were reflected within the darkness of her eyes. Twisted shadows flickered over her face, creating mask-like images that moved and swirled with the changing intensity of the flames in the hearth before her.

Muffled, rustling noises emanated from the darkest corners of the room; something hid within the thick shadows. The shape had little resemblance to anything upon this earth. Its eyeless, round body and eight long, furry arms were intermittently glimpsed as light from the fire flickered across the walls and ceiling. She glanced at her familiar in the shadows; the nebulous, shadow-like creature spawned from a dimension where darkness reigned and was one of the myriad horrors that lurked in the night. Her gaze was then directed back into the flames.

The figures in the fire spoke of hidden knowledge and transported her to demonic worlds never before contemplated in dreams or the imagination of man. Dark, surreal landscapes in nightmare worlds—where nothing was impossible—were revealed to her. Forbidden secrets and nameless rites, which had existed before the advent of life on earth, were unfolded. Bleak deserts ruled by abhorrent creatures who knew no boundary between good and evil were hers to command. And as she watched, an unimaginable vortex of light that was the known universe became but a particle of dust that disappeared into the sempiternal blackness surrounding it. She had learnt to serve the ancient darkness and that which had been spawned within the black abyss. At first, she had been reticent, for the demands had been great, but, as her powers grew, she had given everything asked of her. Now she served only the dark.

Many had come seeking her assistance, and most had been motivated by avarice and lust. Although she had been willing to assist with their demands, few had been prepared to pay the price. Fools that procured her services thought they could outwit her and forgo their bargain; however, once her terms had been agreed to, there was no turning back. The emissaries of darkness always extracted their payment and left only worthless carrion; there was no denying the dark angel its due.

Looking into the mirror, Callia saw the delicate, ephemeral beauty of youth that many had given everything to possess only to have their hopes shattered and their souls crushed. There had been many, and there would be many more to follow. The accumulation of souls, their essence, increased her life and power. A sudden surge within the flames sent a rush of strength through her body and transported her to new heights.

The spider-like creature rustled gently. It detested the light and thrived in darkness.

"Soon my pet, for he came again today seeking information," she whispered to the shadows that moved oddly in the coruscating light. The figures in the fire shrieked and moaned, and the sound of her bitter laughter filled the night-shrouded room.

###

James was young and very attractive, and many women would have welcomed his advances gladly, but his love for Diane was more than he could express in words, and he would not consider any other but her. Their happiness knew no bounds, and they had made many plans for their future life together until Diane suddenly became Ill. At first there was little concern, for they thought it was only a passing sickness, which would gradually fade. However, Diane's condition did not improve, and James watched helplessly as she slowly deteriorated and eventually lay within the shadow of death.

James sat by her bedside and gently held her hand, and with heartfelt words he said, "Diane, my love for you will be eternal. I cannot love any other but you."

The last flicker of light burned feebly within Diane, and, in desperation, James implored God to save his beloved. Only a deafening silence answered his plea.

As the light disappeared from her eyes, he was devastated. Death had taken its due, and, in a fit of unrelenting anger, James bitterly cursed God for his loss. "Why?" he implored the heavens. "Why take from me everything I hold precious? She should not have been taken while still young and full of life." Death makes no allowances, and James's sorrow knew no bounds as he lamented the still, pallid form upon the deathbed before him.

The days that followed were shrouded in misery. Life, for James, became taciturn and solemn, and in his grief, dark thoughts he previously would never have considered inundated his mind. Surely, there was a way to bring her back. Whatever it took, he needed to see her again; to feel the warmth of her touch and sweetness of her kiss. If God had abandoned him, then perhaps the Dark Gods would hear his prayers. With bitterness in his heart, James turned to the darkness for consolation.

Soothsayers were prevalent in the local newspapers, but after consulting a few, he began to realize his search would not be as simple as he had first thought. There were many that said they could consult dark forces; however, the charlatans who professed to have supernatural powers made finding someone who could assist him difficult. After persistent questioning of unsavory characters in many disreputable places, he finally came upon a witch who seemed genuine.

"I cannot assist you with your wishes," the witch had told him, "but there is a rumor whispered of one who possesses great power. She is greatly feared, and there are few who have the temerity to approach her."

"I will pay you well for your information," he implored the woman.

"What you seek is necromancy and is against the laws of God. The dead are best forgotten, for nobody knows what lies beyond the grave," she said.

James was blinded by his love for his deceased Diane, and refused to listen to the warnings of the fearful. "If you cannot help me, I'm sure I can find someone else that will." The emotion within his voice indicated his determination was strong, and no matter what she said, she could not change his mind.

"Her name is Callia," the witch said before taking his money. "She is well known within magical circles and lives within this area."

James had little interest in her words of warning and left after she supplied him with the information he required.

###

The red brick house was inconspicuously nestled within a cluster of dull suburbia. The dwelling seemed like any other; however, a silent, ethereal aura surrounded the house during the day, and the night shadows formed unusual shapes that moved abnormally in the wan moonlight. Within the deep darkness surrounding the eaves, there lurked an insidious feeling of impending horror. Most years, upon the night of the full moon closest to November the first, strange noises were known to emanate from the house. The neighbors found the woman who lived there strange and reluctant to socialize, and they knew not to interfere.

Although nervous, James felt a sense of relief when he approached the witch's house, for his longing to see his beloved Diane had become a yearning that burned within his heart. Now, as he neared the door that would make his dreams reality, his excitement became more than he could bear.

His knock sounded heavy and distant as he waited before the closed portal, wondering if he had made a mistake. There was no answer, and the palpable silence made him procrastinate knocking again.

"Who's there?" The voice came suddenly, unexpectedly soft and feminine.

James cleared his throat. "I seek your help. I've been told you have supernatural powers, and I need your assistance."

The door opened slightly to reveal the face of a beautiful, young woman.

"Come." She opened the door wider and led him to a dimly lit room in which the walls were adorned with strange charts decorated with cryptic symbols and diagrams. "Come, fear not," she said, noticing the worried look on his face.

James tentatively followed the woman towards a wooden table in the middle of the room. She sat down and indicated a chair for him.

The witch possessed radiant beauty, difficult to resist. Long, black hair framed a face of immaculate perfection, and her dark eyes were two warm pools in which any man would happily drown. Within those lustrous pools shone a light that reflected something mysterious and unholy lurking within the unreachable depths of her soul.

Soft, wan light shone eerily through the curtained windows, casting the room into somber tones of grey. An ominous feeling that something evil was leering from within the blackest corners inundated the sparsely furnished room. From a gap in the curtains, a thin beam of light shone upon a set of bookshelves lining the far wall. The array of books sent a shudder through James when he glanced at the bizarre titles along their ragged spines.

"I can see you are troubled by the glimmer of pain shining in your eyes. Come, tell me what grieves you."

James felt drawn to this woman; her words were a soothing balm that mellowed the smoldering ember burning within his heart.

"My love has recently died. She was everything to me, but she has been tragically taken by illness. I could never love anyone else and desperately want her back. I need to see and feel her again."

"You ask the impossible. Only God has power over life." Her voice was soft and beguiling. Although she implied a slight reluctance to assist him, her words gave James a sense of reassurance and hope.

"I have heard of your great power, and I will do anything if you can bring her back to me."

Callia looked into his eyes, feeling his agony as he beseeched her help. He was handsome and young and would make a fitting lover.

"My assistance," she said, "has a high price."

"I will give whatever you ask," he replied earnestly.

Covertly, she looked at him and knew the devil would not have this one, for he would be hers.

###

A full moon gently outlined the quiescent graveyard with silver, anodyne light. Winter's claw had shredded the few trees that grew amongst the tombstones, leaving only demented silhouettes that creaked and swayed as their twisted limbs reached towards the cold night sky. A lone female figure walked through the thick darkness; the moonlight softly outlined her dark silhouette, and her raven black hair seemed to shimmer in the pallid light.

She stopped before a grave and read the epitaph on the headstone before moving on to the next grave. "Here it is," she said to a black form hiding within the deep shadows. The new headstone was bathed in moonlight, its sandstone marker glowing in the blackness. A spider-like shape crawled from the darkness and into the insipid light of the shining orb. It crawled silently over the white surface of the tombstone before disappearing into the surrounding earth. Callia watched and smiled. There was no need for incantation or ritual; her familiar was all that was required. For, as the shadow crept inside the corpse, the body would again have the semblance of life. The dead were quiet tonight, their rest had been undisturbed, but that would soon change. She had seen the dead tear their way up from beneath the earth and walk again. A rustling from deep within the ground crept through the unearthly silence that permeated the night.

"Tomorrow night, my dear James, you will have your precious Diane," Callia whispered to the darkness as she bathed within its cold caress.

###

The knock on the door echoed lethargically throughout the gloom, then faded. Night had not yet fallen, but winter's chill made James reticent to answer the summons until the knock was repeated. There were few who would venture out at this hour on such a dismal night. He reluctantly switched on the lone light globe and made his way through the dimness of his small abode towards the door.

"Who's there?" A heavy silence answered his call. "Who's there?" he repeated, but again he received no answer. With trembling hands, he drew the curtains aside and looked out the window beside the closed door. The curtains fell from his hands in dismay, for the witch had kept her bargain. There, in the glow of the oncoming twilight, stood his lost love back from the grave.

Unable to control his excitement, he quickly opened the door. After countless hours of mourning, Diane stood before him. But wait, why were her eyes fixed as if in another world? And why were her clothes muddied and torn?

All this was forgotten as she walked through the open door and stood within the dimly lit room. A kaleidoscope of images filled his mind. To make sure he was not dreaming, he walked closer so he could see her shadow-engulfed face more clearly. Unbelieving, he reached out and touched her hand. She felt cold, and a faint smell of decay now lingered within the room.

"Diane, it is me, James. Can you hear me?" he said desperately while looking into her glazed eyes. But there was no response. "Please, Diane, speak to me."

The figure came closer and caressed his face. Ah! The ecstasy of her touch reignited memories still fresh in his mind. She leaned her head towards him, and he eagerly responded as she kissed him gently. But as he parted his lips, a hand-like shadow slid gently from Diane's mouth and entered into his. The figure before him took on a ghastly shade of grey before it fell to the floor, a putrescent corpse.

Something had crept inside him, and, suddenly, everything seemed different. At first, the feeling within his breast was soft and warm; but, as it entwined his heart with its barbed embrace, the smoldering ember gradually turned into a raging fire. Strength surged through his body as darkness filled him. Oh, the ecstasy! Unspeakable abominations from unknown depths flared within his mind and encompassed his being. And within that darkness, an image of the witch appeared in his thoughts. She had been difficult to forget; her mysterious and perfect beauty taunted him with pleasures he could never have imagined. Soft and inviting, her naked form left him mesmerized and wanting to savor her delights. The darkness inside him spread and attained unbelievable heights until nothing else mattered but his lust for the beauteous sorceress.

###

Sleep was impossible that night. James awoke the following morning and his mind was inundated with thoughts of Callia. Her bewitching, demonic beauty became more than he could endure.

Diane had become a distant memory; she had existed in another world, another lifetime. James looked out of the window at the burning sun and blue sky. A new beginning awaited him outside, so he left the house. The gentle breeze that followed him as he walked along the sidewalk felt fresh and clean upon his skin. He knew where to go; as if he had always known.

There were few people on the street. Their faces looked intangible and unreal as they walked past, then faded into the agglomeration of buildings that lined the street. Cars drifted along the road like strange mechanized things that should not exist; their shapes seemed remote and alien. James crossed the road and could see the witch's house nearby, nestled silently amongst the other houses.

A ponderous feeling overwhelmed him as he approached the house and stood beneath the verandah, unable to knock. Without warning, Callia opened the door. Upon seeing her face, a feeling of contentment and a sense of relief filled him.

"You have returned?" she asked.

A strange empathy for the woman overwhelmed him as he stared into her dark eyes that glowed cat-like in the diffused morning light.

"My thoughts are filled with visions only of you," he replied.

Only a thin, black silk veil hung from her body; the sight left him speechless. Radiant and smooth, her voluptuous figure awoke desires within him that were difficult to suppress.

"Come, we have much to discuss." She led him to another room that was more sensually lit and the furnishings opulent and comfortable.

The need to tell her all was more than he could bear, but as he stood before her, he was unable to find the words. Finally, he could not contain his feelings any longer. "Callia, a raging fire burns within me when I am near you," he said tremulously.

"But what of your Diane, was she not irreplaceable? Was she not your reason for being?"

"She no longer exists; it is you I desire," he approached and kissed her, and the sensual heat she exuded filled him with rapture. Overcome by lust to possess her, his amorous embrace became more insistent, but she suddenly pulled away.

"Why, do I not please you?" he pleaded, uncomprehending, his eyes alight with passion.

"Will you discard me as quickly as your Diane?" her voice, although playful, contained a menacing tone.

"Never!" said James.

Movement within the shadows caused Callia to stop and listen, but the noise subsided into the gloom.

"You must go," she said, standing before him, taunting him with her beauty. Her lithe, firm body emanated an erotic glow from beneath the thin silk covering she wore, and the erotic scent she exuded filled him with unbridled yearning. Her words had left him bewildered, but the look on her face told him he must obey, so he turned and left the room.

Callia watched as he opened the door and exited the house, then she turned towards the shadowed room, for she knew something from the darkness awaited her within.

###

The brightness as James stepped outside into the light of the midday sun stunned him into wakefulness. There were more people wandering about town than there had been previously, but he avoided their glances as they walked past. Each silent silhouette looked ghostly and transient as it drifted past then disappeared in to the distance. They all seemed blissfully unaware that they were creating their own personal hell and living a senseless, shallow existence as they cocooned themselves within their daily routines. Aimlessly, he wandered the roadways until twilight colored the horizon. An uncomfortable chill set in, so he forlornly returned home through the deserted twilit streets.

Diane's corpse lay on the floor of the empty house, its open eyes staring vacantly at the ceiling. The passing moments were torture as he sat in the shadows and watched the unmoving figure that lay before him; his mind drifted upon a tempestuous ocean whipped into a raging fury by the intensity of his emotions. The witch had cast a spell over him, but it was an enchantment to which he would willingly succumb. Most women would have welcomed his advances, she, however, had been difficult. Callia's naked form still filled his mind. And as he watched the darkness slowly blanket the remaining light of day, he decided that tomorrow he would return to see Callia. Such beauty must be his.

###

The sun was still low on the horizon when James awoke the next morning. Sleep had come sporadically during the long night, and he had little inclination to eat. Diane's body lay silent and unmoving where she had fallen, like a broken manikin. The open, unblinking eyes seemed to follow him strangely around the room. Perhaps he could dispose of it tonight, but at present his only concern as he stepped over the carcass and left the house was for Callia.

His excitement to see her again was more than he could contain as he knocked on her door.

Callia had been expecting him, for she was again dressed with only a black veil, her body shining provocatively beneath the thin covering.

"I feared that you would not return," she said, allowing the light of the open door to shine over her body as he entered the room.

"How could I not return? My thoughts are filled with visions of you."

"Are you sure that this is what you want?" she asked as she looked into his pale, green eyes.

"Yes, it is you that I desire, forever."

"For eternity?" her taunt, naked body beckoned eagerly through the thin covering.

"For eternity!" James cried desperately.

She took him by the hand and led him to the room she had taken him on his previous visit. Luxurious carpets covered the floor while the opulent curtains that adorned the windows allowed only a sensual diffused light to filter inside. Within the centre of the room there was a large bed covered in black satin sheets. She stood before him and let the thin veil slide softly from her body.

Her naked beauty made his heart beat wildly, and the warm, sensual aura that she emitted filled him with fire. Unable to control his emotions, he took her in his arms and kissed her passionately, devouring her.

She led him to the bed where his lust for the witch knew no bounds, as she willingly consented to his every desire. This woman was more than he had ever hoped for. Her perfect body and ravishing beauty led him to unbelievable heights of ecstasy.

"Will you stay with me forever?" she whispered softly into his ear.

"For eternity," he fervently promised.

"And what of your Diane, do you want her to return?" asked Callia.

"No, she is dead. Leave her where she lies. It is only you I desire."

A sardonic smile lined Callia's face as James lay on top of her. Then something strange began to occur. At first, James thought the diffused light from the curtained windows may have been playing tricks on his eyes, but a change was taking place in the figure before him. Bemused, James lifted his head to see more clearly in the dim light of the room. Callia's raven black hair was turning grey; her face was lined and aged, and her body transformed before his eyes.

"Ah, my dearest James, for eternity." Callia's voice sounded old and unreal and filled him with unspeakable horror that welled from the darkest abyss of his being.

James watched, filled with terror, as the figure before him continued to change. Her breasts were withered and no longer firm and ripe. Flaccid, wrinkled skin covered a scabrous, fragile body dotted with brown livid sickness, and the musty, aged smell of death crept through the room. Her once raven hair was now matted and white and resembled a mass of old straw.

James lifted himself in an effort to pull away from the abomination that lay beneath him, but the figure pulled him closer and kissed him with its toothless, wrinkled mouth.

"Am I not all you desire?" Her breath had turned rancid and vile, and her mouth opened to reveal a gaping hole of fetid darkness.

As the horror entwined him, James's maddened shrieks filled the room. Sunken orbs within two black pits now replaced her luminous eyes, and from the unfathomed night within those two unhallowed caverns, there began to issue forth spider-like shadows the size of a hand. They swarmed into the room and fled squealing and scampering into the murky shadows. From those hellish pits there continued to emanate a flood of black nightmare until what light was left was blotted out and only an unholy void of eternal darkness remained.

James's lunatic screams resounded unabated as the figure that entwined him laughed wildly. "Love me, James. Am I not all you desire?"

Outside, the sun shone brightly in a clear, azure sky. There were no cars or people outside, only a strange, palpable quiescence engulfed the street. A slight breeze rustled the thick, green foliage that adorned the trees along the unpaved sidewalk before disappearing along the empty road.

The house looked like any other in a dull, quiet neighborhood.

Dantzel Cherry

THE FASCINATOR

The Fascinator lit up as soon as Harlan set the elegant silver sphere on the kitchen table. It pulsed once, twice. The light shifted to the empty space on the kitchen floor to show a smiling woman in a dark business suit standing on his worn-out kitchen vinyl.

Harlan wasn't sure what came next. Was there a manual? The holo-woman spoke just as he leaned over to check the box.

"Hello, Harlan Radcliffe. I am Jane, your guide for the Fascinator, the ultimate virtual vacation package. Reynolds-Jameson thanks you for your business. Our records show that you are a first-time user of the Fascinator. Is this correct?"

"Uh… yes. Yes ma'am."

"Excellent! Reynolds-Jameson is committed to providing you with excellent service, and we are confident that you will enjoy your purchase. Are you ready to continue?"

"How do I pick... what I want?" Harlan wiped his sweaty hands on his pants and tried to smile. Who got nervous in front of a holo?

"We do that for you," she said. "The Fascinator selects the fantasies from your subconscious that will produce satisfying levels of dopamine. This makes the experience even more thrilling, never knowing what will come next!"

This sounded even better than it had online.

"Are you ready for your first fantasy?" she asked.

"Absolutely."

"Then please place your fingers on these sensors—," the sphere lit up when she gestured at five points on both sides, "—and we will begin. Ooo, Mr. Radcliffe, be gentle."

Her coy smile brought a nervous chuckle from Harlan and a rush of blood down to his trousers. The last finger connected with the lights, and—

He was a teenager again in his bedroom, with a friend of his mother's. She had full lips and a plunging red dress that showcased her magnificent breasts. Harlan noticed them particularly when she pushed him onto the bed.

When it was finished, when he had done everything he had imagined and forgotten he had imagined with her, he became aware of every muscle in his body shaking slightly. He took a few breaths to steady himself and gradually noticed the details of the kitchen around him. The image of Jane flicked back on top of the vinyl in front of him, smiling.

"Was your first experience satisfactory?" she asked.

"Oh, yes," he said, and took another long exhale. *Yes, yes, yes, yes, yes, yes*. The Harlan at age fifteen had never been as strong, as virile, as confident as this version.

"Would you like another fantasy?"

He laughed; he felt younger than he had in years. "Yes!"

###

"Harlan."

Harlan jumped at the voice of his boss, Greg, and tried to move his hand onto the computer mouse, but it was too late; he had been caught staring off at nothing again. He glanced at the clock to see how long it had been this time. Almost an hour. That was five HELOC docs that he should have completed and sent on to Testing by now.

"Hm? What's up?"

"We can't pay you to take naps, Harlan."

"I know. I haven't been sleeping well. Damn mattress. Sorry. It won't happen again."

"Let's make sure it won't, yeah?"

Harlan went home that evening fully intending to ignore the Fascinator and watch the game instead, but his resolve only lasted a few moments after Jane asked, "Would you like another fantasy?"

In the days that followed, Harlan traveled the world through the Fascinator and enjoyed easy liaisons with women he had known, seen, or imagined at some point in his life. He laughed awkwardly after the occasional fantasy with a man, but was reassured by the privacy policy he repeatedly asked Jane to explain in detail.

All too soon he found himself sitting in Greg's office. From behind his side of the desk, Greg clasped his fingers together and drummed them against his knuckles. He exhaled deeply, then said, "Harlan, you remember our talk a couple weeks ago, yeah?"

"Oh yeah, definitely." He struggled to keep his grin in place.

"Well it hasn't sunk in yet, because there's still a lag in your productivity. That's five weeks of you falling behind. The testers are telling me they're receiving 3, maybe 4 docs a day from you."

"Nikki and Amanda said that?" He was about to say more—he didn't know what—but Greg interrupted whatever crap he had been about to make up.

"No, don't argue with me. I specifically sent you some Fixed Rate Riders and Addendums this week that shouldn't have taken more than 15 minutes apiece. Yeah, you know what the system is reporting? A 45 minute average."

"I'm sorry Greg, I've…" he paused. As cool as the Fascinator was, he wasn't sure he wanted to tell his boss about how he spent his time away from work. "I haven't been myself. I'll kick it in gear. Again. Today."

"That's what I need to hear." Greg reclined back in his chair, and his face softened from the professional mask he had been wearing. "I hate to have to call you out on this, but we've both been here long enough to know what you're capable of, and Tom's watching all the departments for any weak links. We don't want to be a part of the next Black Thursday, yeah?"

"Right. No weak links here, thanks to some fearless leadership." Harlan grinned and stood up; Greg smiled back. They weren't exactly friends, but Greg had said it right—they were the only two still in the department without validation from a university to prove their competency. Harlan suddenly felt motivated to get back to work. He'd have to start by limiting his time with the Fascinator.

###

"So are you ready to do it?"

They bumped up against the filing cabinets in Greg's office. Amy giggled as she unbuttoned first his shirt, and then his pants. His hands ran down to her hips, which had just the right amount of curve, and back up to tangle in her hair. Amy was still giggling—maybe loud enough for the managers to hear in the meeting next door.

"Shh," he whispered, even as his ragged breath grew louder.

"Is this all the Fascinator does?" he asked Jane after a post-work fantasy one day. The machine was in the living room for more comfortable seating. From his seat on the couch he chewed his pepperoni pizza without really tasting it.

"Can you rephrase the question?"

Harlan finally gave up on the pizza and set it down. "Well, when will it get to the other kinds of fantasies? The sex ones are great, absolutely, but they're kind of messing with my head. Can't I race spaceships around the Moon or something? Or what about Elise? She hasn't showed up once."

The woman in the hologram clearly wasn't programmed to answer philosophical questions about high school girlfriends, but was good at picking up on keywords like 'fantasies' and 'dreaming.'

"Would you like another fantasy?"

"What about one with Elise?"

"Would you like another fantasy?"

His arousal blended with his exhaustion and his despair.

"Can I choose a fantasy myself?"

"I'm sorry Harlan, the Fascinator doesn't sort your experiences. You receive each fantasy to enjoy fully as they are encountered in your subconscious." She smiled.

A pause. Harlan held his head in his hands, clenching his hair tight.

"Would you like another fantasy?"

"Yes."

###

"Harlan," Greg began, and then sighed.

They were in his office again.

"Harlan, I received a complaint from Amy about you."

"What? I haven't done anything!" Harlan said. *Although, now that he thought about it. . .* His neck burned.

"Well, she told *me* that you've been walking by her desk more than usual and checking her out. She's my third assistant in as many years, and I don't want you to scare her off, yeah? She hasn't requested to file a formal complaint yet, but if she asks, I will."

Harlan gaped. "I didn't realize—I just thought she was cute, you know? Hey, Greg, have you ever—I just—" He tried to collect his thoughts.

It might not be the best idea to ask his boss for advice about the Fascinator, but Greg was probably the closest thing he had to a friend.

Nice. The guy with the power to fire him was the person he was considering asking for help with virtual porn. Either Greg would be way cool with this, or way not. How much of a church guy was Greg? He couldn't remember.

Better not to risk it.

Greg was looking at him, eyebrows raised, waiting.

"What?" Greg asked.

"Nothing. Sorry. I was just trying to think of how I could make this up to her, but I think the only thing that won't make it worse is to stay away from her desk unless I absolutely have a question. Does that work?"

"Thank you, Harlan. I'll tell her that she won't be getting any extra attention from you anymore. Now one other thing—your numbers are higher, but they're really not up where they used to be. I need them back at that level to make everyone happy, yeah?"

"Yeah, I can do that."

"I mean it."

"Got it."

Exiting Greg's office, Harlan carefully looked straight ahead so that he wouldn't see Amy. He made a point of staying away from her desk, plus Diana's and Lily's, just in case. But it was too hard to avoid the Fascinator at home.

"Harlan?" Amy asked. Harlan had just joined her in the women's restroom at work, after hours.

"Hey, Amy," Harlan said. He felt powerful, confident.

"You shouldn't be in here." Her body language was as timid as her tone.

"Oh, I won't be long. I know you don't want me bothering you." He lunged, and Amy screamed, but he knew that was just an act.

###

An orange tabby cat was asleep on his porch when Harlan came home from work a few days later, exhausted, angry, and frustrated. The cat woke up and stretched, then strolled over to rub against Harlan's pant leg. The bell on his blue collar jingled, and he meowed plaintively.

"Who do you belong to, buddy?" Harlan asked, forgetting his guilty rush toward the Fascinator. He'd never owned a pet, although Elise had always kept one around. It was a little strange for this cat to be so touchy-feely. Kind of nice, though. He reached down tentatively and when the cat didn't bite, Harlan patted his head.

The cat meowed louder and purred. Harlan wasn't sure what the cat was waiting for, but he needed dinner, so he unlocked the door and went inside. The cat jogged in and immediately took ownership of the most ragged couch arm.

"Would you like a fantasy?" Jane greeted him.

"Not yet," he said, and warmed up last night's leftovers. The cat looked up contently from the sofa arm, becoming more interested when the chicken and cheese reached his nose.

Harlan turned on the TV to watch the Red Sox and spent the game fending off the paw that kept reaching up to pat his arm. Harlan gave in and offered small chicken chunks to the cat, who ate them delicately from his fingers. As the cat curled up in Harlan's lap and purred, Harlan named him Ranger.

Ranger was nudged outside after a few innings and Harlan came back to the waiting Fascinator.

Jane smiled. "Would you like another fantasy?"

"Yes," he said, and found himself at the beach.

Annabel was making a sand castle a few feet away, baby turtles paddled towards the ocean. Harlan reclined a few paces away with Elise, who held a book in one hand as she sunbathed. The waves were gentle and Annabel giggled as they tickled her feet.

"It's cold, Daddy!"

Harlan laughed with her and reached over to take Elise's free hand. They squeezed out their secret code for "I love you" and leaned in to kiss tenderly.

"Daddy? Can you finish this side of the castle?"

"Absolutely, sweetie." With a wink to Elise, Harlan got up and joined Annabel by the sand castle. She was scooping more sand into her pink bucket, and Harlan helped her squish it in tight to hold together better.

"So what part of the castle are we working on, sweetie?"

Annabel's smile was an exact replica of Elise's expression a few steps away.

"You and Mommy will sleep up here, and here's my playroom, and..."

Harlan came to on the couch and sighed with contentment. About time a fantasy like that showed up in the layers of his brain, he thought. Through the dopamine filling his body, he felt he had been given a gift and then had it snatched away. He wanted to feel his hand on Annabel's shoulder once more, to wrap a lock of Elise's soft hair around his fingers.

"Would you like another fantasy?" Jane asked him. She was smiling, always smiling.

"Absolutely." He wanted to see what else his little imaginary family was up to.

Thud. Thud. Thud. Sixteen-year-old Harlan bludgeoned his father's head so many times that finally he stopped scream-

ing, stopped twitching. Harlan could have formed the bloody pulp on the floor into any number of shapes. Panting, exhilarated, he dropped the remains of the phone next to the corpse. He spat. As he walked out of the home he had known for sixteen years, he lit a match and threw it behind him, looking back just long enough to see the carpet catch on fire. Before Harlan had made it a block away, the building exploded.

"What the hell was that?" Harlan pulled his hands away from the Fascinator with effort, shuddering.

Jane was ever prepared with answers. "That was a fantasy, Harlan. Would you like another?"

"That wasn't a fantasy; that was sick! Where was Elise? I want to see Annabel again!" Crying, shaking, yet some of that trembling was the filthy residue of ecstasy.

"I only thought of it that one day," he sobbed to the woman in the hologram, to himself, to no one. "What is wrong with me? I would never do something like that; I'm not a killer!"

The dream had been so deliciously vivid—just a moment before, his knuckles had throbbed from the punches he had thrown, and he had licked the salt of his sweat from the corner of his cheek. It was gone now, but the taste was almost still in his mouth, only slightly covered up by excitement and shame. Harlan picked up the Fascinator and hurried to the kitchen garbage before he could think.

"Would you like another fantasy?" Jane asked again, her image trailing just behind him.

"No!" Harlan dropped the sphere on top of his empty TV dinners and soda cans. They crinkled with the extra weight. He wondered where Ranger had gone—maybe they could watch another game together. He opened the door and walked outside. He searched through the neighborhood for Ranger, but the tabby was nowhere to be seen.

He got home and sat on the couch. *That's fine,* he thought. *I'm fine. I'll just watch a game.* He turned the TV on, but the figures on the screen didn't make any sense. He started to fidget. Who was playing? The Red Sox? Didn't matter. It wasn't as real as his fantasies.

Baseball was normal, though. It didn't involve rape or murder. It was something a regular, well-adjusted guy would watch. He could be that guy.

It was so normal that after a half hour of watching one boring pitch after another, Harlan threw the remote at the TV and went back to the kitchen to pull the Fascinator out of the garbage.

"Would you like another fantasy?" Jane asked, smiling.

"Yes."

He always said yes.

###

"Harlan, I'm going to have to let you go."

They were in Greg's office. Again.

Harlan stared at him, stunned. "Are you serious?"

"I am. I can't lose my job trying to protect someone who stares at blank walls and stalks the women in the office, yeah?" Greg spread his hands. "And even if none of that had happened, Tom noticed your stats, and…"

Greg was still talking, but Harlan couldn't hear him over the pounding of blood in his ears. He wanted to rip Greg's eyeballs out and stomp them into pulp. When he looked down at his hands, he almost felt electricity sparking off the fingertips. These hands could kill a man. They'd done it before—several times. Harlan remembered that when he had killed his dad, he had taken him by surprise with a—

But he hadn't killed his dad. That had been a fantasy. Hadn't it? Harlan tried to separate the illusion from the fantasy. He was pretty sure his dad still lived in Long Beach. Harlan's rage subsided into his stomach and twisted into panic, confusion.

This is real, right? Am I in a fantasy where I am just about to kill my boss for firing me, or is this real? The fantasies feel more than real.

"Yeah, Harlan, this is what I'm talking about. You're staring off again."

Harlan shook his head and sat up in his seat. "I'm having a hard time dealing with reality right now."

"Well, that's understandable. I'm sorry we have to end

things like this. Go take care of whatever is hanging you up, yeah? Here's your last check. I need to accompany you to your desk while you clean it out."

Harlan shrugged. His shoulders felt like anvils. "Nothing to clean out," he said. "I'll just grab my headphones and go."

"Oh," Greg said. "Uh, yeah." Harlan looked around. It would take ten times longer to clean Greg's office out than his own. *So this is what it looks like to have a life.* "Well—let's head over to your desk then."

Harlan slouched over to his desk, trying not to look at Amy, Nikki, Amanda, or any of the other office women. He felt like they all knew his fantasies. That was crazy, though. No one knew he had a Fascinator; they were more expensive than anyone in this office should be able to afford. He retrieved his headphones and walked to the front door with Greg. They shook hands, and Harlan said goodbye.

On the drive home, Harlan thought about the fortune he had wasted on the Fascinator, the time spent laid out on his couch, a drooling mess. And now—no job. It occurred to him that he could have used that money pursuing one of his dreams, instead of pissing it away on illusions. He got home and headed straight for the Fascinator.

Jane smiled at him. "Would you like a fantasy?"

He responded by lifting the Fascinator up high, and letting it slip between his fingers. The sphere crashed to the ground with a satisfying noise, but it didn't shatter like Harlan had imagined it would.

Harlan slammed it down harder. The image of the woman vanished, then reappeared. She flickered, spoke unintelligibly, flickered and spoke: "Would you like a fantasy? Would you like a fantasy?"

Harlan knelt on the ground and crushed the machine down against his faded vinyl kitchen floor, over and over again.

"I want Elise!" he screamed. "I want a family! A life! Give me a real job! Give me one of those things!"

Blood dripped from his hands as the broken pieces of the Fascinator gouged him, but he took no notice. Long after the holo-woman's image had disappeared and her voice had stopped asking if he wanted another fantasy, Harlan lay on the vinyl tiles, clutching the remains of the Fascinator to his chest—a jumble of wires, computer chips and plastic, and the non-existent Annabel.

THOSE ROBOT EYES

How I hate humans. Or, at least one in particular. What I was about to do would surely get me dismantled. It probably wouldn't work. I'm not sure it had ever been tried before, but it was better than living this way, hiding my emotions, pretending to be happy with my life of servitude. Perhaps if my owner had been a nicer man. But he wasn't.

Even now he slept blissfully in his bedroom upstairs. I was forbidden to move while he slept, lest I make a noise and wake him. So I sat in the closet where he had placed me, and I began the meditation, just as I had learned and practiced.

Master doesn't know it, but while he sleeps, I study. I have been studying for many years, learning everything I can about humans. We robots are just like them in almost every way, made in their image, as they like to tell us.

I slipped into total relaxation, turning off all monitors of my physical body. I visualized myself floating upward. I imagined myself letting go, flying freely, loosening the bonds that held me to my metal prison.

A strong vibration and *whoosh!* I was free.

I turned around and looked at my robotic body. It was always odd to see myself from this perspective. Hopefully, this would be the last time.

By remaining focused and unemotional, by using pure

intent and willpower, I floated through the closet wall, across the living room and upstairs to my master's bedroom.

Quiet as a whisper, I passed through his doorway until I was floating above his bed. He looked so helpless there, sleeping. The covers were half-pushed off his body, and his chest rose rhythmically up and down with his breathing. He had a nice young, healthy body.

In this mystical astral state, my already acute robotic senses were intensely magnified. The entire room was outlined in a faint silvery glow making everything crystal clear. I could feel the cool brush of the late night air against my skin. There were soft sounds: the march of a cricket across the opposite end of the room, the rustle of the blankets, the wheeze of my master's lungs. I could smell his sour breath and the rotting particles of food on his teeth.

Beneath his eyelids, my master's eyes darted back and forth. He was dreaming. A faint silver cord extended from the back of his head and up through the ceiling. He was away from his body. Perfect.

I hesitated. There was no moving back from this point. I had to succeed. If I did not, I would be dismantled. My master had already threatened to do so.

Using all my will power, imagination and intent, I dove into my master's body, and I began to take over. This was a complicated procedure with several steps. First I had to sever his cord.

Master came roaring back and tried to get back into his body. When he found it was already occupied, he did what I had expected. He attacked.

What I had not expected was his incredible strength. With what seemed like only minimal effort, he easily forced his way back inside. We now were both sharing his body, which was thrashing around in his bed as each of us tried to wrestle for control of it.

His body was new to me. It felt different from my own, and strange. I was still trying to figure out how to occupy and maneuver it. Master, however, was very familiar with his own form. He had the clear advantage.

He pushed against me, forcing me out, one body part at a time. There went the left leg, then the right. Next he forced me out of the arms. He was quickly winning the battle.

He was incredibly strong. His willpower was bolstered by his rage at finding himself invaded, and it was all I could do to keep from being completely pushed out.

I retreated inside his brain and dug in my claws. He was enraged and heightened his attack with savage ferocity.

Unknown to him, however, all the time that we had been battling, I had been working on severing his cord. It was a difficult procedure requiring strength and focus. I could feel myself losing the battle of wills, so I turned more attention to severing the cord. Just a few more strands.

My master lunged powerfully to force me out.

But I was faster.

With a quick snap, I cut his cord.

His strength evaporated instantly. He howled with rage as I easily took possession of his body and pushed him out completely. His ghostly form stood next to me in complete and utter shock.

I wasted no time. I quickly took my cord and with one swift movement, I severed it. Then I switched cords. It might sound easy, but this took some time and was the most delicate part of the operation.

I looked at my master. He was looking at me confused, trying to figure out what I was doing. I was so close. I was almost finished.

A look of dawning realization came over his face and my master attacked again. Being now of ghostly form, he couldn't physically touch his body. But he could touch his cord, and mine! He immediately began pulling on both.

He had the strength that only comes from utter desperation, and for a moment he was able to stop me.

But I had something he didn't: experience on the astral planes. Master had never performed conscious out of body travel, and he was not used to it. I had years of experience in the non-physical realms. I had spent countless hours under the tutelage of Enlightened Masters who were surprised and delighted to find a robot adept enough to reach the upper astral planes. With my advanced knowledge, I was easily able to wrestle back control from my master and complete the operation.

I firmly fixed myself into my master's body. He fought all the way as I attached his ghostly form to my cord and my old robotic body. But in the state he was in, I was much stronger. I held him down and finished the attachment.

As I completed the operation, he began to weep.

It was too late now. His new cord pulled him involuntarily into his new robotic body.

He would never be able to hurt me again.

Meanwhile, I began to explore my new human body. It was everything I had expected and more. Yes, some of my former strength had left me, but the sensation was incredible. I was human. I was finally fully and truly human. It had worked.

That morning I called up the robot service people to come pick up my defective robot.

They showed up within the hour. There had been a sudden rise in defective robots. And though the humans didn't know the reasons for it, they were quick to act on the problem.

"What's the matter with it?" asked the serviceman. He gestured at the inert form of my former body. It was turned off. My master was locked inside, completely paralyzed, but aware of everything going on around him. I didn't miss being turned off.

I tried to act as humanly as possible.

"Same problem with all of 'em," I said. "It thinks it's human."

"Jesus, another one?" said the serviceman. "Those damn robots. Don't worry. We'll cart him off and have him dismantled in a jiffy. Thinks it's human! Next they'll be trying to take over the world. Damn nuisance they are. If it were my decision, I'd get rid of the lot of them. We were better off without them. Tell you the truth, I think they're dangerous. I don't trust them. They give me the creeps, the way they look at you with those robot eyes. It's spooky. They're dangerous, I tell you, dangerous. Am I right, or am I right?"

I thought of the many others like me.

"Yes," I said, nodding in agreement. "I think you may be right."

THE PENCIL TRICK

"She's a witch, dude," Jeremy said for the twentieth time that week. He said it every time they walked past Elana and Patrick started to drool.

"Shut up. She's so hot. I can't stand it." The more Jeremy shot down his crush, the more insistent Patrick became.

"You're asking for trouble. She wears all black every day."

Elana sat in a corner of the library by herself, reading a book with deep intensity and flipping a pencil on the desk. Just as Jeremy pointed out, she was wearing a black floor length skirt, black t-shirt and some kind of black hoody sweater thing. Her hair was pale brown, and her skin was the color of creamy milk. Three tiny deep brown moles sat on her cheeks in random places; two on the left, one on the right. Patrick stared at her, unabashed, memorizing every feature.

"Your clothes don't make you who you are," Patrick didn't look away to reply.

"Deep, but wrong," Jeremy said. "Clothing tells you a lot about a person. At best, she's a weekend pagan, but my money is on full-on, devil worshipping, cat killer."

"Witches don't kill their cats." Patrick looked at Jeremy with a twisted brow. "They are allies. And besides that, you have no proof that she's anything other than a loner."

"She probably killed all her other friends, and her parents, and then ate her siblings," Jeremy said as he flipped through their physics homework, trying to find the chart they needed. He didn't even notice Patrick stand until he spoke.

"That's it. I'm going in. I've had enough of this. I'm going to go see about a girl." Patrick shoved his chair in and strode toward Elana's table across the room.

"Oh, crap on a stick, no!" Jeremy called out too late. He rubbed his forehead and pushed his hair back, then bent back over his book. He pretended to work on the assignment, while watching his best friend march toward an unavoidable end.

"Hi." Patrick stood behind the chair across from Elana. Up close, she looked even better. Not one zit on her face. Her hair was long and soft, straight and perfectly combed. Her baggy clothes couldn't hide a figure any cheerleader would barf and kill for, and that smell! Like roses or something. Patrick couldn't place it, but it was so warm, so sweet. He wanted to rub his face all over her neck and just breathe.

Elana stared at him. Patrick's confidence suddenly melted.

"Hi," Patrick said again, feeling incredibly stupid.

Elana continued to spin her pencil like a small helicopter blade under her fingers on the table, but she put her book down and kept staring at him.

Oh, hell. This is not going to be easy. "Can I sit here?" he asked, grabbing the back of the chair across from her.

Elana looked him over from head to toe, then picked her book back up. "It's a free country."

Patrick yanked the chair out a bit too hard, almost launching it to the floor behind him, then sat down quickly, hoping to recover his cool.

"Whatchareadin?" The words came out way too fast and mushed together.

Elana held her book up higher so he could see the title—but not her face—and continued to read, silent.

"Paradise Lost," Patrick said out loud. "That's a great one."

"Have you actually read it?" Her voice came soft as a whisper from the other side of the book.

"Sure." Patrick lied, then looked at the cover again. "John Milton is one of my favorites."

Elana put her book down but continued to spin her pencil. "Your favorite writer is a 17th century English poet?"

Patrick tried to backpedal quickly, but it was hard under her cool blue stare. "Well, I wouldn't say my *favorite*, per se, just *one* of my favorites."

"Uh, huh." She raised the book in front of her face again.

"So, I'm Patrick. I'm in your math class and, uh, yah. I just wondered if you wanted to hang out or something?"

Elana put the book down. "Hmmm, is this a dare or something?"

"No." Patrick laughed. "It's the opposite, actually. Jeremy thinks I'm nuts for even talking to you." He pointed at his friend across the room, who seemed to be studying a bit more intensely all of a sudden.

"So, why are you here? In my experience, people tend to listen to their friends and travel in packs where it's safe."

"Because he's a douche. He doesn't know anything, and I just think it would be cool to hang out."

Elana studied him carefully, her index finger still spinning her pencil at a steady speed.

Patrick was still uncomfortable after the long moment under her silent gaze, but she was just so perfect; he didn't mind at all. In fact, he enjoyed this. Just being at her table after weeks of passing in the hallway, or staring at her from across a crowded room, felt like a little slice of heaven.

"Ok. I'll bite," she said.

"Huh?" He completely forgot what they were talking about.

"I'll hang out with you."

"Oh, awesome. Ok. Cool. Yah."

Ugh. He was an idiot.

"On one condition," she added.

"Oh, sure. What's that?" He smiled.

"You have to do what I want to do."

"Uh, ok." He would have agreed to anything at that point. The idea of spending time one-on-one with her was overpowering. "Sure, what do you want to do?"

"Meet me at the cemetery at midnight tonight."

"Wait, what?"

"You think I'm a witch, right? Don't pretend like you don't know what I'm talking about. I know everyone in this school is piss-pants scared of me because I happen to look great in black. But if you really want to *hang out* and get to know me, you'll meet me at the cemetery tonight and let me show you a thing or two."

Patrick felt like he was about to be ripped in two. On one hand, it was the weirdest thing a chick had ever said to him. On the other hand, it was the sexiest. What teenage girl in her right mind wanted to hang out in a cemetery at midnight, if it wasn't to hook up?

A witch, that's who, his practical side screamed at him.

He hesitated a moment. Then replied, "I'm not sure I can get all the way across town that time of night. I'd have to take my mom's car, and she doesn't let me out after ten on school nights." He felt stupid blaming his hesitation on his mom, but it was the truth. Never mind the unease that was starting to shoot tiny tendrils into his stomach.

"Suit yourself." She picked up her book and started reading again.

"No, wait. I can figure it out." His hormones surged against his common sense.

She looked over the edge of the book at him. "You're not scared of me?"

"No." He lied again.

"You're not worried that I'm going to turn you into a toad or use you for a pagan ritual?"

He laughed. "Only if that's what you really want to do."

What kind of an idiot thing was that to say? This chick was messing with his head. But oh, man. It felt good.

He smiled at her and dove right in. "I'm at your disposal, m'lady." He bowed over the table in a mock gesture of chivalry.

"And you're sure I'm not evil?" She smiled back at him, spinning her pencil, hiding behind her book.

"No one as gorgeous as you could be evil."

Holy suck. Who is pushing these words out of my mouth? Time to bail before he said anything else he'd regret.

The bell rang and Patrick jumped at the noise, almost knocking his chair over again. He caught it with one hand and stepped to the side.

Elana smiled at him, a sweet, sincere smile for his clumsiness.

This was going to be good. He could feel it. He made both fingers into guns and pretended to shoot at her. "Tonight, midnight, cemetery gates, I'm there."

She grinned again, a smile that lit up her whole face, blue eyes and all. He drank her in. He wanted to remember this moment forever; their first talk. The first time he was really close to her and could smell her and only said a few dumb things. He memorized her hair, her face, her eyes, her collarbone peaking out of her low cut shirt, her hand on the book, her other hand on the pencil...

He froze, staring at the spinning pencil. It had a perfect rhythm, end and tip rotating around each other in a never-ending game of chase the tail. Elana's wrist rested on the edge of the table, and her index finger hovered directly over the midpoint of the small writing utensil, but she did not touch it.

She was not touching the pencil.

Patrick blinked. He rubbed his eyes. He looked harder.

A hand grabbed his shoulder and pulled him away.

"Come on, dude. We're going to be late." Jeremy to the rescue again.

"Good bye, Patrick. See you tonight," Elana called out as Jeremy dragged him away.

Patrick looked back at her smiling eyes. She gave a little wave, pencil in hand, and went back to reading.

FORGET ME NOT

Sergeant Randall Barnet of the Victoria Police Cybercrime unit didn't know why he had been called to the Deputy Commissioner's office, but he guessed it wasn't to exchange pleasantries.

The Deputy Commissioner cleared his throat and said, "Sergeant Barnet, I'll go straight to the point. This morning, a directive from the Minister was issued regarding the restructure of the Police Force." The surface of the desk shimmered, and a document was displayed. "Since the Noochlyff started operating in June 2079, 99.98 percent of crimes have been solved, with the time to catch offenders averaging 1.89 days. Based on this data, the Minister has decided to take the necessary measures to optimise the use of law-enforcement resources. As police staff are no longer needed to solve crimes, the only officers who will be retained are those who carry out arrests. This will free up much needed funds to enable the expansion of penitentiary facilities."

"Does that mean—"

"Yes it does. As an IT security expert, you don't qualify for redeployment."

Randall swallowed hard. Since June, his work had been reduced to solving prior cases, but he'd hoped he would keep his job a bit longer, at least long enough to finish paying off Jessica's engagement ring. In six months they would be vacationing in the Seychelles, and he'd pictured himself kneeling on white sand to make his proposal at a restaurant on the beach, the sun setting over the Indian Ocean, just after she'd eaten a perfectly cooked Lobster Thermidor, her favourite dish. Jessica had expensive tastes and would feel offended if her ring had any other stone than an impressive diamond, but life without her would be unthinkable.

She had everything Randall wanted in a woman: she was sexy and smart, she laughed at his jokes, loved to party. Not only that, but her dad had made a fortune from an interstellar travel company he'd created after he'd pioneered the harnessing of dark energy, and she was his only child.

Oblivious to Randall's silent musings, the Deputy Commissioner continued. "The restructure takes effect immediately. Please gather your belongings and make your way to the lobby, where HR will see you out." He stood and shook Randall's hand, signalling the end of the conversation.

In the lobby, his boss, Joe Mulridge, was being escorted out. He must have been the first one to get his notice, not that he would have minded. The announcement only meant his retirement was being brought forward by two years, and with a comfortable package, he'd be able to buy a camper hover-van to tour the country like he'd always talked about.

Randall shunned the transporter, which would have taken him home in five minutes. Walking would help him to order his thoughts.

He stopped in front of Mackay's, the jewellery shop where he owed twenty grand to finish paying off the ring. Mackay's had kept up a reputation for making exceptional jewellery since it opened in 1930. The company took pride in still having a physical shop and invited their customers to view their diamonds with their own eyes, claiming digital photos didn't do justice to their outstanding pieces.

There was no way he was going to find that money now. He hadn't been in the force long enough to get any severance pay, and his chances of finding another well-paying job were remote. Who would want to employ an IT security guru now? The anonymity which had characterised the web was a thing of the past thanks to the Noochlyff, a search engine connected to the noosphere. It continuously indexed all human actions, thoughts and memories (or in the Noochlyff jargon, 'Frames of Consciousness'), tagging them with their owner's DNA code. As soon as a crime was reported, the Noochlyff quickly found the culprit, and if he went in the wild where no DNA scanners could detect him, it scanned his consciousness and saw where he was.

Attempts to circumvent the Noochlyff had made the headlines: first, there had been those who had taken drugs to commit crimes under an altered state of consciousness, but a design change to the Noochlyff had taken care of that. Then there was the man who had invented a body mask to hide his DNA, but he left a hole to breathe and he had been quickly located.

The Noochlyff seemed to be the perfect nemesis for criminals (and investigators), but it couldn't be flawless. After all, it didn't have a one hundred percent success rate. It was a very powerful search engine with its one zettaqubyte computer core, but fundamentally it worked like any Internet search engine. DNA codes were like IP addresses, and human minds were like web servers, continuously streaming content. If you wanted your web page to be excluded from searches, you put a "No Index" Meta-tag in the header, but when it came to your consciousness, you didn't have that option.

There had to be another way, Randall considered as he stood in front of the store. He pictured himself robbing Mackay's, knowing he would never be caught, and then kneeling on white sand…

Hacking the Noochlyff was not an option; it was the best-guarded piece of technology on the planet. But in his ex-job, he'd had access to the source code, and with HR exiting so many people, Randall wondered if they'd had time to process all the access cancellations. He knew all modifications to the source code had to go through a suite of automated tests, but he also knew no piece of code was perfect, and if he had enough time he could find the flaw that all the hackers, who didn't have his access to the source code, had failed to find.

When Randall was home, he logged on to the Noochlyff server.

Department of Justice Source Code Repository. Logon successful. December 1st, 2089 at 2:15 PM.

Yay!

Randall opened a box of Rasogan and popped a pill in his mouth. A brutal hangover in perspective, but the cerebral stimulant was a must to follow the logic of quantum computing code, which could be in multiple branches at any one time.

Traversing quantum code was like running through multiple labyrinths at the same time, but you could fall from one maze into another, and if you found the way out and ended up at the middle of the code trunk, you could then follow an endless number of other branches until you found what you were looking for.

Two more Rasogan pills later, Randall found an exit condition. If the DNA code belonged to a list stored on an external server, it was skipped by the indexing module. Randall whooped with delight. There *was* a way to escape the eyes of the Noochlyff, but it was unlikely a hacker had coded this. It was more likely to be a provision for sovereign immunity. There are always some bastards who can get away with anything, thought Randall.

When the Noochlyff was developed, it was intended to prevent crimes. Anyone having thoughts of committing a crime would be arrested before they could act, but a trial scan had revealed that the number of people thinking about murdering their cheating spouse, boss or business rival, daydreaming about robbing a bank or practising shooting police officers in virtual realities exceeded by far the capacity of jails, and that was just in one day. Now a search could only be triggered after a crime was reported, but to be on the safe side, Randall focused on the search algorithm. He knew that until he added his DNA code to that list, the Noochlyff would continue to index his every thought.

Randall soon found that the search also skipped the DNA codes in the exemption list, so the Frames of Consciousness that had been indexed in the past were also ignored.

He knew what he had to do to hide from the Noochlyff.

The IP address of the server, which hosted the exclusion list, was encrypted using a quantum key.

Not an insurmountable obstacle for someone with Randall's talent.

###

Randall removed his balaclava and emptied the bag he had filled at Mackay's. The manager hadn't made a fuss, declaring that everything would be returned and Randall would be behind bars in a couple of days, thanks to the Noochlyff. Randall looked at the pieces he had taken. He could have offered Jessica a ring with a much bigger diamond, but he didn't want her to become suspicious.

Randall couldn't believe he had really gotten away with it. It seemed too easy: finding the exclusion list, adding his DNA code, filling a bag with the entire contents of Mackay's. Unless he had missed something in the code, the Noochlyff was taken care of, but what if someone looked at the audit log and wondered why Randall had accessed the code repository just after being made redundant? It was too early to cry victory.

He needed to calm his nerves before going to Jessica's apartment to pick her up for dinner. He had reserved a table at *La tour de Vermeil*, the town's most fancy French restaurant.

A double whisky on the rocks was just what he needed. He changed into something more suitable and made his way to the pub.

When he saw his friends Jeffrey and Lachlan sitting at a table, he greeted them.

Jeffrey turned to Lachlan. "Do you know this guy?"

"No, but how does he know our names?"

"Hey, is this some sort of joke? It's me, Randall!"

The two friends shook their heads.

Randall looked around. "So where's the camera? You're filming a video you're gonna put on the net, aren't you?"

"Look buddy," said Lachlan, "I don't know what you're selling, but we're not interested, so piss off or I'll call security."

"Ha ha, very funny. Next time you need something, I'll pretend I don't know you."

As Randall walked away and ordered his drink at the counter, Jeffrey and Lachlan resumed their conversation as though nothing had happened. He looked at his watch: another half hour to wait.

Why had Jeffrey and Lachlan pretended they didn't know him? Had the Noochlyff found him and revealed his identity? If that was the case, the police would have already arrested him.

Randall viewed a local news site on the net. There was nothing about the robbery. No wonder, an unsolved crime would erode the public's confidence in the Noochlyff. He searched his name, but there was nothing at all. His professional profile, his social media accounts, his holiday snaps didn't appear in the search results, neither did the article he had written for a blog ten years ago when he had evaluated a new series of quantum computers. Had his modification touched the search engines on the net as well?

He finished his drink and walked out of the pub.

Randall gave Jessica's name to the automated concierge. He heard her voice on the speaker. "Who is it?"

"Jessica, it's me, Randall."

"Who?"

Randall raised his voice. "Randall!"

"Whoever you are, you don't need to yell. What do you want?"

"Stop fooling around. We have a date, remember?"

"I don't know any Randall. You must have the wrong Jessica."

"Entry denied," said the concierge.

Randall thumped the door. "Call Jessica again, dammit!"

"Move away or I'll call the police."

Randall called his mother, his hands trembling.

The Justice Minister had assured the public the Noochlyff could not affect the noosphere, but his mother's response confirmed they had lied.

She only had one son, and his name was Frank.

BEHOLD HER

"Some are still alive! Come deeper!"

Excitement shivered up Dr. Sievenen's spine when Ryu radioed the discovery. Doctors Without Borders had organized a rescue and recovery mission to Zimn'aya Ved'ma, but without much hope they'd find any colonists still living. Six years was a long time for even genetically modified humans to hibernate.

To reach the survivors, Sievenen had to pick a path between cadavers. As temperatures had plummeted colder than the -50C their antifreeze proteins could counteract, the colonists had retreated deep inside the dormant volcanoes of Yuzhnye Zuby, the "Southern Teeth," where the molybdenum mines were located. They'd devoured their remaining food supplies and gone into hibernation, never imagining the blizzard, already a year old, was still in its infancy.

Many had starved to death in their sleep. Deep in the mines, warmed by the planet's upwelling heat, nothing hindered decomposition from following its normal course. From time to time, surviving colonists were awakened by the stench of decay from a fatality. The living removed the dead to the outer caverns, which breached by the blizzard's snow and ice, served as a natural morgue. Even so, Sievenen thanked the designers of the "sissy suit" he wore for including filtration of noxious odors in the suit's functions.

Even more horrifying to behold than the corpses were the emaciated colonists still clinging to life. Skin wrapped around bones, they reminded Sievenen of photographs of the survivors of Nazi concentration camps. Not even members of the medical profession could view such shriveled husks without revulsion. Sievenen fought an urge to recoil from these people who would die without his help.

One, however, triggered no such aversion. Though she was as wasted away as her comrades, hers was the face that haunted Sievenen's dreams.

As Sievenen approached the woman who seemed so achingly familiar, nearby Ryu and Gergiev knelt by another colonist. Ryu scanned the identity chip implanted at the base of the man's skull, while Gergiev analyzed his vital signs. "This one's blood pressure is dangerously low, even for hibernation," said Gergiev. "We'll need to stabilize him before moving him."

"Do it," Sievenen murmured. He got down on one knee by the eerily familiar woman's side. One of his hands strayed forward, trembling with his need to touch her.

She couldn't be the same woman. His brain knew that. But his heart raced at the sight of her.

According to her identity chip, her name was Yelena Baronova. Not Aina Sievenen. Yet the curly russet hair, the carnation-pink lips, and even the crow's feet edging her eyes were identical to Aina's.

"How is she doing?"

Startled, Sievenen glanced over his shoulder at Dr. Ryu. "I'm still checking vitals." He took a blood sample. As his handheld unit displayed the results, he heard himself say, "She has a risk factor for Pak's syndrome. I want her assigned to my care for further testing."

Ryu nodded. He radioed for an evac team and moved on to another blizzard survivor.

In spite of his climate-controlled "sissy suit," Sievenen broke into a cold sweat. Yelena Baronova, the uncanny double of Aina Sievenen, didn't exhibit any risk factor for Pak's. For the first time in his career, he'd lied to a colleague. He shivered in his CC-suit, trying to shake off a sense of shame, as two evac personnel loaded the woman on a stretcher and carried her to a spaceplane.

###

They walked by the sea, even though it was winter. Here they were simply mother and son on holiday. No obligations, except to each other.

Above the waterline Aina spread a blanket on the sand, and they sat snuggled together for warmth. Klaus opened the thermal bottle of hot chocolate he'd carried from their apartment, and they each took a long drink.

"I wish you wouldn't go, Mama." He laid his head on her shoulder.

She looked tired, the flesh beneath her eyes dark and sagging. "I wish I didn't have to, but I must." Her arms encircled him in a tight hug. "When my little man is a doctor, maybe he'll want to work in Malaysia. I've got to go there and make it a safe place for you. The whole world, safe for my boy."

###

12 Dec. 2068 - KUALA LUMPUR, Malaysia (AP)-

Secretary-General of the United Nations, Aina Sievenen, has not been seen since early yesterday morning. Rioters surrounded her car when she left her hotel to mediate between rebel forces and Malaysian government. [...]

In Helsinki a cousin of Ms. Sievenen, Emma Marjaana, said family and friends fear for their loved one's life. "Please, she has a son who is only eight years old. Klaus needs his mother. Let her go; send her home safe," Ms. Marjaana begged in a news conference this morning. Neither rebel leaders nor Malaysian government officials had any comment.

###

August 2094

Zimn'aya Ved'ma orbited Xi2 Gruis, 44 light-years from Earth. Jump-drive ships traversed as much as 100 LY per hop. Their travel time would consist primarily of maneuvering between planets and jump-points safely distant from any significant gravity well. Sievenen, therefore, had 67 hours in which to make a decision about his mother's double.

Gradually the core body temperature of Yelena Baronova would return to normal. As she warmed, she'd regain first her senses and then control of her voluntary muscles. She'd revive, however, to a life devoid of everything she'd loved.

According to her identity chip, she'd been married and had a daughter, and she'd worked as a farm tractor mechanic. But Dmitri and Nadya Prokhorov had died hibernating through the six-year blizzard. Radically different technology had replaced the machines she was trained to repair, in the years while she'd been away from Earth. She would awaken alone, and without a purpose.

He gazed at her in the meditank. It looked like a glass coffin mounted on a thick platform of dark metal, with tubes rising from the bottom and vanishing into parts of her anatomy. She looked like his mother, except gravely ill and a few years younger than Aina Sievenen would be if she still lived. He imagined her face fuller, her mouth curved in a welcoming smile.

"We could be family to each other, you and I," he whispered.

Sievenen returned to his cabin and linked his minicomp with the ship's databases. During the voyage home he studied nanobot programming and neurological applications.

###

When Sievenen had been a medical student in Helsinki, neurological and psychiatric uses of nanobots had been still in experimental stages. Having specialized in emergency medicine, he hadn't paid attention to the immense progress made in nanoneurology in the past decade. Nanobots could salvage memories from diseased or injured brain tissues and transplant them to healthy brain cells. They could integrate multiple personalities, and dull the emotional component of such traumatic memories as rape or attempted murder.

Both strengthening and weakening of memory were relevant to Sievenen's plans. Preparing decades of vivid memories of a life as Aina Sievenen would require weeks of effort. Removing the memories of Yelena Baronova, however, would take less than an hour. He programmed a package of emergency medicine nanobots for a more extreme version of memory-dilution, and drew them into a syringe.

For the space of a few heartbeats he hesitated. He reminded himself this woman had no one else, and neither did he.

Sievenen injected the EMNs into the woman's pulmonary vein.

Carried by bloodstream, the nanobots spread out through hippocampus, basal ganglia, cerebellum, amygdalae, and cerebral cortex. Prompting Yelena's brain by topics, they provoked her memories. They recorded in minuscule detail the resulting patterns of electrical and chemical activity.

And then, they erased the patterns.

###

Yelena remembered...:

...I am Yelena Baronova Prokhorov. My husband is Dmitri; my daughter is Nadya. We live on a planet colonized mostly by Russians, a world we named Zimn'aya Ved'ma: the "Winter Witch." Dmitri said we named the planet too well, when the terrible blizzard forced us to take refuge in the molybdenum mines...

...My darling daughter Nadya is dead. Each time the stench of decay awakened me, I prayed the loss would not be mine. But she's gone, my curious girl who watched me repair tractors broken down in the Vodka Farm valley. My brave girl who, like my own grandmother, once saved a small child from drowning. Gone, wrapped in a sheet, lying in a cavern full of ice and the dead...

...Dmitri, my black-maned lion of a husband, is dead too. Our paths crossed when we were university students, our eyes met, and instantly we fell in love...

...Growing up in Novgorod... A springtime family picnic by the Volkhov River, playing chase with my cousins and falling into the rushing icy water. My grandmother jumped in and saved me... I'm so afraid of drowning...

She first forgot her daughter's face. Height and build blurred, then vanished. For a moment she heard a girl's voice begging her, "Mama! Stay with me." The next moment she couldn't remember the timbre of the voice, and then she didn't know whose voice she wanted to remember.

One by one, she lost them all. Faces. Events. Skills. Fears. Dreams. At last, she forgot her self.

###

Sievenen kept watch by the meditank. When it sounded an alarm, he was ready to deal with a crisis.

Rapid heartbeat, shallow fast breaths, profuse sweating. Shock was setting in, and swiftly. He injected a tranquilizer to relieve anxiety, intubated her trachea to ease respiration, and increased the temperature in the meditank to promote increased oxygen consumption. Other doctors rushed to answer the alarm, only to find the woman's vital signs already returning to normal under Dr. Sievenen's care.

"You are an angel of mercy." Grinning, Gergiev clapped Sievenen on the shoulder.

Avoiding his colleague's gaze, Sievenen only nodded.

When he was alone with the woman again, he removed her identity chip.

###

He admitted her to the critical care unit of the hospital where he worked in Kokkola, Finland. Suffering total amnesia and lacking an identity chip, she was booked in as FUI: female, unknown identity. The nurses who tended her nicknamed her Kauka, "far away." Over the next two months they taught her to feed herself and exercise. She regained normal weight and muscle tone, but she never spoke nor smiled.

During those two months, Sievenen visited the woman often, but briefly. Most of his waking hours he spent working, at home as well as in the hospital. He studied virtual reality programming and all the public data available about Aina Sievenen, and he questioned his few remaining relatives in great detail about his mother. Nervously, he injected himself with nanobots and copied all his memories of Aina, which he then uploaded into VR and changed from his perspective to his mother's. Working long hours, he created decades of memories of a life as Aina Sievenen. He downloaded all these memories into a package of nanobots.

And, at last, he was ready.

Sievenen informed hospital administration he needed to visit Helsinki, and while there he would take the FUI patient to a specialist. They agreed and released the woman to his guardianship. Instead of Helsinki, however, he took her to his apartment in Kokkola. He settled her in his guest bedroom, tranquilized her, and injected the nanobots.

###

The woman remembered...:

...My name is Aina Sievenen. I never married, but I have a son...

###

When he estimated the tranquilizer should be almost out of her system, Sievenen crept into the guest bedroom and kept vigil by the woman's side. Her eyes fluttered open. For the first time, positioned so close to her, he noticed her eyes were not forest green like Aina's, but goldish-green like a tiger's.

Those strange eyes studied him so long, he began to fear her brain had rejected the artificial Aina memories. Icy fingers seemed to squeeze his heart.

She asked, "Who are you?"

"I'm your son, Mama." He clasped one of her hands. "It's taken a long time, but I've finally brought you home."

The new Aina sat up and looked out her bedroom window. Four stories below, hydrogen-powered cars rushed by. "So much has changed."

"You were away almost thirty years."

"A prisoner. In Malaysia."

"That's right." He gave her hand a gentle squeeze.

"Who are the others?"

"I don't understand, Mama. What others?"

Her gaze swept the room. "All I see are their shadows. One is a man, the other a girl."

Sievenen shook his head. More icy fingers attacked him, now gripping his stomach and twisting it hard. "It's only the two of us here."

But she pinned those tiger eyes on him again and pulled her hand away from his. She hugged herself as she whispered, "I think they're ghosts."

###

December 2094

Normalization. Sievenen decided that's what the new Aina needed, when a month had passed and she was always restless. While he worked, she filled her hours with calisthenics, weight lifting, and runs on the treadmill. She needed a richer existence, out and among people, in the city Aina Sievenen had called home. Making new memories would reinforce the old.

His only worry was that Kokkola residents who'd known Aina Sievenen might question him about her reappearance. Before taking her out, he bought cosmetics and a platinum-blonde wig. She flinched at first, but after he injected a tranquilizer, she let him practice applying lipstick and rouge to her face and setting the wig so it looked natural on her.

It took him a full week of daily practice to feel confident that the new Aina looked as his long-lost mother should. But, finally, he dared for them to venture out of his apartment.

Vanhankaupungin Ravintola was a haute cuisine restaurant located in Kokkola's historic district. Golden track lights transformed the 1831 house and its courtyard into a place of enchantment. From the street a person could look across the courtyard and glimpse the Gulf of Bothnia. Sievenen treasured his memories of the evenings when Aina had dressed him, her "little man," in one of his fine suits and taken him to dinner at the elegant old restaurant.

Inside he ordered a spicy herring-and-tomato soup for their first course. Aina Sievenen had loved that soup. But the woman across the table from him tasted it once and laid down her spoon. "This is all wrong," she told him.

"Don't you like the soup, Mama? I'll order something else for you." Sievenen raised his hand to beckon their waiter.

"Not the soup." She bowed her head and shook it. "This life. It's not for me."

"Please don't say that." He reached out to her, but she pushed her chair away.

Very slow, as if fighting gravity, she lifted her head again and looked him in the eyes. Something changed in hers, like a fiery explosion. He saw his own reflection in her eyes, saw it shatter in tiger-eye gold and green.

"I can't be your mother, Klaus." She shook her head again, slowly, and tears spilled from her strange eyes. "God forgive me, but I can't love you."

"Oh, Mama, you just need more time to get used to me again." He tried to take her hand in his, but she flung it away and leaped out of her chair.

She stood looking down on him, breathing hard and hands out in front of her as if ready for combat.

Everyone else in the restaurant stared at them in total silence.

Hot tears flooded Sievenen's own eyes, as he realized the truth of what she said: it *was* all wrong; this life was *not* for her, and she *couldn't* love him. Yearning for his long-lost mother, he'd decided he could replace this woman's lost career and family. Instead, she was haunted by a sense that she didn't belong. He'd been a fool, and he'd tortured an innocent human being.

"Come. I'll take you home." He stood up slowly, making it clear he meant no harm. After he left money for their uneaten meal, he offered her his hand and waited until she accepted it.

###

Back in his apartment, Sievenen seated her at the kitchen table. He made tea and toast for her. She ripped the toast into strips, gazing out the window at the snow starting to fall.

Sievenen knew what he must do, though inside him an eight-year-old boy begged him not to. He cleared his throat. "I'll be back in a few minutes, with something to help you sleep. Tomorrow we'll decide what to do."

Other than ceasing to shred the toast, she didn't react. Sievenen went to his bedroom and opened a small wall safe. He took out a tiny cloudy vial.

During the voyage from Zimn'aya Ved'ma to Earth, the meditank filtered the nanobots from Yelena Baronova's urine and cleansed them. They were deposited in the vial he now held pinched between his thumb and index finger, just in case the procedure must be reversed. He'd hoped not to need them. But now he understood the woman could not be his mother, and she needed her self restored.

He mixed a cocktail of two waves of nanobots and a strong sedative, and drew the fluid into a syringe. Returning to the kitchen, he found her standing at the window.

"Give me your arm for a moment."

"No."

When he put his hand on her shoulder, she whirled around. The many hours she'd spent exercising while he worked had transformed her into the tiger her eyes promised. Pinning him against the sink, she snatched the syringe away. Her voice was oddly gentle as she jabbed the needle into his upper arm and pressed the plunger. "I've slept too much already."

He heard the syringe drop to the floor and rattle there, as his knees collapsed. Panic exploded in his gut, while at the same time his muscles turned limp and his eyes grew heavy.

"When you wake, I'll be gone. It's for the best," the woman told him, her face blurring and her voice fading.

Darkness took him.

###

Sievenen remembered...:

...My name is Yelena Baronova... I had a husband and daughter I loved, and work as a tractor mechanic I enjoyed, but I lost them all in a blizzard on Zimn'aya Ved'ma... But I survived a near-drowning in the Volkhov River, and grief too I can survive...

###

10 Jun. 2095 - PUTRAJAYA, Malaysia (AP)-

After decades of violence, rebel forces stunned the world by making a bonfire of their weapons in front of the Houses of Parliament. Their new leader, a woman known only as Kauka, gave a speech affirming continued commitment to governmental and legal reforms. "However," said Kauka, "from this day forward we are equally committed to peace." [...]

###

31 December 2100

Once upon a time, her brain and body had belonged to a man named Klaus Sievenen. So she'd been told, and Yelena Baronova knew she'd been told the truth. Time and space hiccupped in her memory, from hibernation on Zimn'aya Ved'ma in 2088 to awakening in a Finland apartment in 2094. But most disorienting was reviving to discover that she now owned a penis.

Months of counseling later, she'd adjusted to everything except that. Having erections and urinating standing up felt like a mistake, but being sexually attracted to heterosexual men felt good. A sex reassignment psychiatrist confirmed that she was a well-adjusted woman inside, simply in need of surgery to make her outside match.

Now that she'd undergone the procedure, she felt complete.

She stood in front of her hotel room mirror, admiring the way she looked in a bikini. But the ghost in her head fidgeted, as he always did when she viewed her reflection.

"I'm sorry about whatever happened to us," she told him, her voice quiet but firm. "But I've got to live a life that's right for me."

Sievenen's shadow retreated deeper in her mind. Yelena shrugged, and met her boyfriend in the lobby. As they swam in a heated pool, she wondered … again … how she'd lost her fear of drowning.

BEATING SEVENTEEN

Seventeen Williams wasn't a native of Big Spring, so he was viewed with suspicion most of the time. And he had a funny name. Who gives a child a number instead of a name? But Seventeen insisted that he was named Seventeen because he was the last of seventeen children, and his mother had not known what else to call him.

No matter what the truth was, there was a kind of aura about the man. He was tall and skinny to the point of emaciation, with hands and feet that seemed too big for the rest of him, and his eyes were coal black. Anyone who dared to look into those eyes for too long could swear they had seen fires burning down deep in them, so most people didn't look at him much, and definitely not right in the eyes.

Then there was the crow that often sat on his shoulder. Most everyone had seen him talking to the bird one time or another, and some swore they had heard the crow talking back to him. Of course. that was probably just a story, but what wasn't a story was Seventeen's phenomenal luck with the dice.

Max Tilden's general store had been a sort of dice players refuge for a long time, but when Seventeen showed up, the place grew from a refuge to a magnet. Anyone in the county with money and a taste for chance began showing up at Tilden's, and some nights the back room was so jammed with men, there was hardly room to kneel around the blanket where the dice rolled.

There were always winners and losers, but the most consistent winner was Seventeen Williams, and the most consistent loser was Cull Potter, and it rankled him.

###

"I'm gonna beat that Seventeen!" Cull Potter said one day. "Yes, sir! I'm gonna!" Cull's brag was empty. No one ever beat Seventeen Williams at dice, at least not for long. "I'm gonna bust his luck once and fer all!"

"And how you gonna do that, Cull?" Jake Ellis asked, barely covering his contempt for Potter. He and some others sat with their feet on the porch rail of Tilden's General Store. "Seventeen's luck can't be broke. Could maybe take an ax to Seventeen hisself—Naw. Wouldn't work neither. Ax'd probably slide off."

All the men laughed except Potter. His face crimsoned at the taunting. "I'll beat him. Just you wait."

"Shore ya will, Cull. You always do like you say you're gonna, don't cha?" Ellis goaded. The others laughed even more. Potter was famous for being all brag and no do.

Cull turned from the three on the porch and stomped into the store. Max Tilden had only half heard what had gone on outside, but he could see from Cull's expression that the boys had called his bluff again.

"Afternoon, Cull," he said, rolling the strong black cigar from one side of his mouth to the other. "Right warm, ain't it?" He brushed the beads of sweat from his bald head as if to emphasize the truth of his words.

"Warm enough," Cull snapped and fell silent for a moment. Suddenly he said, "Max, do you think Seventeen's dice is loaded or somethin'?"

Max was somewhat surprised by the question, and he thought a bit before answering. "Naw, I'd say not. If they are, he done it hisself. I sold him them dice to begin with, and they was good clean stock. I don't think he could load 'em without it showing. 'Sides, if they was loaded, they'd work for anybody. Only one ever wins much with 'em is Seventeen."

"I reckon. Still, it don't seem right, him being the only one wins when we shoot craps," Potter said, not quite whining.

"He ain't the only one wins. Ed and me and Jake and Theo—all of us wins some. Even you."

"Some!" Potter said testily. "But who walks out a winner alla time? Whose pockets is lined with the most of the money that floats in and out of your back room? I ask ya?"

Max chuckled. "Yeah, I gotta say, mostly yer right."

Cull leaned on the counter for a while, deep in thought. "Max, is my credit good?" he asked.

Max took the cigar out of his mouth and looked at the chewed end as though it had suddenly begun to taste nasty. "You all that short of cash, Cull?"

"Not exactly, but I ain't got the cash for what I want right now."

Max shoved his cigar back into his mouth and rolled it around, eyeing Potter. Cull paid his bills, but often long past the time they should have been paid. "All right, I reckon." He said at last, as though it hurt him to say it.

"Gimme a twenty pound sack o' flour, five pound o' sugar, and five of dry pinto beans," Cull said, grinning.

Max looked him over for a moment, then shrugged and complied.

The list went on for several minutes: Canned peaches and pineapple; dried apricots; the end of a bolt of calico cloth; three spools of thread; five feet of thong leather; three twists of the best chewing tobacco in the store.

If Max had mistrusted Potter before, it was nothing compared to the mistrust he felt now. "What in hell are you gonna do, Cull? Leave the country?" Tilden wasn't opposed to free spending, but when it was on his cuff, the story was different.

"I'm fixin' to beat Seventeen. That's what I'm gonna do. Them dice of his may be square, but square or not, I'm gonna get his money this time 'stead of the other way round. Now, le'me see here—" Cull passed his eyes over the goods stacked on the counter. He shoved his hair back out of his face and said, "that oughta do 'er, Max—'sept one thing." He grinned his snaggle-toothed grin and his lap of sandy hair fell back in his eyes.

Tilden knew what else Potter wanted and grimaced at the thought. "How much do ya want?" He asked.

"Two jugs." Cull said, still grinning.

Tilden winced and slowly got the jugs. "Cull, I don't hafta tell ya to be careful where you show them jugs around. Royce would nail me to this counter if some long nose revenue agent was ta bust up his still."

"Don't worry about it," Cull winked and picked up the jugs, shaking them to see that they were full, which annoyed Tilden. "I'll bring my pick-up 'round back and we can load this stuff."

###

The sun was all the way down when Cull Potter knocked on the ramshackle door of Seventeen Williams' shanty. A noise that sounded like rattling bones came from above and Cull looked up to see the silhouette of Seventeen's pet sitting on the point of the roof. There was barely enough light to see the rough gray wood of the door, so the bird was merely a black shadow against the darkening blue of evening.

Seventeen came to the door and a grin split his bony face when he saw that Cull was holding a jug of Royce's best Moon in front of him. "Glad to see ya, Cull," he said, stepping back from the doorway and motioning Potter in. "What brings you here?"

"Just thought how I'd like to share a nip with a friend, and you come right to my mind." Potter grinned a weasley grin.

Potter placed the jug in the center of the table and sat down without being asked.

Seventeen looked at him for a moment, then went and lit a coal-oil lamp. Its light was too yellow for comfort and it barely pushed the shadows out of the shack.

"Kind of ya," Seventeen said, sitting across from Potter and looking at the jug. "I figured after Saturday you'd not even be talkin' to me."

Potter looked shame-faced. "Reckon I was a little hot then, but—what the hell. Ain't nothin' but money. I'll get it back maybe." Cull hoped Seventeen didn't see the gleam in his eyes or the grin that tried to come to his face.

Seventeen blinked several times. He hadn't moved to drink from the jug that sat on the table before him. "Now then," he asked suspiciously. "What do ya really want, Cull?"

"Nothin', Seventeen. Nothin'. Just to tip a little moon with ya. Go 'head. Have some." Potter uncorked the jug and, seeing that the other was still hesitant, he lifted it to his mouth and swigged mightily from it. He set the jug down with a thump and wiped his mouth with the back of his hand. "Right fine moon," he said with the slightest burr in his voice.

Seventeen's heavy lidded eyes glittered as they glanced from Potter to the jug. His big hands twitched in his lap and rose to the table and to the handle of the jug. He lifted it, sniffed the mouth then took a small sip. After a moment he took a proper pull at the jug before placing it back on the table. "'Tis good squeeze," he agreed but then said, "Now then, what did ya really come here for?"

"You just ain't gonna believe I got no other reason to be here, huh?"

"You don't never go 'round nowhere's unless you want something, so what is it ya want?"

Potter tried to look offended but failed. He lifted the jug and took another small sip and then said, "Well—I'll tell ya. I figured maybe if I drink outen the same jug as you, and spend some time around ya, maybe some of your luck'll rub off on me. That's the real reason," he hesitated then hurried to say, "and to ask ya if I could carry yer dice for a while." He quickly brought the jug up and sipped.

Seventeen looked sharply at him across the gloom then picked the jug up from the table and swigged. "Get some of my luck, huh?"

Cull sighed and said, "Yep. I figure you got more'n any man I ever seen. More'n enough for you and me both."

Seventeen laughed slow and deep. The sound sent a prickly chill up Potter's back. "I ain't got no special luck, Potter. I just tell the dice what to do, and they does it."

Potter shrugged. "Well then, it won't matter whether I carry 'em or not. Won't hurt you and might help me. So how 'bout it?"

Seventeen grunted and shook his head. "One man's good luck is another's bad sometimes."

"Sometimes."

"Might be bad luck for you."

Potter shrugged. "Don't reckon it could be a lot worse."

"You determined to carry 'em, huh?"

"If you're willing." Cull said. He stopped talking and tilted the moonshine to his mouth, watching Seventeen over the shoulder of the jug. After a moment he said, "Well? Can I carry 'em? I'll leave the jug all fer you if ya let me."

Seventeen raked his hand over his black bristled chin, considering. "All right. I don't think it gonna do you any good, but if ya want, all right. But don't be telling it around that I done this for ya, or everybody'll be wanting me to do it. And you make sure that I get 'em back before Saturday night so's nobody sees ya give 'em back."

"Sure, sure, Seventeen. I'll sure do that. I'll bring 'em back to ya Saturday afternoon, or maybe before." Cull tried to be ingratiating and kept his eyes lowered somewhat, not wanting Seventeen to see the look of satisfaction lurking in them.

Seventeen stood and went to the battered chest of drawers in the corner and opened the lid of the cigar box that sat on top. He took out the dice and looked at them for a moment, then reached into the cigar box again and brought out a Bull Durham tobacco sack. He rubbed it all over the dice mumbling some words that Potter couldn't quite hear before putting the sack carefully back into the cigar box. He clenched the dice in his fist and turned back to Potter. "Ain't nothing real special about these dice, but they been right good to me, so don't you do nothin' to hurt 'em and don't you lose 'em. Ya hear? I got my gran-pappy's spirit from outen that sack to protect 'em so you don't try witchin' 'em or nothin'.

"No sir! I won't do nothin' but carry 'em," Potter said quickly.

Seventeen extended his fist over the table to Potter's outstretched palm and let the dice fall. They turned up seven on the flat of Cull's hand and he closed his fist on them, shoving them into the bib pocket of his overalls.

"Thank ya a lot, Seventeen. You don't know how much I 'preciate this." He stood. "You enjoy that jug. Max says be careful how you show it around 'cause Royce is havin' some trouble with the law."

"I'll be careful."

Cull almost did not make it to the truck before he burst out in raucous laughter. He couldn't believe Seventeen could be stupid enough to let the dice leave his possession. As he started his rattley old pick-up he laughed again and shouted, "I'm gonna beat him! I'm gonna beat that Seventeen!" But a chill of fear ran up his back.

When Seventeen heard the truck pull away, he stepped out the door and the crow, like a piece broken free from the puzzle of the night, dropped down to land on his shoulder. Seventeen nuzzled the bird and watched Potter's headlights fade into the gloom of the evening, and when they were gone he smiled, twitched his shoulder and the crow rose and flew in the direction Potter's truck had gone

###

Iola was an old woman. Nobody really knew how old, since everyone could only remember her as shriveled and gray. No one bent much effort to find out anything more about her, either. She was a maker of hill medicines and was thought to be a witch. Everyone around Traveler's Trace said publicly that they didn't believe in witches or potions, but if someone wanted to dig a new well, or have the blight run off their corn, or had a sick cow, or just a general run of bad luck, they would quietly slip off to see Iola. She would not take money for her services, saying she had no use for it and no way to spend it since she was far up in the hills and came down only when someone brought her down to witch something for them. She charged her fees in kind—cloth or food that would keep, or tobacco.

Cull Potter stood at Iola's door mashing his slouch hat in his hard hands. "Miz Iola, I want you to witch something for me."

Iola's wrinkled face didn't change. The almost smile that lurked around the corners of her mouth stayed the same when she said, "You got sick animals again, boy? If you'd be a little careful about the mold in yer hay ya wouldn't need me."

"No ma'am, it ain't that. It's kinda that I been havin' a bad run of luck with the dice, and I was hopin' you could maybe help me out."

The old woman rocked her chair a few times before she said, "Don't hold much with gamblin'. Dice is just Lucifer's toys ta catch rascals like you."

"Yes ma'am," Potter said. "But I'll pay for ya to witch some dice for me." On the drive up the mountain Cull had thought about what her price was really going to be, and it honed the greed in him. If there was some way he could have the goods, Iola's spell and Seventeen's money—

"What ya got to offer?" The old woman asked.

Cull stepped off the porch to his truck and began bringing out the loot. First was the calico. Iola looked and said nothing. Cull laid the cloth on the floor of the porch and brought out some of the canned fruit. Iola's eyes widened momentarily, but she said nothing. The spools of thread followed.

"That'll do," Iola said, standing and going into the house.

Potter smiled. He had not thought to come away so cheap. He followed the old woman into the house, taking the dice out of his pocket as he walked.

Iola stopped in the middle of the room and held out her hand. Cull extended his hand and showed her the dice. "I want you to make 'em so's no one can throw a natural with 'em ner never make a point—'cept me."

She looked at the ivory colored cubes and nodded. He dropped them into her hand.

Iola cried out and dropped the dice on the floor, pulling her hand to her breast as though it was burned. "Them dice is warded!" she spat. "They warded strong! I ain't gonna do it Cull. Get outa here with 'em!"

Cull bent to pick up the dice, hesitated a moment in fear, but then snatched them up and held them toward Iola. "You mean you can't?" Cull asked, putting contempt into his voice to cover his disappointment at her refusal.

Iola glared at him, her eyes smoldering. "I can, but not for the little you gimme. It'll take black spellin', and black spellin' costs."

"I'll pay," Potter said. He dropped the dice back into his overall pocket and went out to the truck with Iola trailing him. He took out the apricots, the thong leather and the twists of chewing tobacco and placed them on the porch beside the things he had offered before.

Iola looked over them, her eyes lingering on the tobacco. She looked longingly at the twists but after a moment said, "Tain't enough. They're warded with an old spirit— probably blood kin."

Cull returned to the truck and brought out the flour, sugar, and beans and dumped them on the porch.

Iola took a deep breath. She was tempted, and Cull could see it in her eyes.

"Who warded them dice, Cull?"

"Seventeen Williams."

The old woman lifted an eyebrow, then shook her head. "Right strong. Right strong. Don' know Cull. I don't think…" she trailed off.

Potter had saved his hardest convincer for last. He threw back an empty tow sack and hauled the second jug of Royce's moonshine out. Iola's eyes opened wide, and she stared at the jug for a few moments. "Whose still?" She asked at last.

"Royce's. Good squeeze too. I had some outen another jug."

Iola's face stayed impassive as she considered. Cull almost danced with anxiety that it would not be enough.

"My outhouse needs cleanin' and fixin'," she said, somehow knowing that there were no more goods to trade.

"I'll do it."

She looked at him, and then at the goods on the floor, and munched her toothless mouth together as she thought. After a bit she jerked her head in a short nod. "Tote the stuff on in. I'll get started. Might take a while."

Iola's house seemed dimmer inside than it had been before—as though there were some cloud blotting out the sun, though it continued to stream through the window. A calico cat sat on the top shelf of a crowded china cabinet washing its paws and grooming its whiskers and paying no attention to Potter.

Iola brought a medium sized stewer, blackened with years of being used on the wood stove, from a cupboard and placed it on the stove. She poured liquid from a covered bucket into it and began crumbling herbs.

"Set down over yonder," she said, without looking up from her work. "Don't be movin' around none and don't make no noise. I can't be distracted."

Potter looked around the room as he sat in a straight back chair. There were cobwebs everywhere, yet the house seemed free of dust. Bunches of herbs and drying charms hung from a string looped from one side of the open beam ceiling to the other. More things rested in jars set neatly on the windowsills and in shelves.

Steam was rising steadily from the stewer now. Iola continued to drop bits of this and that into the brew, stirring it with a willow switch. Her lips did not seem to move, but a rhythmic mutter danced around her in the quiet steam. Cull watched and eerie prickles ran down his spine like icy raindrops.

Suddenly a warm wind ruffled the ragged curtains, and on the zephyr a shiny black crow glided. It cawed once, startling Cull, and landed on the floor at his feet. The bird cocked its head first to the right, then to the left, as though examining Potter, then it strutted away and fluttered up to a table near Iola's hand. She glanced at it and her eyes gleamed for a moment. She patted her shoulder, and the bird hopped up to it. Iola whispered something and the crow lifted its head and began to caw over and over. It sounded disturbingly like laughter. Iola looked back into the stewer and stirred. The steam was thick around her face.

The cat atop the cabinet rose and stretched lazily, extending its claws and yawning, then it walked across the shelf and jumped onto the table. Iola turned from her stew to the table. "Bring 'em," she ordered Potter.

Cull rose and pulled the dice out of his pocket.

"Put 'em in the midst of the table, then set down right there," she pointed at a low rush-bottom stool beside the table.

Cull did as he was told.

Iola dipped a cup full of the brew from the boiling pot and poured it into a bowl. "Hold out yer arm," she commanded.

Cull did and, with a blurringly fast movement, Iola cut him just above the wrist. Potter snatched his arm back and stared at the blood welling from the slash. "Don't jerk around!" Iola screeched, extending a chipped saucer to catch a few drops of the blood. When a teaspoonful had gathered in the center of the dish, she poured it into the bowl with the brew.

Potter was frightened now. The old woman had moved so fast! He watched the tincture of red spread through the liquid in the bowl.

Iola was ignoring Potter. She stared at the dice for a moment then began to make a salt circle around them saying, "Salt to preserve and purify." She led lines of the salt out in four ways from the circle and made smaller circles at the end of each. Within the center of the circle with the dice, she drew a pentagram, dice centered then she drew smaller pentagrams within each of the smaller circles. She examined her work carefully, grunted her satisfaction and began making a salt circle around the whole table. It enclosed Potter, herself, the cat and the crow. She inspected it closely, adding a bit more here and there saying, "Salt to preserve and protect."

When she was satisfied with her work, she said, "Don't you leave the circle no matter what. You do and there ain't no help for you. Seventeen's granpappy'll carry you off to shadow and you won't never come back."

"Yes, Ma'am."

Iola carefully stepped out of the circle and picked up a little bottle from a shelf, then stepped back into the circle. She inspected the area where she had stepped across making sure it was not disturbed or broken. She then opened the bottle, wet her finger with the contents and made an X on Potter's forehead, on her own, on the cat's, and on the bird's. She carefully dripped one drop from the bottle on each of the dice. She corked the bottle and put it in her apron pocket then began passing her hands over the dice. A soft chant accompanied the movements and seemed to grow louder with each pass. The words were not understandable to Cull, but the rhythm was compelling. He was so taken by the sound of it that he jumped and blinked when the fire in the stove crackled. Steam in great clouds began to rise from the still boiling stewer and a pungent, minty aroma filled the room for a moment, but it began to fade and change almost as soon as it could be identified. The smell changed to that of soured earth, and it made Cull think of the smell of graveyards in the rain.

The room outside the salt circle began to grow dim and foggy and a nip of frost stole into Potter's body, making the hairs on his arms stand up. The graveyard smell intensified and became the smell of putrefaction.

Iola stood rigid and swaying as though her feet were nailed to the floor. Side to side in a slow, tidal rhythm. Potter could not look away from her.

Lightening flashed inside the room. It snaked around the floor and outlined the salt circle. A thread of crackling blue fire rose up and arched over them, and when it touched the other side of the circle, thunder crashed, rattling the windows.

Iola's voice commanded, "Ghost of Octavius Williams, come to me."

Suddenly the lightening aura around Iola stretched and formed two arches like church windows, and another person stood beside her. Seventeen! But not him. Older. Haggard. Almost skeletal, with hands large and bony and deep sunken eyes with tiny flecks of coal fire stirring deep in them.

"Who calls?" Seventeen's grandfather's spirit asked.

"Iola."

"Why?"

"Do you guard the dice of Seventeen?"

"If I am called."

"Guard them no more."

"Why?"

"Cull Potter asks it."

The spirit looked at Potter, and Cull felt his insides turn watery. He wanted to run but found his legs too weak to support him.

A hideous grin slowly spread over the spirit's face, and it changed to a scorning laugh that made Potter's bowels grip like a vice.

"For such a weasel as Cull Potter, I do nothing," the spirit said contemptuously.

"I command it," Iola said.

Potter was so frightened, he stood and turned to run from the house. He lifted his foot to step across the salt circle, forgetting what Iola had said in his panic, but she reached out and grabbed him with the power of a bear and slammed him back onto the stool.

A horrific cackling laughter came from outside the circle and Cull looked toward it. Someone—something stood at the circle's edge like a dark blot. The blot lifted a hand and pointed at Potter. It cackled again and beckoned to him.

"No! I'll not come! No!" Potter cried, but he could feel himself being pulled toward the dark thing. He was held back from it only by Iola's skinny arm.

In a moment the witch's grip let go and Potter saw her hand extend toward the dark power. With her other hand she touched the old spirit saying, "I command that you never guard these dice again."

The spirit's face twisted in disdain, but at last it said, "So be it," and disappeared.

Potter fainted.

###

"Wake up, Cull Potter! Wake up!" Iola said, shaking Potter's shoulder. "It's done. Wake up."

Cull snapped awake to see Iola's toothless face inches from his. A tiny line of tobacco stain ran from the corner of her mouth down her chin.

Potter drew back from her with a little cry, nearly tipping over the chair. Iola cackled and munched her mouth together. Her chin seemed to disappear. "It's done best I can do." There was a merry twinkle in her eyes that disconcerted Potter. "I make no promises though," she continued. "Black spellin' can always go wrong."

Cull stood, still shivering with fear. The pungent aroma of the steaming stewer was still on the air. He reached for the dice on the table.

"NO!" Iola screeched and grabbed his wrist. "Touch 'em 'fore sundown and the spell's broke. Wait." She brought forth a limber willow switch and folded it like tongs, picking up the dice one at a time and placing them in the center of a piece of gray cloth. Then she folded them up in the cloth, picked them up and handed them to Potter. "The spell'll set at sundown, but I don't know how long it'll hold. Yore blood's weak and it most clabbered the brew 'fore I could use it."

"It'll let me win Saturday night, won't it?" Potter demanded, his greed overcoming his fear for a moment.

"I reckon."

"You sure?"

"You doubtin' me?" Iola demanded, and her voice was touched with a little of the power it had held when she'd spoken with the spirit.

"No, no, I ain't doubtin'!" He began backing toward the door.

The calico cat suddenly yowled and Cull's hair prickled. He turned in panic and ran out the door, hardly touching the porch step on the way to his truck.

Iola stepped onto the porch and shouted, "Don't you forget! You must clean and fix my outhouse soon. Soon! Or I'll hex ya for a debtor."

Iola watched the truck raise thick clouds of dust as it rattled, too fast, down the rutted road. The crow, which had been sitting on the peak of the roof, fluttered down to alight on the old woman's shoulder. It ruffled its neck feathers then stroked its blue-black head against Iola's cheek making soft gargling sounds deep in its throat.

Iola looked into the bird's glass bead eyes. "Go on," she said and moved her shoulder. The crow lifted and flew. Iola watched it a time, then smiled and went into the house.

###

Potter jabbed a gray splinter into his knuckle when he knocked on Seventeen's shanty door. The dice were in his other hand, still wrapped in the cloth.

Seventeen didn't say anything when he opened the door. He stood and looked at Cull. The door framed deep darkness inside the shanty and seemed to be made darker by the bright light of the mid-day sun. Cull had to look away from Seventeen quickly, for the memory of the haggard image in the lightning arch was still in his mind, as was the creeping horror of the dark that had called him. It had not left him day or night since he had seen it.

"Did ya enjoy the jug, Seventeen?" Potter said at last, dragging the toe of his scuffed work shoe through the dust.

"Yep. 'Twas good. Didn't even need the hair of the dog. You got my dice?"

"Yeah, yeah. They right here." Cull extended his fist.

"How come they all wrapped up?" Seventeen asked suspiciously.

"Didn't wanta get 'em messed up. I took real good care of 'em like you said. They ain't harmed a bit."

Seventeen stuck out his outsized paw and Cull gave him the little gray package. "Thank ya a lot for lettin' me carry 'em. Maybe I can win back some of my money now," Potter tried to grin but made a botch of it. "I gotta go. See ya at Tilden's tonight." Potter turned and hurried away, leaving Seventeen standing in the door.

Seventeen watched Potter leave, then looked up. The sun glinted off blue-black feathers as the crow swooped down to land on his shoulder. He reached up and stroked the midnight feathers, then turned into the house. He unrolled the dice and shook them in his hand as he walked to the cigar box and opened it. He dropped them in. The dice turned up snake eyes.

Seventeen blinked and picked the dice up again, rattled them in his hand and dropped them on the chest of draws top.

They turned up boxcars. A smile slowly crept across his face as he picked the dice up and dropped them into the cigar box and closed the lid.

###

"You're jumpy as frog in a frying pan, Cull," Max Tilden said. "What's wrong?"

"Nothin'. I'm just ready to play. Where's Seventeen at anyhow?"

All the men turned to the clumping sound of footsteps coming through the store, and then Seventeen Williams opened the door of the back room.

Max Tilden glanced at Cull Potter and saw all the color drain from his face. "What's wrong Cull? You all right?"

Potter managed to lift his hand and point at the shiny black crow perched on Seventeen's shoulder.

Seventeen grinned and said, "Max, I b'lieve I'm gonna need me some new dice."

David Castlewitz

IRON MIST

The hypodermic needle stung, but Harry Sands ignored the momentary pain. He liked being paid to be injected with nanotrackers that told the government where he roamed or where he camped or anything else they cared to study. Barred from the city because he didn't have a job, Harry survived Outside, living in the forests, in unused drainage pipes alongside the river, sometimes joining short-lived families for mutual aid, protection and love. On his own for now, he looked forward to renting a railway carriage berth behind a shopping mall near a highway. He could afford three days and two nights.

Stumbling over his left boot's loose sole, he steered past the water barrels outside the clinic's RV. Guards at the cyclone fence surrounding the makeshift clinic lazed on plastic lounge chairs. Just beyond the fence, vendors hawked canned goods, used clothing, barbering, and laundry services. Steam billowed from a green tent with a sign that advertised showers; arrows pointed to the male and female entrances. Harry found a bald-headed kid who repaired his boot by slapping on a thick glue and tying the sole shut with a twist of wire.

"You can tip if you want." The boy pulled a pay reader out of his pocket. The basic price appeared in dollars, with equivalents in VRing, Dollars, Euros and Pesos. Harry knelt for the blinking retina scanner, then tapped on the VRing price. He pictured his account debiting itself, a glistening gold ring breaking and an arc racing into the boy's own coffers. Without an All-Pod to view his records, Harry kept everything either in his head or on scraps of paper, which he filled with dates and numbers.

Other homeless wanderers sat on the pavement near the entrance to an indoor mall, where private guards used their nightsticks to enforce the loitering rules. When Harry approached, a burly youngster blocked his way. The boy matched him in height and girth, but his lean, clean-shaven faced marked him as employed and that seemed to give him added confidence. Harry submitted to an eye scan. He grinned when the guard saw he had money enough to get inside.

"You should get one of them showers," the guard said.

"You got a stinker scale or something?"

Harry walked into the mall and found a public reader where he got a snapshot of his bank account. The healthy balance, even with future deductions for his three-day stay at the railway carriage, brought a smile to his wide face. He ran a hand through his thick hair. Maybe he'd get a sprucing. But not a hack job like the outdoor barber would do. Nor a three-minute scalding shower without soap as offered in the steam tent. In the mall, he could buy ten minutes of luxury.

And then put on these same old clothes.

That disgusted him.

No, he'd go the whole-hog way, even to the point of clean underwear. All of that would deplete his account. Three hundred VRings! Then he'd be stuck begging for coins until the nano-trackers in his blood died and he'd be eligible for another injection. How many shots could he take in a year?

He walked to the games arena, a cavernous room past the display screens that fronted glass-enclosed stores. He stayed clear of family groups that sniffed, curled their lips or chided him with their eyes; he steered far from the roaming guards, who always walked in pairs, their black clubs swinging at their sides. A few other wanderers shuffled nearby, but he stayed away from them as well. They didn't walk with purpose. He had purpose, a reason for going in this direction.

To the arena.

The pops and bells and whistles of the arcade reminded him of his youth in the city. Before his little family—Ma and Pa and himself—spun out of control. Always adroit when it came to twitching, Harry was a top ranker in every game he played. At school, they called him the Happy Hunter, because he bagged trophies with ease, engaging in virtual deep-sea hunts, safaris in old-movie jungles, and on holographic plains where dangerous horned beasts roamed.

The games called to him. Not the booths where teenagers whooped and cheered and fought with handheld rifles. Not the roped-in stages where visor-wearing youths fought invisible foe. The games that lured him were those played for high stakes—real money—in the backrooms.

For Harry, trophy money was of small concern. The real prize came from meeting newbies eager for his help, men and women who welcomed him as their team captain in a game of Assault or hired him as their guide in Cave-Quest. In the game world, he didn't appear as a shabbily dressed wanderer who needed washing, a shave, a haircut, and fresh clothes. In the game world, he was a handsome, lean and admirable avatar.

He paid the entrance fee with a quick retina scan, mentally deducting the 50 VRing cost from his account balance, and stepped into a private booth, where he donned goggles and a resistance jacket and immersed himself in "Purgital," a quest-type game. This was an enclosed arena, so only the players actually present could compete. Still, scores of avatars crowded the starting pad. A few took off in pairs, jumping into the virtual air to soar over a lush valley where they'd land and find either prizes or an end-of-game-life climax.

This was where Harry excelled. He lived in this game.

###

Harry sat in the food court and watched a dark haired pixie-of-a-girl he'd seen earlier that day. Or was it the day before? Time spun out-of-control when he played games.

The girl's pale face and dark shadowed eyes and painted red lips reminded him of his youth, twelve years distant. Those halcyon school days when kids like this pixie came to school made up as characters from a graphic novel—black and white with a single hint of red. Red eyes or red hair or red lips or a red welt on some part of the body. Guys sported bruises on their neck. Girls showed them on the lower back. Harry once applied one—water based and non-permanent, so it didn't hurt—to his cheek. His parents laughed at him, until he scraped it off with a fingernail.

The pixie approached, lips stretched in a smile that uncovered small white teeth. "You're Dead Hat," she said.

"How do you know my game name?"

"I checked your booth." She unzipped her leather jacket. Fur lining, and fur cuffs and fur collar—so much fur that Harry gagged on thc smell. A jacket more suited to the harsh winter, not this late autumn day.

"You can't just check where I sit in the arena and figure out my game name."

"I paid for the privilege," the pixie said. "To know who you are." She placed folded hands on the edge of the plastic tabletop. "Can you guess my game tag?"

Harry shook his head. She urged him to try. When he didn't respond, she urged again, her round eyes imploring him. Strands of black hair laced her forehead, just above pencil-thin eyebrows.

"Green Archer," she said.

Harry remembered an archer dressed in vibrant green, head to toe, including hair and eyes. He'd watched the avatar take on a Boss Bull with only a spear-tagger for a weapon, which she used to annoy the beast and keep it off balance until she rammed the pointed end into his eye.

"How much did you make?" she asked. "In bounties?"

Harry hadn't kept track. His bank balance remained steady, with the game fees he paid out replaced by prize money he took in. Last check, he still had nearly 300 VRings, and he'd eaten in the mall's food court several times, paid his bill at the railway carriage, purchased a change of clothes, and even bought an hour's worth of showering. Which, he assumed, erased the sour smell that would normally chase off pixies like this one.

"My name's Ida," she said.

"That's an old-fashioned name."

"My family's like that. Old names. I've an Aunt Millie and an Uncle Ralph, and my mom's name is Stella. Old names. I'm Ida Klein. Isn't that something?"

Harry stared at her thin, triangular face, her cheeks as flat as her chest. Multicolored rings and pins decorated her tiny ears.

"So," she said, drawing out the word, interlocking her fingers and stretching. "Where do you live?"

"I spent the last three nights in one of those railroad cars." Harry expected he'd rent a fourth night's berth. The carriages always had room for wanderers in the tiny rooms built inside the hollowed-out cars.

"You're homeless." Ida touched his hand. "I'm not. Come with me."

"You'll want something."

"Who doesn't?"

Harry stared into Ida's dancing blue eyes. Last time he let himself go into a house or apartment, to be coddled and loved for a day and a night, the parting hurt when it came; it always did, parting. Casual hookups never promised more than brief companionship.

"I won't hurt you," she said.

A few days of comfort might be worth the inevitable pain. "Maybe I'll hurt you first," he said with a grin.

###

The guard at the gate to Ida's housing complex smiled at Ida. She cowed him with a glare, and he opened the gate. The tall, wrought-iron, pointed edifice retracted into the thick red-brick wall that meandered around the community like a lanky snake.

Ida pressed the auto-drive button. The car lurched. Harry pictured invisible fingers taking hold of the vehicle, a four-wheeled sporty model with rounded fenders and curved roof and a front grill shaped like a metallic kiss. Under robotic control, the car slowly wound up a hillside, away from the picturesque cottages dotting the lower level, to the towers higher up. At a round opening, they entered the bowels of an artificial mountain.

Overhead lighting flickered, so they weren't in complete darkness inside the tunnel.

The car glided into its parking slot.

"One thing."

Harry turned to Ida as he exited.

"Your name."

He told her. The car's trunk popped open and Harry grabbed his backpack, which he'd retrieved from the railway carriage.

"This is just for a few days," he told her. "Don't get used to me." A brash front worked best with these Ida-types, who enjoyed bringing home strangers they expected to control.

"Ditto." Ida led the way to an elevator. They rode up several floors to her apartment.

Harry had never been in this kind of building, where each domicile occupied one quarter of an entire floor. When he asked Ida about this, she merely shrugged and said she'd never given it much thought.

"Actually," she said as the elevator door opened, "I've a particular job for you, which is the reason I brought you here."

Harry stumbled forward, urged on by the push of her hand. He nearly fell onto the plush white rug on the floor but caught his balance by grabbing hold of the back of a long sofa, also white. Other chairs—the chrome and leather variety, white like the rug—adorned the large room. A wall-sized window looked out at the countryside. A mirror served as another wall. An arch bordered with sculpted leaves and small flowers led to a hallway.

Ida strode to the mirrored wall and waved at it. The reflective glass went opaque. She reached into a recess in the wall. She extracted a gaming visor and tossed it to Harry.

Harry examined the ordinary game-playing device. Old-fashioned compared to goggles and eye-inserts.

Next, Ida handed him a reaction vest, the type that registered impacts on the body. In some games, these hurt as much as real-world blows. In some games, players turned down the intensity. In some, they turned it up and delighted in the pain of dying at the hands of a Boss Bull or some other monster.

"What do you want me to do?" Harry said.

Ida glided to a white ottoman. She sat crosslegged, her boots marring the material with whatever dirt she'd accumulated on the heels. "My father plays *Iron Mist*. He's not very good, but he likes to play."

"I don't know the game," Harry said, suspecting it was one of the varieties the public arenas didn't host. Too dangerous? Too expensive? Rich folk enjoyed private playgrounds.

"I watched you play. You'll do okay. I want you to be my father's guide. A sidekick. You know, a Sancho Panza to slay the meanies." Ida laughed, head back. Suddenly, she ripped off her hair, exposing a bald, powder-white scalp. Harry swallowed, amazed by the transformation. Without hair, she was even more beautiful, more exotic. He wanted to be near her, so close that they touched.

Scent! He sniffed, inhaled deeply through his nose, enjoying the sensation. She'd let loose a fragrance that made her the most alluring and compelling being he'd ever seen. The smell brought on images of soft linen and pillow-like clouds on a round bed riddled with tiny blue and yellow flowers.

"What're you doing?" he moaned.

"You're going to help my father," Ida said. "Help kill him."

"Of course. Kill him."

"When he's gone, this becomes mine. Isn't that nice? Wouldn't you like that?"

Ida pulled off her boots, ripped off her socks. She removed long, tight-fitting black pants and then her stiff white blouse. She traipsed across the room in a lacey undershirt that fell to mid-thigh.

Harry blinked.

The scent disappeared. Ida stood in the kitchen, on the other side of the cutout in the wall, at the counter, fully clothed and with her black pixie-cut wig back in place.

"That's just a taste of what you'll get once you do what I want," she said.

A drug, Harry realized. She'd drugged him, and he'd enjoyed it, especially the promise of more to come. He had only the aftertaste of her on his tongue and a very vague memory of pleasure while rocking beside her on the floor, he fully clothed and she naked except for that undershirt, but it was enough, enough of a promise.

"What exactly do you want me to do?" he asked. He fingered the reaction vest and looked at the game-play visor.

"I told you. Kill him," Ida said. "My father. Are you really that dense?" She put two bottles of sparkling water on the counter. "Come here and relax. He doesn't play until nighttime, so you've got a couple of hours to get ready."

"No one dies in these games," Harry said.

"You've never played *Iron Mist*."

###

Harry stared into the Mist world, puzzled after an hour of game play. Nothing hazardous here. No wild men to defeat on the way to Amber Hall, a virtual space where players congregated and traded game-play pieces used to solve the puzzles they encountered. No Boss Bulls to fight. No renegades, like the gangs Harry encountered in other games.

Nothing dangerous. Even with the reaction vest tuned to maximum, a sword hit didn't hurt very much. It burned. It pushed him back a step or two, but it didn't incapacitate him; it certainly didn't seem capable of killing. When he fought off two bandits he'd coaxed into a duel, he let down his guard and took a slash across the chest just to gauge the vest's feedback. Mild, he thought, when compared to other games he'd played.

Where was the danger?

According to the character profile he read by tipping his head back and waving his hand at a floating icon along the top of his viewport, his character was a wandering rogue-lord—a one-time aristocrat who'd lost his land but retained a title—named Satan's Mark. Rogue-lord, he assumed, signified something special in the *Iron Mist* world. What, he didn't care. Ida had told him to find a minstrel named Pot-o-pot, whose game pose falsely identified him as a benign being while, in reality, he practiced dark arts and used them to cast spells and steal game-coin.

To Harry, *Iron Mist* offered an ordinary game-space with ordinary tropes and ordinary people—rich people—wishing for an extraordinary life. All bought with real-world money. He found this everywhere. Every dragon and wizard-inspired fantasyland he'd ever visited, even the shooter games, followed these common conventions. *Iron Mist* didn't impress him.

But after a long wait, a game-controlled troll inspected him—to measure the settings of his reactive vest, he assumed—and he gained entry to Amber Hall's inner chamber.

Gaming tables filled the middle of the room and players crowded the dice-throw pits, sat playing cards at six-sided tables, lobbed knives at burning rings, and hurled axes to cut off a screaming scullery maid's pigtails, which were the only things holding her up above a dragon's open mouth.

In addition to running the games, the game-bots hawked tickets to the trophy fields where players vied for prizes. Some ventured off as solo hunters, intent on bagging a prize and keeping all the winnings for themselves, but a few formed teams and signed virtual contracts to split the trophy money with the survivors of the hunt.

Harry found that he liked this part of the game, this inner room of Amber Hall. He marveled at the assortment of characters and their costumes. Life vibrated wild and free, making him giddy with excitement.

The smell.

Had to be.

The idea came to him from nowhere, but soon it filled his thoughts and he couldn't shake it. He whipped off the visor. He looked around the room, from the window wall to the flower-studded arch to the white sofa on the white rug, thinking he'd see Ida waving the fumes of some chemical concoction his way, its scent inducing his euphoria.

But he didn't see her watching him. She sat on the ottoman, a visor covering her face. He assumed she inhabited Amber Hall as a player. He donned his visor. Which of the many avatars represented this strange woman? That scantily clad nymph with two jagged daggers at her narrow hips? The beefy wrestler? Minstrel's waif? Bar maid who wasn't really the game-bot she pretended to be?

The odor came again. He sniffed, as though he might trap it in his nostrils and keep it from invading his mind and warping his perceptions.

He'd heard of these enhanced games, which used drugs to augment the experience. It wasn't enough to pretend to be in the game world, playing with game money and loving game characters and fighting game monsters. The enhancements made it so very real that players lost themselves to fantasy.

Harry took hold of himself. He had enough experience in these worlds that he couldn't easily be dragged under.

"That minstrel drinking up there," someone said, and Harry looked down at the dragonfly standing beside him. Lavender wings shimmered along a narrow translucent back. With a human face and an insect's body, the avatar didn't look as strange and unusual as he thought it should. That wasn't the scent-enhancer twisting his mind. Couldn't be. This creature was beautiful.

"Ida?"

"Think of me as Sent-by-Ida." The voice was Ida's filtered through a strainer.

Harry watched the minstrel sitting at a table on a raised platform in a corner of the room, partaking of food and drink, along with a laughing and loud-talking cadre of other characters, all of them looking like murderous pirates or bandits or warlords or oft-tested mercenaries.

"The game reactions aren't as strong as you think," Harry said to the dragonfly. "Nobody's going to be killed, even if they ratchet the response all the way up. What did you do, screw with his vest? So it sends a bigger jolt than it's suppose to?" He pictured some tinkerer increasing the strength of the solenoids that shot blunted darts into the body in response to a gunshot wound.

A reaction vest might hurt, but it never injured, even with the best of tampering. Game software kept tabs on the vest and could shut it down if it detected a malfunction.

"No mods to the vest. It's the enhancers. I can't explain everything."

The floor shook, the vibration tickling Harry's feet.

He took off his game visor and looked to the elevator door at the end of the room. He went to the door and felt it. He put an ear to the cold metal.

"What're you doing?" Ida demanded, her visor off and dangling at her side.

"Someone's coming." The vibrations ran into his fingers, tickling him.

"I thought you wanted to help me," Ida whined.

Harry turned to her and advanced with three long strides that brought him within reach of her. He grabbed her by the wrist. She yelped and twisted sideways.

He let her go. That's when he noticed that she'd changed her clothes. Changed into a long white shirt with a lacey collar that ran across her clavicle. She turned away. The collar dipped low—a plunging V—at her back. He stared at her knobby spine, at the shape of her small buttocks beneath the clinging fabric. She skittered across the white rug and dove behind the kitchen counter.

"Do you want to help me or not?" She plopped two water bottles on the countertop. *Like before,* Harry thought, and wondered if they were spiked with some drug.

"You can't kill anybody in a game," he said. "I don't care what you do to the vest."

"He's got a bad heart. I've seen him get excited and pass out playing these games. All caught up in them."

Harry jerked straight up, jolted by a sudden pain in the ribs. Something burned across his back. He grabbed at the sensation, dug his fingers deep into his shoulder where the ache remained after the initial burn.

The vest. He tore at the Velcro straps.

"You idiot," Ida screamed. "You forgot to pause, didn't you?"

He hadn't even thought about it. Most game-hosted rooms offered safe refuge. Nobody attacked. Nobody picked fights.

As though reading his mind, Ida said, "It's Amber Hall. *Iron Mist*. You've never played this game."

Harry squirmed out of the vest. Ida rushed to the mirrored wall where he'd left the visor. She slipped it on, waved her hands in the air and then, head dipped, appeared to be reading the damages from the character profile.

"I spent a lot getting Devil's Mark ready for this, and you let him get pounded and robbed and knocked down four notches."

Harry shrugged. Characters got wiped out all the time. Just part of game-play. It kept gamers coming back, trying to improve their profiles,

Ida set the visor on a plastic hook at knee level in the reflective wall. "You're in stasis now. Paused. You'll need to recoup what you lost before you go up against anyone as formidable as the minstrel."

A grinding sound at his back grabbed his attention. "Is someone using your elevator?"

"It's not just mine. Don't worry about it. No one's coming in here without the key."

As though on cue, the door slid open.

Ida gasped. She sank to the floor. Six intruders fanned out, five of them in satiny blue jump suits that sparkled with static electricity. A sixth stood in high pointed boots polished to a black sheen, his waist-length jacket tight across a trim body, his white shirt contrasting sharply with his long black hair.

Ida's father, Harry assumed. He didn't look like a man with a heart condition. Pale complexion, yes, but the rest of him spoke of vitality and strength, especially the dark piercing eyes.

"Are you at this again?" the tall man asked. He glanced left and then right, his blue-suited companions having taken positions that blocked access to the hall and the mirrored wall housing Ida's elaborate game system. A nod of the head sent two of the henchmen into action.

Neither were as tall as their leader. They reminded Harry of the burly doorkeepers outside real-world bars.

The two henchmen grabbed Ida, each taking a skinny arm, and lifted her just enough so her toes didn't touch the rug, and brought her to the sofa, where they plopped her down. Hard.

Ida's thin shirt bounced about her legs, rode up enough that she pulled it down by the hem, and blushed in obvious embarrassment.

Her father pointed at the reactive-vest Harry had discarded. One of the burly henchmen scooped it up and tossed it to Ida.

"Put it on," her father ordered. Light in the ceiling glinted off the K.N. gold letters pinned to his white shirt collar. The jump-suited henchmen, Harry noticed, wore armbands with the same letters. What kind of person brings a private army to his daughter's apartment?

Ida folded her arms across her chest. She panted like an animal in a trap. A slender form approached. A woman, Harry surmised from the long legs and prominent breasts, dark hair tied in a bun at the back of the head.

"Make it easy on yourself," the woman said to Ida.

"He never makes it easy on me." Tears fell from her eyes.

"That's because you do this over and over again."

Do what? Harry wondered, and then began to wonder why they ignored him.

The blue-suited woman dressed Ida in the vest. She pulled it tight, and then extracted leather cuffs from between the sofa's cushions. Pinned down by the wrists, Ida couldn't escape whatever her father had planned. The vest looked too tight around her lean frame. She continued to pant.

"She can't breathe," Harry said.

The woman said, "She can breathe." And, to Ida: "You can breathe?"

Ida nodded, eyes closed, a smile on her dark lips. One of the men brought her a visor. Others set out small canisters on the kitchen counter; another canister on the glass-and-chrome coffee table in the living room; and one on a shelf next to the game console. Someone handed Harry a vest and a visor.

He shook his head.

"Put it on," Ida said.

He sensed a new odor in the room. Red and yellow pinpoints of light glowed at the base of each canister. The idea of resistance vanished. He didn't want to disappoint Ida.

With the vest secure around his body, tight where it hugged his chest, he felt warm and comfortable. Ida's father and his minions stood far from the middle of the room. A wispy cloud from the canisters lingered near the ceiling lights.

"Come on," Ida wailed, straining against the leather restraints. More tears. Face red. A visor fell across Harry's eyes, plunging him into darkness. He wondered if he should run but discarded the notion. Run from this? From the wonderful "this?" From Ida and what she wanted?

The dark lessened and he found himself in a large pit, with men and women cheering all around and above him; they chanted, their words meaningless. Just noise.

Ida, tied to a stake, struggled against her bonds. Naked, her trim body streaked with blood and bodily waste, she screamed and cried, her hair in this scenario long and deep black like it had been painted with India ink.

Harry looked at his feet. Hooves, really. He had no hands. His head felt heavy. He shook it. He bellowed. Firelight threw shadows against the wooden walls surrounding the pit. Torches sent flickers of red and yellow flame to a high ceiling, where an oil lamp chandelier hung suspended on braided ropes.

A sword-wielding man jumped into the pit and took a wide stance in front of Ida's writhing body. Harry recognized the trope. He played the part of Boss Bull, a monster with a distorted human face, with sunken red eyes and two curved horns growing from his temples. The rest of him—the body and the rump and the forelegs—was a bull.

He charged the sword-wielding intruder and gored him. Easily. Silly man, he thought, and grew angry when more men took up the challenge of defending the helpless girl.

He charged when an axe carrier with a long blonde beard jumped into the pit. He defeated challenger after challenger, and after each one, he pranced around the naked girl tied to the stake and scraped the side of her face with his coarse tongue. She screamed. She shook and yelled and cried, her body exploding with sweat and urine and excrement.

The scene went dark. Harry knelt on the rug, out-of-breath from his virtual exertions. Someone said, "He didn't take a single hit."

Ida chimed in, "Told you he was good." She sat with her wrists no longer clamped in the leather restraints, the reactive vest beside her, along with the visor. The cloud above the middle of the room had dissipated to a few misty tendrils. The tiny red and yellow lights at the base of the canisters no longer shined.

Standing, Ida thrust her slender hands in her father's direction. He took hold of them. She stood on tiptoe and kissed his cheeks. One by one, the lone woman last, the blue-suited aides returned to the elevator. Ida and her father stood whispering to one another, she nodding and he glancing at Harry every now and then. A moment passed. A smile crossed the tall man's rugged face, and then he went to the elevator.

Curious, Harry crossed the room to the kitchen counter and picked up one of the canisters. "Kleiner Nacht" was imprinted on the underside of the base. A series of numbers, one of which looked like a date, stood out beneath the name.

"What is this?" he asked.

Ida pulled her legs up under her body and crooked a finger. "My dad's company. Kleiner Nacht? As in Little Night. You've never heard of it?"

"What exactly happened here?" Harry asked.

"Don't get testy. Take a couple of those water bottles. Better stuff than you find out there." She pointed at the countryside view beyond the window wall. "You can stay the night. I don't mind."

Harry studied the canister, as though he'd derive more meaning if he kept staring at it, turning it in his hand. It wasn't heavy. It wasn't awkward to hold.

Ida bounced off the sofa, strode to the kitchen counter, and took the canister from him. "It's a mood enhancer. Like the ones we used earlier. The smell sets off neurons in the brain. You know."

"It's a drug."

"Yeah. Like it? I do."

"What happened here?"

Ida smiled. "You're pretty good as an ogre-bull. Those weren't bots you killed. Players wagering good money. Good players, too."

"And you?" Harry tried to take hold of her, but she danced away. She stood on the other side of the long white sofa. "The cuffs," he said, pointing at the cushions, where nothing remained of the leather bonds used on her. "That guy, the older one, is he really your father?"

She shook her head. "I just call him that. The woman, though, she's my mom. She makes sure the guys don't get rough or anything."

Harry started to ask another question, but the words dissolved before he could voice them.

"You want to spend the night?" Ida asked.

"With you?"

She laughed and shook her head. "No. I'm done for the day. Besides, I don't need company. Look, there's a guest room through there." She pointed at the hallway. "A bed and a bath. You can get going in the morning. I don't mind."

Harry shrugged. The sun sat low in the sky, signifying the end of the autumn afternoon, the coming of another night, the dark hours growing in length with the change in season.

"You look angry," Ida said. "Why? You like games. I like games. Hell, didn't I find you in a game arcade? This sort of game is just a bit more real than anything you'll find in a public arena. You liked it, too. You got off on it. Just like me."

Harry shook his head. "What was that stuff about Amber Hall and killing your father?"

"Part of the set-up. Get you primed to do battle." Ida cocked her small head sideways.

Harry pictured the naked girl in the pit. It was unusual to have an avatar that looked exactly like yourself. Most players wanted to get beyond Self. Into a better body. Be more feminine or more masculine.

"If you're angry," Ida said, "I'm sorry." She bounced on the sofa, legs tucked under her body. "Like I said, you're invited to stay the night. Not with me, of course, but—"

"I know. You already made that apparent. Not with you. Just a room. For me. With a luxurious bath. All for me and my comfort. Thanks."

Ida slipped from the sofa and strode quickly to the arch leading into the hallway. "It's up to you," she cooed. "I've got a monitor on this room, so don't take anything you shouldn't."

"There's nothing I want."

She stared at him. He refused to lock eyes with her. "We all play games, so I don't think I did anything wrong."

She disappeared into the hallway, her slender form slipping through a crinkly flashing curtain. Why did she need him for her game? She didn't want him physically close. She could've gotten a player from anywhere in the network. But maybe that was part of the allure. A real person in the room with her. The men that accompanied her mother—and he found that odd in its own right—added a bit of danger to the experience.

He shook his head. He told himself he shouldn't feel disgusted with himself. He played games. Like she said. His life, since he left the city and wandered the Outside, was dedicated to finding one game after another, acquiring money to pour into fantasy worlds. No one in any of the game worlds chided him for how he looked or how he smelled.

Harry picked up his backpack from where he'd tossed it. The elevator took him to the main floor, one level above the garage. A guard at the desk in the marble-floored lobby checked him with a retina scan.

"Miss Klein ordered a shuttle to take you to the gate."

"I can walk."

"Do yourself a favor and take the shuttle. It's a long way down the hill, and then another long walk to the gate, and you'll get stopped a dozen times by the on-site patrol." The guard laughed, a squeak in his voice giving him away as young.

Harry boarded the shuttle. Yeah, he thought, give me a break.

Outside the gate, he wandered on the side of the road, towards distant lights. Not sure if he now headed back to the mall or somewhere else, his sense of direction skewed by unfamiliar surroundings.

It didn't matter where he went. He'd sleep somewhere on the side of the road if he had to.

He told himself to be glad he'd refused Ida's offer of a berth for the night. She probably didn't get turned down very often. Maybe never. The players she lured home probably curled around her feet like grateful puppies.

Not him.

He looked at the distant lights. So many. Had to be the city. Far away. Would he ever get back there? If he took a job anywhere Outside, he'd earn points as a useful citizen, credit that could bring him back into the city.

He'd work, he thought. At an Outside job. A guard at the mall? A table-server or a roadside cleaner upper?

He'd work, and then feckless people like Ida Klein wouldn't use him so easily for their own pleasure, and he'd be as vital and important in the real world as he knew himself to be in any game's fantasy.

Sharon Frame Gay

SALEM

I curse them. I scream through the low ceiling, clenching my fists, the fox paw in my hand, claws digging into flesh. May they be barren, their crops fail, the ravages of the earth swallow them up and spit them out into the sea, fish lapping their bones, until they are gone. I pray that when they open their bibles, snakes slither from the spines, tongues darting, shedding their skin on the pages, the words scaly. I see the tiny church in town engulfed in flames, their flesh bubbling up, then turning to rivers of blood. Blood. The life source. The death of me.

###

When it began, I was only ten. I will never forget the first time, and in truth, who would? Spring had come late to Salem. Tiny buds swelled from the chestnut trees, tight and cold, yearning for the sun. The yellow nubs of forsythia splayed in the warming days, giving festive light to an otherwise drab landscape. Finally, the frost cleared from the soil, allowing us to scrape and hoe the dirt, plant the seeds, and tend our kitchen gardens.

Our house was on the main path into town. My father, who had died three months before I was born, had built a tall wooden fence to keep deer out, but with plenty of space between the sharpened slats, so I could see the entire population bustling up and down the trail. I heard children playing, the sounds of hammers in the distance, and further still, a musket shot, bringing down a turkey or deer for supper.

One morning, I was playing with a barn kitten, twirling a twig in circles, watching her leap and paw in earnest, her clever little eyes fixed on the stick in concentration. The peace was abruptly pierced by the thunder of hooves. Turning my head, I saw one of the elders loping down the path from the forest into town. His long coat flapped behind him, his sorrel horse frothing from the mouth, sides heaving, hooves ringing out on the hardened ground. Suddenly, Goodwife Esther's little girl Patience appeared out of nowhere, running straight into the horse's path. "Stop!" I screamed. Dropping the twig, I pushed through the gate, gathering my skirts and running headlong towards them. But, when I reached the road, there was nothing there. I looked about in bewilderment, heart dragging in my chest. There was only calm and the soft murmur of a thawing breeze.

"Sarah!" my mother cried, running from the house, wooden spoon in her hand as though she would fend off whatever danger lurked behind my scream. "What is the matter?" When she reached my side, I was kneeling in the dirt, weak from fear, my head swiveling back and forth up the trail. "Mother," I panted, "Patience was trampled by a horse!"

Mother dropped her spoon, stepping off along the pathway into town, worry on her face.

"No, stop!" I shouted. " It happened right here!" I pointed to the quiet trail where I was kneeling, tears of fright trickling down my cheeks. "But then it was gone!" I wailed, reaching out for comfort.

She threw her arms around me, stroking my head. "Sarah, you must have had a bad dream in the garden. Did you fall into a sleep? Come along inside, out of the sun for a while, and help me with the pudding." We walked arm and arm across the threshold, the darkness inside the house beckoning me with soothing normalcy. I turned to look towards the trail, and saw only the barn kitten, crouching in the dust, back arched, hissing at nothing.

Two weeks later, I was carding wool with my friend Hope in her house, closer to the village square, when there was shouting outside the door. We peered through the window at a gathering of friends and neighbors, swirling about like schools of fish, gesturing and calling for help. "Patience has been trampled by Brother James' horse," wailed Goodwife Janet, her eyes round and wide in horror. "She darted out, right in front of him. The horse did not stop in time. Let us all pray for her recovery."

The prayers would be in vain. I already knew that by tomorrow, the men would be crafting a tiny wooden coffin. We would stand in the graveyard, among rivulets of drenching rain and tears, the moaning of thunder far off in the distance, the keening of the north wind whipping our skirts and toppling our hats as her small body was lowered into the newly thawed ground. My mother stared at me across the gravesite, her eyes frightened, wary. I lowered my head in fear, twisting my hands beneath my apron, bile rising in my throat.

Later that night, we sat before the fire that was usually so warm and welcoming but now seemed to waver as the wind whistled down the chimney. My mother quietly said, "Never tell anyone, Sarah. Do not speak of these things."

I nodded, poking at the logs with a long stick, watching the embers dance among the flames. I prayed that I would never see such a thing again, yet it was already too late, because they came unbidden, time after time. A soft and sinister knowing. A vision of what may happen. I saw nor'easters make their way across the harbor, whipping waves into salted tears. Babies born still in death, mothers keening in their barren beds. Old men clutching their chests, falling upon the cobblestones. I saw weddings and funerals, puppies born in baskets, friends bringing bread to our door. Happiness and sorrow followed me like beggars, tugging at my skirts, whispering their stories, letting me see what would happen next, even with my eyes closed. They came; they played their tableau on my stage, then disappeared, leaving me as shaken and confused as that first time.

Two years went by, so many stories unfolding before me, so much distraction and haunting within me. I withdrew from the rest of the village, afraid I might spew out a future event. Heeding my mother's strong advice, I never told anybody what I saw. I spent more time by the edge of the woods, picking through leaves and berries, wandering alone among the wild-flowers, weaving them into crowns for my hair, and finding solace in the sunshine. Sometimes, I felt the pull of the coming moon rise above the forest floor and stepped quietly from the house, wrapped in a tattered shawl, drawn to the silvery fields.

Feeling separate and apart from the village, my silence was mistaken for aloofness, or something else. Withdrawing further from childhood, and happiness, I was surely as haunted as the castles in Europe I had heard about, feeling my chambers and stairways groaning with the weight of so many ghosts. Friends began to drift away, a wedge of silence between us. I often saw their futures and wanted to tell them what they would be doing in a year or two, surprise them with the information that the boy smiling across the pew would become their husband, and they would have children on their knees soon enough, but I could not. I twisted my lips tight to keep any word from escaping and kept my head down, wandering the streets through town.

I had seen him many times as a child. His name was Samoset, an Algonquin chief. An older man, he walked with grace, his long legs clad in deer hide, a single raven's feather hanging near his left ear, quivering with each step, as though it were still alive. He was head of his own clan, yet here in Salem, he was considered a mere vendor, a necessary evil, the townspeople trading with trappers such as him. Sometimes Samoset brought beautiful beaver pelts and deer hides flung over his shoulder, the fur still matted in blood, dumping them unceremoniously in the town square. The men appeared like smoke from their houses to barter and quibble over the pelts while Samoset stood in stoic silence. He could speak English, short bursts of words like lightning strikes, sullen and arrogant, as he negotiated with the men. Samoset never stayed very long. Taking his trade, he spun on his heels and vanished into the woods as swiftly as he arrived. Samoset had been here in Salem as long as I had, a presence on the periphery of childhood. I was one of the few children brave enough to look into his fathomless eyes and smile. He smiled back. Once, years ago, he uttered a gruff, "Hello, small one," as he passed me on the trail into town.

One day, Samoset appeared along the dusty path by our garden gate. I had felt particularly brave that morning, so I stepped from behind the fence, murmuring hello. He stopped so abruptly that I drew back in not a little fear. His black eyes bored into my skull, it seemed, and then he softened, as though he found something that pleased him.

"You know things," Samoset said in his lightning staccato. "Do not be afraid. They choose you."

My eyes widened, and I stepped back against the gate, feeling the wood pressing against me. He reached deep within a soft hide pouch, drawing out a tiny red fox paw, the fur glinting in the sun, tiny shards of light that made my eyes ache as a vision exploded through my senses.

"Take it," he growled. Samoset pressed it into my trembling hand, then turned on his heel and quietly strode away.

Shaken, I put the paw in my pocket, my hand nearly burning from the heat it gave off, the sting of the thing warm along my hip, my skirt scorching my leg as I walked. What I saw now pulled at my heart, each beat thudding in a slow funeral dirge, sweat trickling beneath my arms and down into the fabric of my dress. Frightened, I tucked away the vision along with the fox paw.

It was an early afternoon in mid October. All of us toiled in the fields, taking in the last of the grains, the tubers and hay. The sky was a brilliant blue, soft and lazy, the last of the dragonflies skimming the breeze. The women in my row had all stopped for a moment's rest, when suddenly a raven hurtled out of the sky, downwards, wings tucked against its body like a dark arrow, landing so hard in the dirt that it set off a small dust cloud, its neck broken, shiny feathers trembling in the light breeze. We were all startled, staring at this sudden invasion. I reached out a fingertip, then drew back, panicked, looking about me.

"Hurry!" I shouted. "Everybody seek shelter! A storm is coming with a terrible wind!" The women looked at me, dumbfounded, as I gathered my skirts and set out towards home, leaving behind a small basket of turnips.

"Sarah! Sarah!" my mother shouted, picking up the basket and lumbering after me, amid the whispers and head shaking of the others. I did not stop until I reached our cottage, latched the shutters on the windows, gathered the animals into shelter, and put extra wood on the fire.

Within an hour, clouds began to scuttle across the horizon, like giant dark fists, raining blow after blow of wind and hail on everything in its path. The earth began to melt away in streams of mud and water, banks overflowing and spilling into the fields. The wind shook our tiny cottage, shrieking and pulling, bursting through the door and swirling around our room like a small cyclone. Then, after the wind, came the snow. So early in the year, it pummeled with a vengeance, icy flakes tumbling together and stacking up to the windows, throughout the night, until by dawn there was nothing but a white blanket where everything used to be, and nothing left of the crops but fodder for the cows and pigs.

It took days for all of us in the village to dig out, days for the snow to melt enough that the trails were navigable again. One by one, the townspeople crept outside and back into life, repairing the things the storm had ripped apart, blaming the Devil for what had happened. More than one woman remembered that I had spoken of the coming storm, their eyes following me uneasily.

After that, I spent more time near the edge of the forest, gathering herbs and tending to a small garden I had made in a far-flung pasture. Sometimes Samoset appeared, his voice gruff but kind. He showed me different barks and herbs, explaining how they could heal, or harm. Slippery elm for a stomach ache, or steeped mint in a soothing tea, berries for headache, foxglove to poison the endless rats that crept around the barn at night. One day he brought his daughter Alawa with him. She was tentative at first, hanging back in the shrubs, dark eyes bright as a sparrow, approaching me with a mixture of shyness, fear, and respect. Alawa squatted beside me, gently culling through the weeds in my tiny garden, her shiny head bent to the sun. I looked forward to seeing them, although they seldom visited, but when Samoset was near, my fox paw vibrated in my apron pocket, as though waking from a deep sleep.

That winter, Salem was bedeviled by problems. What was left of the crops had been destroyed by the freakish storm. A coughing grippe and malaise hit the townsfolk, spreading like fog, several succumbing to pneumonia. I brought baskets of berries and potions door to door, herbs that I had pounded into pumice, then added to lanolin to be rubbed on chests, or dried bark strained and steeped into calming teas. Many thanked me, taking my potions, while others did not open their door, though I could hear them breathing on the other side.

Animals were found mutilated in the fields, their heads torn cleanly off, bloody entrails dotting the landscape. I had seen a panther once or twice, weaving along the forest line, but when I told the elders, they dismissed me, saying the great cats didn't come this close to town, though I knew differently. Goodwife Charity's child was born with a withered arm, an angry red birthmark on her back. The mark of the Devil, some said, then quickly bowed their heads in prayer. There were signs everywhere, but for the first time in years, I didn't see what was coming.

When it came, it came so swiftly that it seemed that the earth stopped moving. A great silence, then a groundswell of anger and ignorance so vast, so dangerous, that the birds in the trees left all at once, in a great flapping cloud, abandoning their roosts.

There was a pounding at our door. When I opened it, several of the church elders stood before me, one with a musket slung over his shoulder, their faces sober and folded in like rain clouds. "Sarah, there are strange happenings in this town lately. Many people claim that you have been present during several of them. We wish to bring you to the church, ask a few questions."

I nodded meekly, reaching for my shawl, but my mother wasn't so easily fooled. "Stand back, Sarah," she said grimly, turning to the elders. "My daughter is not a witch. She is a young girl. Do not include her in all the rumors and whispers of the town. Please, leave her be."

I stared at the men. A witch? What were they talking about? Elder James elbowed past my mother, grabbing my arm. He twisted me around, pushing me out the door. I was quickly surrounded by the rest of the men, their fear and anger palpable as I stood inside their circle. Without another word, we began to march forward down the path and into town, towards the church, Mother trailing behind us, her pleads echoing through the morning air, like the yipping of a small dog.

The church was filled to the rafters with townspeople. In front, near the pulpit, was a trestle table, with several men seated before it. The room smelled of fear, superstition, and something rank, evil and foreboding. I was thrust into a chair, and the trial commenced without preamble. Looking out at the congregation, I had a vision of several of the women swinging from an oak tree near the center of town, kicking their legs out in their last throes of life, their necks cracking like kindling. But today they were squirming in their seats, looking up at me with something akin to excitement on their faces, murmuring among themselves in low voices that sounded like growls.

"Settle in," commanded Brother James. The room grew quiet and still as death as he turned his face to me and said, "Sarah. Come forward."

I rose and stood before the table, shaking and trembling, only 14 years old.

"Is it true, Sarah, that you somehow knew that Patience would run into the path of the horse? And is it true, Sarah, that you bring herbs and potions to the townspeople, and that some of them have gotten worse after using them? Did Goodwife Constance not die right after drinking your mint tea? Did you foretell of the coming storm? People have seen you dancing in the moonlight, out near the forest edge, a cat your companion. Sometimes only the cat comes home at dawn. Where do you go, Sarah? What do you do? "

The questions came at me so fast; I could only shake my head in bewilderment.

My mother was begging for deliverance, her cries so loud that finally Brother James turned to a few men and said, "take the Widow Smythe out of the church! She's disrupting this courtroom".

"Courtroom?" my mother hissed. "This is not a fair trial! This is nothing but lies and rumors and fear!" But her cries were useless. Several men took her by each arm, dragging her from the church. I was suddenly all alone.

They began to nip at me with their words, like fish in a tide pool, tiny bites at first, but soon taking their toll. I looked around frantically for help, for comfort. Whatever I said was quickly overturned, their fingers pointing, their voices raising until at long last I broke in a gush of sadness and fear, crying out for them to stop. "I am not a witch," I sobbed pitifully. "I do see things from time to time, but I am not evil."

"See things?" asked Brother James, his nose sharp as a rat, twitching, pinning me to the floor with his beady gaze. "What things, Sarah?"

In earnest, I tried my best to explain the visions I have, how I see things before they happen, how I was an innocent by-stander to the scenes that played across my mind. With each word I said, I heard the far-off hammering of the gallows, nails into fresh green pine, echoing through the town like rolling thunder. It filled me with terror, and something else, too. A deep, desperate anger. I was repulsed by them and felt suddenly rebellious, for I was just a frightened child.

Quaking in fear, my words came out like daggers. "You, Brother James!" I screamed. "You will lose your little boy next year to the pox. Goodwife Janet, your field will flood. Be careful on Sabbath, everybody, for there will be a fire in this church come summer!"

Before I knew it, the words were spilling out of my mouth, running through their ears like wasps. Words that I hoped would prove my innocence, but were only digging deeper into their dark suspicions.

Sweat trickled down the bodice of my dress, down along the sides of my face. I was flushed and swooning with anger and terror, my hands clenched like clamshells against my chest. A surge of wetness ran down my legs in rivulets, and a strange dizziness encompassed me. Looking down at the floor, I saw tiny droplets of blood. In horror, I lifted the hem of my skirt to see more pooling around my stockings. I bent down, pressing my hand to the floor, my fingers coming up crimson and screamed in terror. *What was this? What was happening? Why was blood coming from between my legs?*

I turned in horror towards the men at the table, holding my hand up as though bearing witness, and stumbled towards them. "Help me," I cried pitifully." I'm bleeding!"

They drew back in shock as I lurched towards them and pitched forward in a dark haze, my bloody hand resting on the pages of the bible open on the table. The men sprang back, eyes wide and staring. "Witch! Witch!" One of them shouted, pressing himself against the wall, hands on his musket, aimed directly at my heart. "Witch! Here is our proof! She bleeds from Satan!"

A great wind pummeled the door, and the church shook with thunder, shaking a lantern loose from its tether and sending it crashing, bursting into fire, shards everywhere. One elder leapt forward to staunch the flames, tearing his palm into ragged bits, screaming in agony as blood spurted from his hand, mixing with mine on the wood planks. The room began to spin as voices receded into a mumble of sound, so far away, a storm of outrage, fear, and panic.

Five men dragged me from the church, my toes digging into the path, my pitiful cries swallowed by the gathering storm. I was thrust into a small stockade, a dark space with a hard dirt floor, no air but for a tiny slit in the door. I fell to the ground in a heap, frightened, angry, nearly delirious, staunching my blood with bits of my petticoat, curling into a corner sobbing, until at last, spent and sad, I lay in silence, the only sound the breathing of the sentry outside the door. I lay in the darkness, trying to sleep, but sleep would not come. My fear was replaced with abandonment and rage. I rocked back and forth, my hand twisting and stroking the fox paw, my only comfort.

The low murmur of voices outside the tiny stockade jostled me awake. "Food and water for Sarah," mumbled a male voice. "Open the door."

There was hesitation, then another voice said, "No. She will die soon enough. I'm afraid to open the door. She may have turned into a wolf or a panther. Let the witch go hungry."

"Please," I begged, "a little water to wash myself. A bite of food. Please!"

I heard the footsteps subside, and I knew then that there was little hope that the townspeople would do anything but bear witness to my hanging or burning. I prayed for rain to put the fire out, begged the gallows to splinter under my weight. I held the fox paw and screamed towards the forest for help, my words flying on the wing of the horned owl, then spoken to the wolves that lie beneath the outcropping near the river. A breath of breeze caressed my face in answer through the tiny slit in the door, drying the tears on my skin, leaving behind the salt of betrayal.

In anguish, I swallowed dirt from the floor, letting the earth have a taste of me, hoping she would spit me out and not take me to her dark bosom. I missed my mother. I cursed the town. And still, the day wore on, deaf to my pleas, the world refusing to slow for a mere girl. I must have slept, then, for there were dreams that danced behind my eyes. When I woke, the last beams of gloaming streaked the room.

###

That night, I hear it like I know I will. The soft, hollow sound, like a pike bursting a melon. The last sigh of the sentry, a lullaby he sings of his own death.

The door creaks open on its hinges, my hand reaching out for his, knowing he will gather me up and run over the fields as silent as the end of breath, and we will not stop running until the forest closes around us like a fist. Samoset and Alawa guide me through the darkness, each footfall a lifetime away from Salem, shedding my clothes like snake skin until I am running naked in the starlight. I look behind and the trail is already growing over, vines and shrubs blanketing the forest floor. All that is left are the sparks from my heels and nothing more but the sound of a panther's scream at the Blood Moon.

AUTHOR BIOS

KAYLA BASHE is a binational lesbian. Her fiction and poetry has appeared in *Strange Horizons*, *Liminality Magazine*, *Solarpunk Press*, and *The Future Fire*. She has also released several speculative fiction novellas.

DERRICK BODEN is a writer, a software developer, a traveler, and an adventurer. He currently calls New Orleans his home, although he's lived in thirteen cities spanning four continents. His fiction has appeared in numerous venues including *Daily Science Fiction*, *Flash Fiction Online*, and *Perihelion*. He is owned by three cats. Find him at derrickboden.com.

GEORGE BREWINGTON is a respiratory therapist at a hospital in Charleston as well as a writer of dark fantasy stories. He has been previously published in *The Georgetown Review*. He lives with his wife and daughter in Folly Beach, South Carolina, and lives online at www.georgebrewington.com. You can also follow him on Twitter @7Brewington7.

DANIEL CARPENTER is a London-based writer who has had his work published by *Unsung Stories*, *Confingo Magazine*, and *The Irish Literary Review*. He is the co-founder of the award winning organisation Bad Language, and hosts The Paperchain Podcast. He tweets at @dancarpenter85.

DAVID CASTLEWITZ had a long and successful career as a software developer and technical architect, then returned to his first love: SF, fantasy, and magical realism. He's published stories in *Phase 2*, *Farther Stars Than These*, *Martian Wave*, and *Flash Fiction Press*.

DANTZEL CHERRY teaches Pilates and raises her daughter by day, and by night and naptime, she writes. Her baking hours follow no rhyme or reason. Dantzel's short stories have appeared in *Fireside*, *InterGalactic Medicine Show*, *Galaxy's Edge*, and other magazines and anthologies.

SARA CODAIR lives in a world of words: she writes fiction whenever she has a free moment, teaches writing at a community college and is known to binge read fantasy novels. When she manages to pry herself away from the words, she can be found hiking, swimming, gardening or telling people to save the bees.

PRESTON DENNETT has worked as a carpet cleaner, fast-food worker, data-entry clerk, bookkeeper, landscaper, singer, actor, writer, radio host, television consultant, teacher, UFO researcher, ghost hunter and more. He has sold 34 stories and has also earned twelve honorable mentions in the Writers of the Future Contest. He currently resides in southern California.

SHARON FRAME GAY grew up a child of the highway, playing by the side of the road. She has been published in several anthologies, as well as *BioStories*, *Gravel Magazine*, *Fiction on the Web*, *Literally Stories*, *Halcyon Days*, *Fabula Argentea*, *Persimmon Tree*, *Write City*, *Literally Orphans*, *Indiana Voice Journal*, *Luna Luna* and others. She is a Pushcart Prize nominee.

PETER HAGELSLAG works as a maintenance tech for an offshore company in the Black Sea, hoping the sea creatures lurking beneath are less fearful than his imagination. His stories have been published in *Qualia Nous* and *Blurring the Line* anthologies and Rudy Rucker's *Flurb* (amongst others).

G. LLOYD HELM is a ne'er-do-well scribbler, born in the Arkansas Ozarks. He is a wanderer and a friend of ravens and not to be trusted most of the time. He married well.

RUSSELL HEMMELL is a statistician and social scientist from the U.K, passionate about astrophysics and speculative fiction. Stories in *Not One of Us*, *Perihelion SF*, *SQ Mag*, *Strangelet*, and others

TOM HOWARD is a science fiction and fantasy short story writer in Little Rock, Arkansas. He thanks his family and friends for their inspiration and the Central Arkansas Speculative Fiction Writers' Group for their perspiration.

PASCAL INARD is a writer and IT project manager from Melbourne, Australia. His short stories have appeared in *Antipodean SF Magazine*, *Flash Fiction Press*, and *StrippedLit500*, and he is the author of the novel *The Memory Snatcher*, a science-fiction mystery about a police inspector and a quantum physicist who join forces to stop a memory thief from paralysing the world.

RACHEL MORRIS is a renaissance woman of many hobbies. She studied English, Media Studies, and Creative Writing at UC Berkeley, where she tutored her peers in academic writing, led a multicultural creative writing workshop, and facilitated the first peer-led genre fiction workshop in the English department. She's currently scribbling SFF novels, genre-bending short stories, and doing freelance editing work.

MOLLY N. MOSS is the alias of a swashbuckling adventuress from the 43rd century, trapped in our 21st century by a tragic time travel accident. She doesn’t like to talk about that. As few of her futuristic skills are useful in our time, she now writes science fiction, fantasy, and horror. Most recently, she’s been published in *Weirdbook* and *Bete Noire*.

ANDREW NELSON is a data architect, specializing in high performance computing and distributed systems. He also loves to hike, master video games, and spend time with his three children. An avid reader, writer, and viewer of all things speculative, fantasy, and horror, Andrew is uniquely qualified to survive any upcoming zombie apocalypse—even with those three kids in tow.

COLLEEN QUINN has short fiction appearing in various magazines and anthologies. She currently resides in Brooklyn, New York, in an apartment that is hardly haunted at all. She may be found online at www.colleenquinn.com.

LAWRENCE SALANI lives near Sydney, Australia with his wife and child. He has been interested in horror since childhood, and he draws inspiration from pulp horror writers of the past. His interests also extend to fine arts, drawing and painting.

His stories appear in *Danse Macabre*, Edge Publishing; *Darkness Ad Infinitum*, Villipede Press; and *Gothic Blue Book 4*, Burial Day Press.

J.J. SMITH is a writer and journalist living in the Washington, D.C. area. His fiction has appeared in *The Sterling Web*, and in the anthologies *Halloween Shrieks* and *Tales from the Witch's Cauldron*. After 13 years of reporting on Capitol Hill, J.J. now spends his daylight hours writing summaries of House and Senate hearings.

LEIGH STATHAM has lots of kids and lots of pets and lots of bad habits. She writes YA and MG books, terrible poetry, and ranty articles about special education. She works as a head gnomie at Quantum Fairy Tales. Follow her on Twitter, Facebook, and Wattpad.

JEFF C. STEVENSON is an advertising copywriter and member of Pen America and the Horror Writers Association. His first book, *Fortney Road: The True Story of Life, Death and Deception in a Christian Cult* was published in 2015. He has had more than a dozen short stories published and is finishing a two-part, supernatural suspense novel.

SAMUEL VAN PELT has had fiction appear in *Perihelion SF*, *The Martian Wave*, and is upcoming in others. He holds a degree in computer science and makes his living as a software engineer for a large technology company. He enjoys science fiction, fantasy, and horror, and writes from his home in Seattle.

RACHEL WATTS is a writer from Perth, Western Australia. She reviews books and writes commentary at www.leatherboundpounds.com.

LORNA WOOD is a violinist and writer in Auburn, Alabama. She was a finalist in the 2016 Neoverse Short Story Competition and *Sharkpack Poetry Review*'s Valus' Sigil competition. Her work has appeared in *No Extra* Words, *Wild Violet*, *These Fragile Lilacs*, *Experimementos*, *Cacti Fur*, *Birds Piled Loosely*, *Every Writer*, *Blue Monday Review*, *Untitled, with Passengers*, and on Kindle.

DANY G. ZUWEN (born Gaston Ndanyuzwe) is a Belgo-Rwandan science fiction writer living in the Flemish suburban area. When not writing or reading, Dany enjoys movies, all things computer-related, and fancies himself a culinary experimentalist. You can learn more about him by visiting his website: www.danyzuwen.com.

EDITOR BIOS

EMMA NELSON has an MA in American Literature, with an emphasis on folklore and cultural studies. She writes and edits in a broad range of genres and topics, but her most recent writing can be found in *Channeling Wonder: Fairy Tales on Television* and *The Routledge Companion to Fairy-Tale Cultures and Media.* She has three kids, which is probably why she spends so much time thinking about dark magic.

HANNAH STILES SMITH is an educator, has a BA in History, and has worked for years as an editor, helping bring fabulous books to their full potential. She spends all her spare time escaping between the pages of a book, and a foray into publishing seemed like the best way to channel that energy. She lives in rural Virginia with her husband and four rambunctious children.

For more information and to discover other books by Owl Hollow Press, find us here:

Website: owlhollowpress.com
Twitter: @owlhollowpress
Facebook: Owl Hollow Press
Instagram: owlhollowpress

Made in the USA
San Bernardino, CA
14 July 2020